Survivor's Guilt

CASSY ROOP

This book is dedicated to those who have loved and lost,
yet learned to love again.

And also to one of my best friends in the whole world,
Judi Perkins who has shown me
what unconditional love means.

In loving memory of Joseli Mycheila Perkins

Prologue

PURE BLISS

Ellie

I SAT IN AN OLD ANTIQUE wooden chair and stared at myself in the mirror. My palms were sweating, but I didn't dare wipe them on my dress. The beautiful bouquet of flowers I held, filled the room with a sweet and comforting fragrance. I took in my overly large blue eyes and the waves of curls that cascaded over my left shoulder. The same flowers from my bouquet were adorned in my hair giving it an elegant touch.

This was the day that almost every woman dreamed of. The day where she got to wear a beautiful dress, and be the center of attention. I fingered the white taffeta of my dress and reminisced about the day that my mom and sisters went with me to go shopping. The big surprise was on me when they gave me an envelope that contained tickets to New York City. All four of them knew that I watched *Say Yes to the Dress* religiously, even before I got engaged. It was always one of my guilty pleasures. So there was no doubt in their minds that I shouldn't go to Kleinfield's to get my dress.

Everyone was behind me putting the final finishing touches on their appearance while I sat back and enjoyed the view in slow motion. I wanted to savor everything about this day, every moment, so that I could hold onto the memory of it for the rest of my life. It wasn't every day that you got to marry your soul mate. The man of your dreams. The man that even after nearly four years of dating made butterflies appear in your stomach just from walking into the room.

"Are you ready, sweetheart?" My dad asked as he walked up behind me and placed one of his tired, worn hands on my bare shoulder. I looked into the mirror and met his eyes that glistened with unshed tears and could see the pride he held in his heart staring back at me.

"I am. Are you?" I asked as I beamed a smile at him. I had to do anything to keep my own unshed tears from threatening to fall and ruining my impeccable makeup.

"If it were any other man I had to give you away to today, I would say no. But I can honestly say you chose well, Ellie. I know that he will do a wonderful job in taking care of my baby just like I always have."

I had to bite my lip to keep it from quivering. To see the tall, strapping Alan Burnette nearly choked up with his words, was nearly too much to bear. I was definitely my daddy's girl and to know he so willingly approved of my choice in husband meant the world to me.

He reached out a hand and helped me from my seat. My mother fluttered over in her light grey sheath dress and gently pressed one of her soft lips on my cheek.

"You look beautiful, sweetheart. Breathtaking."

"Thank you, Momma,"

I watched as her and my father looked at each other and saw the ever-present spark between them that nearly thirty-five years of marriage couldn't diminish. I only could pray that the same flames continued to burn within us after this day.

One more soft kiss on my cheek and then my mom went to go stand at the sanctuary entrance with the bridesmaids. My father offered me his elbow and I graciously took it as he tucked my arm to his side. I knew he wanted the connection of having his little girl with him for only a few seconds more, before he gave me over to the man I would spend the rest of my life with and I leant my head against his shoulder just as I have nearly all my life.

We walked out of the small room and down the hallway to the sanctuary entrance. I felt a small tremble in my knees and a small sheen of sweat form on the small of my back. I didn't know why I was so nervous. I had never been more ready for anything in my entire life. I loved him with every fiber of my soul and knew that our life together would be perfect. So when the music started to play and all the bridesmaids began their march down the aisle, I took a deep breath and turned to face the sanctuary and came eye to eye with my future husband.

Evan

THE BREATH NEARLY left my body the moment she stepped into the room. Most men will tell you that the moment they see their future wife in her wedding dress, it is like a sucker punch to the gut to see how truly beautiful she is. It was more than that. I felt like someone had picked me up and spun me around fast, to the point my equilibrium was malfunctioning. I was dizzy in the head, yet full in my heart as she slowly, one foot at a time, made her way down the aisle toward me. The room was packed to capacity, yet it was like we were the only two in the room.

I watched as she looked up at her father and him, in turn, looked at her with as much love as I was feeling in my heart for her at that very moment. It felt like it was nearly an eternity before her eyes met mine once again. They sparkled with an unconditional love, shone at me with purpose, understanding, love and respect. She smiled and I felt my stomach bottom out, and when she finally made it to me, my hand trembled as her father extended hers to me to take.

The familiar shock of awareness filtered through me as our hands connected. Skin to skin. Heart to heart. Soul to soul. I never thought I could love anything, much less another person, the way I loved her. She completed me in every way. Made me look at life with a whole new meaning and purpose. And when I saw my future, she was the first thing that would always appear.

"Who gives this woman to this man?" The preacher asked.

"Her mother and I do," her father replied as he looked at her once more and then looking at me with a wink. Most people had nothing great to say about his significant other's parents, but my future mother and father-in-law were two of the most wonderful people I have ever met. They welcomed me with open arms and invited me immediately into their family when we started dating years ago. The day I asked for her hand in marriage, he didn't hesitate to say yes, but instead hugged me like I was his own son and said he couldn't be prouder to give his daughter to anyone else.

We stood facing each other, our hands clasped between us and I stroked the back of her hand with my thumb. Her skin was smooth like velvet and I was anxious to put the diamond ring I had gotten her on her finger before she had the chance to change her mind.

"Dearly beloved—" the preacher began and his words soon faded away for all I could do was focus on her. The way her blue eyes shone at me, and her smile that stole my soul the moment we met.

"Evan has prepared his own vows and would like to say them now," the preacher said as he broke through my daydream of the beautiful woman before me. Her eyes widened with shock because this wasn't something we had planned. We had agreed to just the normal, traditional ceremony, but I knew she deserved more than the standard repeated words. She deserved to hear firsthand how her love made me feel. She deserved to know exactly what was in my heart.

"If I had to choose the exact moment that I fell in love with you, it would probably be the first time I looked into your eyes. You captivated me that day with your beauty, your wit, and your amazing ability to mess up a coffee order."

The crowd laughed as they all remembered she used to work at the only coffee shop in town several years ago.

"If I had to choose the moment when I knew I wanted to spend the rest of my life with you, I would choose that day. You made my heart beat in a way that it never had before. The connection I felt with you was beyond words, which is why I was probably silent the entire time you took my order."

The crowd all chuckled again and she smiled knowingly at me.

"But if I had to choose any other person to spend the rest of my life with, I wouldn't feel as alive as I do today. I love you more than my next breath. I will love you more in this life and in the next. You are the reason I wake in the morning. You are my purpose. I promise to cherish you, guide you and support you. I promise to always be the one to make the coffee, because let's face it, you suck at it."

She laughed as a stray tear cascaded down her cheek.

"I promise to catch each one of your tears before they ever hit the ground, whether they are happy or sad. I will stand beside you in the good times and even more so with the bad. I hope that I can give you back all the joy, happiness, and love that you have so selflessly shown me in our short time together. I will spend every day of the rest of our lives proving to you that I am worthy of your love. I love you."

I smiled at my best friend as I turned to retrieve her ring. When my eyes met hers again, they were glistening and she sniffled to try and keep them from falling. Sliding the ring onto her finger, I was finally able to exhale. It was both a relief and a privilege to place this circle upon her hand.

"Let this ring serve as an ongoing reminder of the commitment that I make here with you today. Just like a circle, this ring has no edges. No notches or stops. It is one continuous loop that goes on for eternity, because that is how long I plan on loving you."

It was my turn to be in shock when the preacher announced that she too had prepared her own vows. It only proved how perfectly in sync we were with each other and I couldn't wipe the stupid grin off my face. Her words cut through me like a knife, slicing deeper into my soul and embedding her there a little deeper. So many people say that words don't hurt, or that they can't heal a broken heart, but I am living proof that her words healed. I walked around broken all my life, searching for the true meaning of my existence until the day that I found it.

It was her.

She was my reason.

My truth.

The one person I would willingly sacrifice myself for.

And as she slipped the ring on my finger symbolizing her commitment to me and the preacher announced us as husband and wife, we sealed our forever together with a kiss.

Chapter One

THE HONEYMOON

Ellie

"BABE! I PUT THE LAST suitcase in the car. Are you about ready to go?" My husband yelled up the stairs where I was looking through our bedroom to see if there was anything I was forgetting. I knew we were only going to be gone for two weeks, but I was a planner. I liked things to be in order. He always laughed at me and would tease me about my OCD tendencies, but I would never hear him complain when he needed something and then found out I had indeed packed it.

This wasn't our first trip together, but it was our first trip as husband and wife. I stood in the doorway and looked at the rumpled sheets of the bed. For the first time, I actually didn't want to rush over and straighten it up. It held a memory far too dear to me as I reminisced about last night. How my husband so wonderfully made my body come alive. How he treasured, worshiped, and caressed every inch of my skin. How with just one flick of his tongue against my nipple nearly set me off. It wasn't the first time we had sex, but it was the first time we made love and truly belonged to each other. He was mine and I was his. I even had the piece of paper to prove it.

"What are you doing?" He asked as he slipped in behind me and circled his arms around my waist and rested his chin on my shoulder. The woodsy smell of his aftershave filled my nostrils and I took a moment to appreciate it by taking a deep inhale.

"Trying to remember if we forgot anything," I replied, placing my hands on top of his. I caressed the ring on his left hand and smiled as I looked at my matching one.

"You know, this is supposed to be our honeymoon. You, wifey, are supposed to be relaxed."

He kissed my shoulder where it was exposed from my tank top.

"And carefree."

He kissed the side of my neck.

"And completely and utterly consumed by being with your husband for the next fourteen days."

He kissed the sensitive spot right below my ear and my breathing quickened. We had spent hours last night lost in each other and I was still gloriously sore in so many areas, but it did nothing to dissipate my want for him. Knowing that he belonged to me and only me, made my body heat even more for him.

"Keep doing that and we'll miss our flight. Aunt Silvia will be waiting at the airport in Miami to pick us up. We wouldn't want to disappoint her by being late."

"It all depends on if her disappointment is only fueled by me pleasuring my wife," he said seductively as he licked my earlobe causing a lightning bolt of pleasure to ripple through me.

"Didn't you get enough last night?" I turned around in his arms and teased as I brought my arms up to play with the hair at his nape. I could spend hours getting lost in the bright green color of his eyes. I watched as the tiny red flakes around his irises danced with mischief as he grinned down at me.

"I could spend every second of my time awake inside of you every day for the rest of my life, and I would never be able to get enough."

"When did you get this mushy? You've been so cheesily romantic since you said your vows to me." I asked arching my brow at him.

"You love it when I'm cheesy," he grinned dropping a slow, leisurely kiss upon my mouth. He tasted like morning coffee and it was a flavor that I had become so addicted to.

"If you promise to be good, maybe I'll let you induct me into the Mile High Club," I teased him and his eyes grew wide with hunger.

"You wouldn't?"

"Oh, baby. I will."

"Deal." And he scooped me up into his arms and I yelped, surprised by his enthusiasm and I giggled as he carried me all the way down to the car.

Evan

I WOKE TO THE FEELING of someone caressing my cheek. When my eyes fluttered open, I looked into the beautiful face of my wife. I must have dozed off just a few moments after we took off from the runway.

"How long was I asleep?" I asked as I rubbed at my eyes with the heels of my hands.

"Only about forty-five minutes," she pretended to pout and it was the cutest damn thing I had ever seen. Sunlight filtered through the tiny window of the airplane casting rays upon her golden hair. She looked just like an angel as she sat looking at me adoringly and I smiled as I leaned over and pressed a soft kiss upon her lips.

I would never grow tired of the shock of electricity I felt every time I touched her, whether it was with my mouth or my hands.

"I was thinking," she said as she slipped her hand in between the lapels of my dress shirt where the top two buttons were popped open. I arched my brow at her, curious as to where her thoughts were taking her as her hand caressed the skin of my chest.

"Just what are you thinking?" I asked her as I reached up and traced her jaw with the tip of my finger.

"I'm thinking that I've had you down on earth, but what about in the clouds?" She bit her lip and I knew exactly what she was thinking.

Mile High Club.

She was spontaneous, and it was something I absolutely loved about her.

"I'm going to go use the bathroom. Meet me back there in two minutes," she whispered in my ear and before I could respond, she unbuckled her seatbelt and was making her way down the aisle. I turned to watch her sinful derriere walk down the narrow aisle of the aircraft. I also wasn't immune to the stares from some of the other men on the plane as they watched her walk by.

That's right fuckers. She's mine.

I tried to mentally count to one-twenty in my head, but my *other* head had different ideas. Trying not to look too eager, I unbuckled my belt and made my way toward the bathroom, all the while my dick beginning to strain against the zipper of my jeans. I was too busy thinking about taking my wife to care whether some of the other passengers noticed my gigantic hard on as I made my way toward the back of the plane.

There were two doors that were labeled *lavatories* as I stood in front of them. Luckily, one said *vacant* while the other one said occupied and I knocked on the one I knew my wife was in. She opened the door enough so I could only see her eyes and then smiled when she saw it was me. Looking right towards the front of the plane, I tried to make sure the flight attendants were busy before I stepped inside and joined my wife.

Her shirt was already off and the button on her jeans undone. The delicate black lace of her bra clung to her breasts like a second skin and I hated to admit to myself that I was jealous of the fabric for getting to maintain its position on her body.

Making sure to lock the door behind us, we stuffed ourselves into the tiny space and lost no time before we began devouring each other's mouths. I dipped my tongue inside her warmth and she didn't hesitate to open for me. I loved the taste of her, so familiar, so comforting. I felt like a horny teenager making out with his crush, as my hands touched her everywhere.

"This is so fucking hot," I murmured against her neck and I freed one of her breasts front the cup of her bra.

"Shhhh, we have to be quiet," she whispered and then groaned as I ducked my head to capture her nipple in my mouth.

"Baby, I'm already wet. We have to do this fast. Take me now," she demanded and began peeling her jeans down her legs. Leaving one foot in and taking the other out, She braced herself against the tiny sink and then lifted one leg to expose the matching lace underwear she wore. She then went to work unbuckling my jeans and pushing them and my boxers down just enough to expose my erection. Instantly going to work, she began to stroke my length, causing me to harden in her hands even more.

"Just slide them to the side, and fuck me," she said looking down at her panties.

Holy hell.

I did even better. I hooked my finger into them and in one swift swipe, I tore the crotch and exposed herself to me. I licked my lips wishing that I could taste her, but knew that we didn't have much time.

"I kind of liked those, caveman," she teased.

"I liked them too, baby, but I'll buy you more."

Lining myself up, I slowly slipped inside of her and our mutual moans filled the confined space. I started slow, but when I heard voices outside the door, I quickly picked up the pace and pressed my mouth to hers to muffle our cries. She was my home. Inside her, she was my sanctuary. With each thrust I reached somewhere deeper into her and knew she was getting close when she bit down on my lip.

"I—I'm going to come," she whispered as she was now panting and it made me work even harder. Sweat rolled down my temples and with a soft cry, her back arched and she surrendered to the release of pressure. One, two, three more thrusts, and I emptied myself inside of her. We stilled together as we tried to gain control over our breathing.

"Welcome to the mile high club, baby," she smiled before kissing me one more time. I withdrew from her and as quickly and as quietly as we could, began putting our clothes back on. I let her exit the bathroom first, so as to not cause a scene with the other passengers nor alert the flight attendants. When I thought I had given her ample enough time to find her seat, I exited and made my way back to sit beside her.

"Wow." She breathed as I sat beside her and reached for her hand, pressing a kiss to the back of it.

"That was amazing, but I plan on taking my sweet time with you tonight."

"And I thoroughly look forward to it," she smiled and laid her head against my shoulder and closed her eyes.

———

I WATCHED HER FROM afar as I ordered drinks for us from a small cabana located on the beach. Her skin shone brilliantly beneath the beaming sun of the Florida Keys, causing her perfect skin to begin to bronze. I admired the beautiful curves of her body as she was adorned in a white, sexy as hell bikini. The floppy hat on her head shielded her shoulders from the forcefulness of the sun as my eyes raked from tip to toe where she reclined in the beach chair.

"Yours?" The bartender asked as he nodded his head in my wife's direction.

"Yep. All mine. I'm a lucky bastard."

"Most definitely," he said looking at me with envy. He was a little older, the light peppering of grey at his temples giving away his age.

"Newlyweds?" He asked again as he went back to mixing the fruity concoction that my wife loved so much.

"We got married yesterday," I said as I smiled thinking about our vows at the ceremony and the image of her in her dress flashed in my mind.

"Congratulations," he said as he sat the drinks down in front of me. I reached in my wallet to pay him and he shrugged me off.

"No charge. In celebration," he said smiling at me. I pulled out a twenty-dollar bill and slid it over to him.

"For you then."

"Thank you sir."

I made my way back over to where my wife was and handed her the pink drink she requested.

"Thank you," she replied as she took a long pull from her glass.

We stayed out on the beach for an hour people watching as we reclined in our chairs that faced the water. I securely held her hand in mine, our fingers entwined, desperate to not break our touch from each other before we retired to our hotel room to take a nap.

***

"WAKE UP SLEEPYHEAD," I said as I caressed the soft skin of her cheek. Her eyes fluttered open and she had a glazed over look to her eyes before she realized where she was.

"No, I'm too comfortable. Come back to bed," she said sleepily as she patted my side of the bed. "Let's snuggle more."

"That sounds so enticing, baby, but if we don't get up and get ready, we'll miss our boat."

She rose up on her elbows and the sheet slid down exposing her breasts to me. When we had retired to the hotel room, it was my full intention for us to take a nap so that we could enjoy our evening out on the sea tonight without being completely exhausted. She had different ideas. We had barely made it into the room before she turned around and jumped into my arms, wrapping her legs around my waist and asked me to make love to her. We spent a few hours going slow, touching, teasing, and finally indulging ourselves in the intense pleasure that only we could give to each other.

"What boat?" She asked as she sat up straighter and stretched, the movement causing her chest to push out before me. When she looked at me she saw the stupid grin on my face.

"You know, we could always just stay here and have dinner in bed."

"You sure as hell have become insatiable since you became my wife," I joked and I scooted closer to her on the bed and leaned in to press a kiss on her lips.

"What can I say? I have a pretty sexy husband," she smiled at me, her eyes shone with potent desire.

I groaned. Nothing would please me more than to stay here all night long and only move when we needed to come up for air, but I had spent quite a bit of money on these tickets and I also knew it would be something she would enjoy.

"I hear they have homemade tiramisu on the boat," I waggled my eyebrows at her. She pursed her lips, trying to hide the smile threatening to form on her face.

I had her. She couldn't resist dessert.

"Then later, when we get back," I said as I kissed her shoulder, "we can have a treasure hunt."

"A treasure hunt?" She asked as she laughed delightfully.

"Yes. See I can play pirate. And I'm looking for your booty."

"Oh my God, Evan. You did *not* just say that!" She said throwing her head back so that her long hair fell down her back and broke out into a fit of laughter.

"Well, wife, you definitely have some treasures I seek. I would like nothing more than to seek your clam shell."

"Stop, stop!" She cried as she hugged her arms around her waist. "I'm gonna pee my pants."

Chapter Two

THE BOAT

Ellie

WE STEPPED ONTO the beautiful fifty-two-foot Bluewater Cruiser just as the sun was beginning to touch where the sky and sea met. Whimsical orange and red hues stroked the sky like an exquisite watercolor painting. The sky was mainly clear except for the few dark clouds off in the distance, but with the magical scene before me, I paid them no mind. The outside deck had a few people scattered about sipping on bubbly flutes of crisp champagne as they admired the sunset.

My husband entwined his strong fingers with mine and led me into the main cabin where the mouth-watering smell of gourmet Cuban cuisine permeated the air. White linen cloths covered about ten round tables that were decorated with white fine china and crystal stemware.

"Wow, this is beautiful," I said gazing around the cabin in awe. I was so excited to get to share a sunset dinner cruise with the love of my life. He amazed me with how romantic he could be. I loved how he could still make me feel giddy after four years together, and how he always thought of me before he made any decision or plans. He knew I would love something like this and it made it even more special.

"Thank you for this," I said as I rose up on the tip of my toes and placed a kiss on his cheek, careful to keep it PG. The way he looked in the dark suit he wore, stole my breath away, and my thoughts were anything but appropriate. His broad shoulders filled out the jacket that tapered at his narrow waist. His sexy as sin ass made his slacks look as if they were made especially for him. His dark hair was slightly tousled from the wind and there was a slight speckling of scruff on his face. He looked almost as perfect as he did on our wedding day.

Almost.

"Ladies and gentlemen, thank you for boarding *The Evening Star*. This is your captain Steve Hurst. On behalf of Key Cruises, we would like to invite you to find your seats as we begin our two-hour dinner voyage."

We made our way over to our table where my husband held out my chair for me to have a seat. Ever the gentleman. Two other couples soon joined us, one set seeming close to our age and another who looked like they had been married for over fifty years. I smiled looking over at my husband and thought that I hoped that was us one day. Still in love in fifty years like we are today, if not more so.

The younger of the ladies sat down next to me. I admired her modern, yet elegant red cocktail dress as I extended my hand to her.

"Hi, I'm Ellison. Honeymoon," I said as I nodded my head towards my husband who was engaged in conversation with the older man's wife. She smiled sweetly as she placed her clutch on the table before reaching her hand out to mine.

"I'm Lilly. And same for us. We just got married two days ago."

"We were married yesterday," I added.

"Congratulations," we both said in unison and then giggled. Lilly's husband was talking animatedly with the old man at the table about deep seawater fishing as my husband tried to listen to his wife go on about how to properly skin a fish. I couldn't help but smile at the situation. The older couple was very friendly, but I could tell that our two men wanted to put their attention towards their brides.

"Think we should rescue them?" Lilly asked me as she nudged me slightly with her elbow. I pursed my lips and then smiled widely.

"Nah. I'm quite enjoying this. It's payback for every time he left me talking to his Aunt Dorothy who would talk about nothing but her bunions."

"Ewww. Yeah. I'd say this is definitely payback," she laughed.

"So where are you from?" Lilly asked me just before she took a sip from her water glass.

"North Carolina. We actually live pretty close to the coast, but we wanted a change of beach scenery so we came to the keys. What about you?"

"We are from Miami, actually. I know, I know, we didn't venture far, but my husband is a pediatric surgeon and he wanted to stay close in case he got the call. One of his patients has a brain tumor. Cancer. She's only seven. He felt that he needed to be close by in case something were to happen."

I hated that word. Cancer. The same word that took the life of my beloved grandmother nearly two years ago.

"That is completely understandable. I admire your husband for wanting to do that. Seems you married yourself a winner." I smiled.

Lilly looked over at her husband who was discussing different bait tactics with the old man, and gazed at him with the same kind of love I felt for my own husband.

"I sure did. I think I won the husband lottery."

I picked up my water glass, "To happily ever afters," I said holding it up towards her. She retrieved hers and clanked it with mine.

"And to finding our princes," she added and then we took a drink of the water.

Twenty minutes into the cruise and waiters appeared at our table carrying delicious smelling food, setting plates down in front of us. We all carried on chatting and getting to know each other as we enjoyed our gourmet meal. The older couple, we learned, was in fact celebrating their anniversary, but it was their sixtieth. They lived in a tiny town outside of Nashville, Tennessee and this was the first real vacation they had taken in over twenty years. They were sweet and very lively. We all laughed at the old man's jokes and again at his wife who rolled her eyes at him playfully, claiming how cheesy he was.

All around us, the cabin was filled with glass walls so that we could see the sunset as the last bit of the sun danced upon the water. I was having so much fun that I hadn't even noticed how far offshore we had gone. I couldn't even see the lights of the keys anymore.

After dessert, which did indeed consist of the most delicious tiramisu I had ever had, we sat around drinking a wonderful vintage dessert wine.

Suddenly the boat shifted causing me to nearly lose the glass in my hand and my husband reached out a hand to help steady me when I nearly slid off of my chair.

"Sorry about that folks," the captain announced only minutes later. "The winds have started to pick up slightly so we may experience some more listing throughout the remainder of the cruise. Try not to worry and continue to enjoy yourselves."

An orchestra consisting of a pianist, a harpist, and a cello player made their way onto the stage and began playing a beautiful stream of music throughout the cabin. Tables were cleared producing a makeshift dance floor in the middle of the room.

"May I have this dance?" My husband looked at me before he stood up and bowed, offering his hand out to me. I blushed and smiled at the same time feeling a bit warm and tipsy from the wine. Then I thought back to how Lilly and I had talked about finding our princes earlier. I noticed that she and her husband had already made their way onto the dance floor along with the older couple. I smiled sweetly up at my husband. I couldn't pass up the chance to allow my body to be molded to his and took his extended hand and let him lead me.

He held me close as I laid my head upon his chest relishing in the beautiful sound of his heartbeat. It was still surreal that God was allowing me to feel this happy. There wasn't anything I wouldn't do for this man. The man who filled every space of my heart and had permanently left a piece of him with me, making us more one than we ever were two.

The boat listed again and I stumbled, but was instantly caught by his strong arms as he pulled me back to him.

"I about landed on my ass there," I laughed. He looked down at me, his face serious, and the peacefulness of only a few moments earlier non-existent in his expression.

"No matter what, Ellie. I will always be here to catch you if you stumble. It may not always be before you fall, but in that case I'll be there to pick you right back up. You are my everything."

Evan

I LOOKED DOWN INTO the beautiful blue eyes of my wife and thought that there couldn't be anything more perfect than this moment. Except maybe when she said "I do." The boat rocked a little forcefully and I held her to me, enjoying the feeling of how her body molded so perfectly to mine. How we fit together like two pieces of a puzzle formed and shaped so that we only had one match.

Each other.

"I love you," I whispered into her ear as I held her closer if possible.

"I love you," She whispered back, nuzzling into my chest. My heart ached with the force of my love for her. The power that this one tiny woman had over me was astronomical.

She looked up at me with tears glistening in her eyes.

"What's wrong baby?" I asked her as I reached up to cup her face in my hands and as the tears fell, I caught them with my thumbs, just as I had promised in my vows.

"I—I need to tell you something."

Dread filled my stomach. What was it that she needed to tell me? The concern on her face nearly broke me and about a dozen anxious thoughts raced through my mind. She bit her lip, glancing down for only a brief second before looking back up at me.

"I wanted to do this in a different way. Tell you with something funny, or clever, but it's eating at me and I can't hold it in anymore.

I know we had talked about it before the wedding and that we were just going to see what God blessed us with, but the day before the wedding I found out..."

She paused looking nervous.

"What baby? Whatever it is, we'll get through it together."

God please tell me she wasn't sick. I just barely got to claim her as mine, and we have many, many years ahead of us.

"Well, I think when we get home, we should look into getting a bigger vehicle."

I stopped dancing with her and just stared down at her with a look of confusion on my face. A bigger vehicle? That's what she had to tell me?

"You know, because we'll be carrying more stuff when we take the baby to our parents house to visit," she continued as the biggest, most beautiful smile spread across her face.

Wait.

Did she just say?

"Did you just say baby? Like as in a *baby*, baby?"

She nodded and I felt like all the breath had been sucker punched from me.

"Are you serious?" I whispered not able to find my voice.

"We are due in about seven and a half months. I guess it was all that practice for our wedding night."

I pulled her into me and wrapped my arms around her as the realization began to sink in and elation spread through me.

"I'm going to be a dad?"

"You're going to be a dad."

"WOOOO HOOO!!!!" I yelped as I fist pumped the air and held onto my wife with the other. Everyone in the cabin turned to look at me as I made a spectacle of myself, but I couldn't give a shit.

"Evan," my wife scolded me as I released her and did some crazy assed Irish jig right there on the dance floor.

"Evan," she said again this time laughing her ass off at me.

"Okay! Okay everyone," I announced. "This gorgeous woman, this perfect person I get the esteemed privilege to call my wife just told me I'm going to be a dad!"

Catcalls and a loud thunderous applause echoed off the glass as I grabbed my wife and bent her backwards in a nineteen-fifties style kiss before up righting us.

I didn't think there was anything that could have made me happier in that moment.

Suddenly, the boat shifted again and this time people fell and some glasses crashed and shattered on the floor.

"Ladies and gentleman. The coast guard has informed me that there is a storm moving in rather quickly. At first we thought that it would bypass us, but it looks to be heading right in our direction. The water is beginning to become too choppy for us to proceed so we will be turning back towards shore. You will be compensated for the time lost on your voyage tonight. We apologize for the inconvenience."

The waiters and other staff on the boat began handing out life vests when the boat began to rock more forcefully side to side. I made sure to keep my wife close to me so that I could help keep her steady. She began to look a little sick and I didn't know if it were from the boat or if she were already feeling the effects of the pregnancy.

A father...I'm going to be a daddy to someone who is going to be completely dependent upon me.

Rain began to pound against the glass windows of the cabin causing a small roar as the boat continued towards the marina.

"Ladies and gentlemen, looks like things are going to start getting rough. We are still approximately thirty miles off shore, so if you would, please find a railing to secure yourselves to until we have made it safely back to land."

I walked with Lilly and child toward the outer edge of the cabin so that we could hold onto the railing like the captain had requested. I secured myself to the railing and made sure she had a firm grip as well, as I held her around the waist. The waves picked up and so did the rocking of the boat.

Normally, situations like this wouldn't bother me, but the fact that my wife and unborn child were here in this situation made my anxiety rise to the surface.

Chapter Three

THE STORM

Ellie

M Y KNUCKLES WERE white with the force with which I held onto the railing. My eyes anxiously roamed the cabin for my husband who had gone to the restroom only seconds ago. Or it could have been minutes. My anxiety had risen to an all-new level when the waves had begun to crash against the glass and caused the boat to toss me, and all the patrons within, around like rag dolls. To say I was terrified was an understatement. We were still thirty miles from shore and the boat could only go so fast with the force of the waves it was having to battle. It was such a stark contradiction to the beauty of the sky and sun when we had first stepped aboard.

One of the largest waves yet crashed against the boat causing it to list to the left and also made me lose my grip on the railing. I went sliding across the floor as my arms flailed around to find something to grasp on to. Several others took the force of the wave with me and were too launched to the other side of the boat. Cries, some ear piercing, could be heard from all around.

"Baby! Baby, are you alright?" I heard my husband yell as he reached down and picked me up and helped me walk back over to the railing where he pinned me between his body and the protection of the rails.

"I'm okay. Don't leave me again, please!" I yelled as the force of the rain pounded harder and I could barely hear myself speak. The lights in the cabin had begun to flicker on and off leaving us in flashes of light and darkness. My hands were clammy from my fear and I had a hard time keeping my grip on the railing.

"I got you, baby. We're fine. We're going to be fine." He reassured me, but I could hear the anxiety in his voice as he leaned in close enough for me to hear.

My heart rate was erratic. My legs trembled like I had done a million squats at the gym from trying to fight against gravity and the force in which the waves hit the boat.

Suddenly, a loud crashing sound rang out and I watched as one of the glass walls gave way and it shattered, spilling shards on the wooden floor of the cabin. Water began to spill in causing the floor to become slick. I had long kicked off my high heels in order to get a better grip, but as soon as the water reached my feet, my husband and I both fell to the ground, still gripping onto the rail.

This wasn't supposed to be happening. I was supposed to be back in my hotel making slow, sweet love to my husband and cherishing him with my body the way he had cherished my heart. I wasn't supposed to be out in the middle of the ocean, clinging onto a rail for dear life as my husband desperately tried to keep us from being thrown all around the interior of the boat.

"Baby, hang on!" He yelled and briefly our eyes met. I could see fear in them, worry about how we were going to make it out of this.

"I love you," I yelled.

"I love you," I thought I had heard him say back, but it was muffled by the sound of a warning alarm.

Another wave.

More glass.

More water as the cabin began to fill up.

The crackling of the captain over the speaker saying something about a hole and taking on water.

Everything began to slow down; time seemed to pass achingly slowly as I looked around at all of horrified faces of all the passengers. Women crying and men desperately clung onto them. I could taste the salt water as it invaded my mouth and felt the spray of the water, soaking my hair and causing it to cling to my head.

People were bleeding from the shattered glass. Either from being in the direct path as it shattered, or falling to the floor and cutting themselves on the shards that were confettied on there.

Through the wind and debris that flew around us, I could see Lilly and her husband clinging to each other for dear life. Tears streamed down my face as more water began to fill the cabin.

When I risked a glance out of the window, my eyes widened in shock as I saw what looked like a tsunami sized wave heading straight for us.

I looked to my husband seconds before it hit us and we were both catapulted in opposite directions.

"Ellie!" He screamed and the sound was so painful, that it made my blood curdle. Water assaulted me and burned my nose and lungs as I inhaled it. Water was now in sixty percent of the cabin and I couldn't find my husband. My legs banged against tables. Chairs floated on the surface along with glass and pieces of steel and wood from the boat.

Where was he?

I couldn't find him.

I yelled, taking more water into my lungs and barking out a deep cough as it burned. I didn't care. I had to find him. I needed to get to him and know that he was okay. My teeth began to chatter as a cold chill raked through me. I swam through the angry water as the cabin was now filling up at an alarming rate. Panic began to set in and I knew I had to get out of the cabin before the boat took me under as it continued to sink.

But I couldn't leave until I found him.

Wave upon wave hit against me, some sending me somersaulting through the water, others hitting so hard, the breath was nearly knocked from me.

I yelled his name.

There weren't as many screams as there were before and things were strangely silent except for the angry roar of the ocean.

"Grab my hand!" I heard someone yell and I turned to see Lilly and her husband both reaching out to me. The boat was nearly completely on its side now and I swam as hard as I could to reach the couple. With every ounce of strength I could find, I finally reached them as we climbed out one of the broken cabin windows.

Even in the darkness, I could see the yellow of life jackets floating in the water around us. Some with people alive, and some with people clearly not.

"We have to get away from the boat or it's going to pull us under when it goes down!" Lilly's husband yelled above the wind and water.

"No! I can't find my husband!" I cried as I turned to go back into the cabin to find him. Lilly's husband reached out his hand and caught me by the upper arm stopping me before I had a chance to go back in. As soon as he did, a large wave hit us directly and in an instant, Lilly was taken away with it. I watched in horror as she fought to stay on top of the water, before being pulled under.

"Lilly! NOOOO!" He yelled, and this time it was my turn to stop him from jumping straight out into the ocean.

Faintly in the distance I could make out approaching lights. I shivered as the wind bit through my skin and my dress clung to me. Lilly's husband and I anchored ourselves to whatever we could find. The tears I cried could have been enough to replenish any water lost by the ocean that was trying to swallow us.

As the lights got closer, and my body began to give way to exhaustion, the last thing that flashed before my mind's eye was my husband. The man of my dreams, and love of my life. And then darkness consumed me.

Evan

BRIGHT, BLINDING LIGHT assaulted my eyes when I finally managed to open them. Immediately, I closed my eyes, fighting the stinging pain against the base of my skull.

"Welcome back Dr. Taylor," a soft voice said and I risked a peek through my lids once more to find a middle-aged nurse standing next to me. She checked my vitals and adjusted the drip on my IV as I stared at her in confusion.

"Wh—where am I?" I managed to croak out in a gravely voice. A coughing fit soon followed and I fought to catch my breath as my lungs burned deep within my chest. The nurse lifted an oxygen mask and placed it over my nose and mouth until my coughing subsided.

"You are at the Lower Keys Hospital, Doctor. Try to relax and I'll go and let the doctor know you are awake."

Quickly she left the room and I glanced up at the TV. Seeing the wreck footage flash across the screen, I instantly searched for the remote to turn up the volume.

"Searchers are calling Sunday's incident a recovery situation for they believe there are no other survivors. At approximately nine pm Sunday, the dinner boat, The Evening Star, sank about thirty miles offshore when it encountered a swift approaching storm. Thirty-two people were on board at the time. As of right now, only seven have been confirmed alive. Nineteen bodies have been recovered and five are still unaccounted for. Police have not yet released the names of the passengers of the cruiser until the next of kin have been notified. We'll keep you up to date on all the latest developments."

I sat up in my hospital bed as tears stung the backs of my eyes. It was then that I noticed the bandages on my arms and that my left wrist was wrapped in a makeshift cast.

"Dr. Taylor, nice to see you awake," an older, peppered haired doctor said as he entered the room.

"What happened?" I asked as I gripped at my aching head, feeling like jackhammers were going off in my brain every time I spoke.

"The boat you were on was hit by hard waves and soon sank

when the cabin took on too much water. The coast guard got to you before the boat was fully submerged."

He approached me and shone a light in my eyes and I hissed as it assaulted my senses.

"I'm sorry. Your head must be splitting. I'll make sure to put in an order for some pain meds. Your wrist isn't broken, but it is sprained pretty badly and we believe you may have a mild concussion."

"How long was I out?' I asked.

"About eighteen hours. We have given you some antibiotics due to the amount of water you aspirated. We want to be sure that is doesn't turn into pneumonia."

The fogginess began to subside and then reality began to sit in.

"Where's my wife? Is she here too? What room is she in? I need to see her."

"Dr. Taylor, as a physician yourself, you know we cannot let you out of the bed. Someone will be in to speak to you in a moment."

The sullen look on the doctor's face before he turned and left the room made my chest tighten to the point I felt like I couldn't breathe. I heard the faint beeping sound of the monitor increase as my heart rate sped up. I tried to inhale and exhale through my nose, begging my body not to go into a state of panic.

Hope.

That was all I had left. As more images from the incident flashed over and over on the screen and in my mind, the only thing I had left was hope.

Hope that my wife was only a few doors away from me.

Hope that we could move past this and continue living our lives together like we were meant to.

Hope that was shattered as soon as the hospital Chaplain entered my room. He didn't even have to say anything before desperate, earth and soul-shattering sobs tore the very breath from my body.

It can't be…

It can't be…

It can't be…

It can't be…

I don't recall if I were chanting it out loud or to myself. I reached for the small bucket on the table beside my best and lost the contents of my stomach into it. I alternated desperate pleas mixed with dry heaves, the more that it began to sink in.

My wife didn't make it.

The last vision I had was a wave sweeping her away from me. The last bit of color I remember was red. The same color of the dress she wore.

"I let go of her! I fucking let go of her!" I cried over and over.

"There was a woman, Allie, Ellie. I don't remember. She was trying to go back inside to get to her husband. They were seated at our table earlier that evening. I was trying to stop her. It's all my fault! I shouldn't have let go. I shouldn't have let go!"

My body violently trembled and I yanked the IVs out of my arm. Thrashing around until the blanket and sheet covering me let my legs free as I tried to get out of the bed.

"Dr. Taylor, please, please calm down," the Chaplain begged as he came to stand in front to me, but I ignored him. I fought through the searing pain my body was feeling, running on nothing but pure adrenaline and denial.

"No, I have to see my wife. Take me to my wife! Please…please… please," I begged and the Chaplain placed his hands on my shoulders slightly shaking his head from side to side.

My head collapsed in my arms and I couldn't stop the tears. I couldn't get past the gaping hole that was now in my heart. My puzzle was missing its most important piece. The one piece that put my entire life together.

My soul was lost without her.

"Lilly..." I cried over and over.

"I'm so sorry, Evan. I'm so sorry," was all the Chaplain could say to comfort me.

Ellie

I LAY ON MY SIDE in the fetal position staring out of the window of my hospital room. I didn't want to move, didn't want to breathe, because it meant that I felt something. I didn't want to feel. I didn't deserve to have oxygen enter my lungs. I didn't want to be here alive on earth when *he* wasn't.

"Mrs. Morris, I'm so sorry, but Jeremy didn't survive the accident," was all I could repeat over and over in my mind. I watched the love of my life torn from me. Ripped away by the very same force of nature that had brought us together. Honeymoons were supposed to be spent enjoying your spouse and celebrating the life you were going to build together, not curled up in a sterile hospital room mourning their death and feeling like every bit of your soul had been sucked right out of you.

Jeremy never would have taken me on that boat if it weren't something he knew I would love. It was all my fault. My stupidity for being a romantic and his stupidity for giving into it.

I felt numb, vacant and empty, as if my very own life had been stripped right from me. I wish it had been. I wish it were me who would have died, that way I didn't have to try and deal with the massive hole in my chest. The desperate need to see his face and hear his voice. I didn't know how to be me without him. He was my soul mate. My key that only had one lock it would fit.

"Mrs. Morris?" The soft sound of the nurse broke through my anguish. I still didn't move, didn't turn to face her or answer.

"Is there anything I can get you? Some food or something to drink?" She asked softly as she placed a gentle hand on my shoulder. I knew if I spoke I would break. Shatter just like the glass did on the boat, yet no one would be there to help me put the pieces back together. So instead, I just lay there staring at the window, allowing the sunlight to burn through my retinas. Praying that it would rid me of my vision so that I didn't have to constantly see the flashes of the incident played over and over before me.

"Well, if you need anything. Just press that red button on the remote and I'll be right in," she offered sweetly before retreating and shutting the door softly.

What I needed was Jeremy. I needed his arms around me telling me everything was going to be okay. I needed him to be okay so that I knew I could go on and be able to function.

Because without him, I might as well be dead too.

Chapter Four

DENIAL

Ellie

RAIN PELTED DOWN on me, matching my mood as I stood there at the cemetery, my heels digging into the soft ground of the Earth. I vaguely listened as the preacher went on about how wonderful of a man Jeremy was, and how he would be missed by so many. They had no clue. Save for his parents, no one knew the real Jeremy like I did. Not only was he adorably handsome, but also had one of the biggest hearts of anyone I knew. He was the type who would give you the shirt off his back if he knew someone was going without. I was eerily calm as the pallbearers had carried his casket out of the church earlier and placed it in the back of a hearse.

It didn't matter. His body wasn't inside anyway.

Jeremy's body was never recovered. It was reported that he was lost at sea and that any hope of recovery was impossible. Swallowed up by the ocean like the raging bitch she was. I hated her. Something so beautiful, yet so ugly as to rip my very life away from me. I wanted to vomit every time I tasted salt. I wanted to scream every time someone asked me if I wanted a glass of water.

"Jeremy Morris was one of the kindest men you'd ever meet. His life was tragically taken far too soon, but God says that he has plans for us both on Earth and in Heaven. The Lord saw it fit that Jeremy's purpose on this Earth was done and called him to be with Him and his angels in the kingdom of Heaven," the preacher said.

"Yea though I walk through valley of the shadow of death…" he prayed.

Shadows.

Death.

Darkness.

That was all I could feel.

One by one, people walked by the empty casket offering me condolences. I had no doubt they were all heartfelt, yet they didn't mean shit. How could someone comfort you when the person you loved more than your own life was laying at the bottom of the ocean while you were alive and breathing?

It felt like ages before everyone finally made his or her rounds and I was left standing next to an empty box that matched the empty hole inside of me.

Only a week ago, we stood in the same little church, in the same little North Carolina town as we vowed to spend the rest of our lives together. Little did we know, that I would be standing in that same church saying goodbye to that same life. Goodbye to my very best friend.

"Come on, baby, I'll drive you home," I heard my father say as he came and took the umbrella I was haphazardly holding over my head from my hands.

Home. I hadn't been there since I arrived back in North Carolina when I was released from the hospital. My mom and dad both flew to Florida to help me bring both my stuff, and my dead husband's things, back home. I knew they were afraid of what my mental state would be when they first saw me. Especially when I kept talking about Jeremy like he would miraculously appear any second.

I found myself listening to old voicemails on my phone so that I could hear his voice. I had already had to recharge my cell several times that day because I would sit and listen to them over and over until the battery would die.

Die just like him.

The charge of his life was gone and with it, my rapidly diminishing energy and will to continue in this life without him.

My father led me by the elbow as we walked to his car. I struggled to fight back the tears as I relived the memory of him escorting me down the aisle in my beautiful wedding dress. The way my eyes lit up when I saw Jeremy standing at the altar waiting for me. I wanted to sprint to him, rather than walk slowly. He was the one thing in my life I was certain of.

I sat stoically in the passenger seat of my father's car as we drove away from the cemetery towards my home. *The home I was supposed to be sharing with my husband.* I thought to myself. The rain flowed like ribbons against the window before vanishing through the wind as the car sped down the road.

"Ellie, baby. Talk to me," my dad's soft voice broke through my thoughts. I felt his hand cover mine and I had to take a deep breath to keep from unraveling like worn strings hanging on by the last thread.

"What do you want me to say, Daddy?"

"I don't know. I guess I just need reassurance that you are okay. I wish there were a way I could take the pain you are feeling away from you. I'd gladly take every bit of it for myself if I knew you wouldn't have to go through this."

Hot tears began to flow down my cheeks but I didn't reach up to wipe them. I let them fall freely, landing in my lap and absorbing into my black dress.

"I know you have a long journey ahead of you, sweetheart. Your mother and I want you to know that whatever you need, we are here. You don't have to go through this alone. We loved Jeremy like our own son. He was a part of you, so he was a part of us."

"Is a part of me, Daddy. He *is* a part of me."

I heard him take a deep breath, but the tremble in it told me he was choked up without me even having to turn and face him.

"Your mom and I think that you should come stay with us for a while. We want to be able to support you and be there to help you in any way we can. Mom doesn't want you sitting in that big house alone."

"I'll be okay. There are so many wedding presents to go through. Thank you cards to send. I need to sort through Jeremy's things and talk with his parents about what I need to do with it all."

He patted my knee like he had ever since I was a child and he was trying to offer courage or reinforcement.

"Just know we are here."

"I know. Thank you."

⁓

I SAT IN THE MIDDLE of the floor staring at all the gifts that surrounded me. His and her towels. His and her coffee cups. His and her customized pillow cases.

His and her…

His and her…

I picked up one of the mugs and threw it at the wall and watched it shatter as it fell to the floor.

There was no 'his and her' anymore.

Only her.

Alone.

Desolate.

Broken.

My chest felt hollow but ached with enough force that I nearly couldn't breathe. Gut wrenching sobs and a flood of tears involuntarily poured out of me as I sat with my arms crossed over me and rocked back and forth.

How could this have happened? How could fate be so cruel as to give me the love of my life only to have him taken from me in the blink of an eye?

I needed to hear his voice. I reached for my phone and pulled up the voicemails again. His low laughter rang in my ears and it was like a soothing balm on my burned soul. The phone fell to the floor after it had once again gone dead. I was fearful that if I didn't listen to his voice, that I would forget the way it sounded.

He can't really be gone.

There was no telling how long I had sat there staring into the empty space of my living room. My body had long gone stiff from sitting on the hardwood floor, yet I welcomed the pain. Any pain, in order to help mask the pain I was feeling in my heart.

I shook my head. It felt so wrong for me to be sitting in our home without him. If felt like abandonment for me to be hundreds of miles away while my husband was in Florida. I felt so disconnected from him.

I got up from the floor and ran up to my room and began throwing things haphazardly into a bag. I didn't care what I was bringing with me. All I needed were a few changes of clothes and some toiletries. For the first time since the incident I felt like I was thinking clearly. There was no way I could stay here.

I ran into the closet and brought down an old box from the top shelf. Opening it, I reached in to retrieve the cash and emergency credit cards that Jeremy and I had stashed away for a rainy day. That coupled with the savings in the bank should be enough for me to get by for a while.

Grabbing the bag and my purse, I belted down the stairs and into the garage to the car. I didn't know what I was doing here to begin with. I never should have left.

I shouldn't have left him.

I needed to go to where my husband was.

Evan

"EVAN, CAN I SEE you in my office, please?" My chief of staff, Robert, asked as he passed me in the hall. I handed the clipboard I was holding to the nurse standing next to me and told her to go in and check on the patient and that I would be right back.

I knocked on the door to Robert's office before stepping in.

"You wanted to see me?"

"Yes. Please close the door and have a seat Dr. Taylor," he said gesturing towards the chair in front of his desk.

He waited until I was seated in the chair with his hands clasped together in front of him on the desk.

"Evan, what are you doing here?" He asked as he looked me right in the eye.

"What do you mean? I was doing rounds. Several of my patients are still recovering from operations and I had a few pre-op meetings with parents—"

"I didn't mean what you were doing while you are here, Evan. *Why* are you here?"

I had no answer to give him. I needed the distraction? I wanted to lose myself in paperwork and visits with patients. Anything to take my mind off—

"For Christ's sake, Evan. You just lost your wife. This hospital is the last place you should be."

Heat flooded my veins as anger began to form within me.

"I'm fine, Robert. I just need to stay busy that's all. I just need to try and go on. The more idle I am, the more I get lost inside my own head and I just can't do that right now."

He looked down at his hands before looking back up at me. When I saw his eyes next, they held sympathy, just like everyone else who I had to talk to since arriving back at the hospital.

"I understand that. I really do. But you gave orders for the wrong med dosage. Luckily one of the nurses caught the mistake before it was administered."

"That was an oversight on my part. I'm thankful our nurses are trained to double check things before administering the medicines." I replied.

"Yes, I too am thankful for that, but it could have been a fatal mistake. Luckily it wasn't. Your head isn't here no matter how hard you try to tell yourself it is. You cannot tell me you can work on patients when you can't even take care of yourself."

"I'm taking care of myself just fine." I bit out through a clenched jaw.

"Evan. You're unshaven, your eyes look dark and clouded like you haven't slept in days. I know coffee and adrenaline are the only things keeping you going right now, but if you are going to be here, I need you at one-hundred percent."

"So what are you saying?"

"I've spoken to the board. We think it is in your best interest to take a sabbatical. Take time to heal and to mourn the loss of Lilly. We all loved her dearly, Evan, so it pains us to see you having to go through this. She was a very special woman."

I fought against the tears threatening to form. I needed this hospital. It was the only place I felt safe from my thoughts. It was the only place I could go to and not think about my dead wife every second of the day. It kept me busy and busy is what I needed.

"How long?" I barked out.

"Indefinitely. Until we see that you are fit to return. You will be put on paid hospital administration leave until further notice."

"You've got to be shitting me?' I rose to my feet violently, sending the chair behind me crashing into the wall.

"Evan, you can't keep walking around acting like nothing happened. You need time to grieve. Time to process. Maybe even get some counseling…"

"Fuck you and your counseling I know what I need and it isn't some goddamned quack telling me how I should feel!"

"We only have your best interests at heart, Evan. Please try to understand that. You are in denial, and until you can come to terms with the fact that she isn't coming back, you won't be able to practice at this hospital. I'm truly very sorry for your loss."

He walked over and placed his hand on my shoulder, but I brushed him off, turning to yank open the door. The force of my actions caused the door to slam harshly against the wall, but I ignored it as I stormed out of his office, pulling my nametag off from around my neck in the process.

Turning around I tossed it to him.

"Lilly would call you a dick for doing this. You all have no right to tell me how I should mourn my wife. She's still here with me. I can feel it."

Then I turned and stormed out of the hospital.

Ellie

"ELLISON MICHELLE BURNETTE! What is Christ's name are you doing?" My mother's voice yelled through my phone as I stuffed my bag in the overhead compartment and took my seat next to an elderly woman.

"I've been calling you for hours, so when you didn't answer, I sent your father over to check on you. Now you tell me you are on an airplane?"

She squeaked into the phone, and I had to hold it away from my ear to diminish the piercing sound.

"Morris, Momma. My last name is Morris. And it's fine. I just need to go back."

She sighed on the other end of the phone and I could tell she was thinking about what to say next. Ever since Jeremy's death, she had been walking on eggshells around me, careful that if she made a wrong step, I would break.

"Sweetheart, I don't see what going back to Florida will do to help you. You need to be here at home where your family and friends can be here to support you."

To me, that was the last thing I wanted. To be surrounded by friends and family was like a constant reminder of who wasn't there in my life. Jeremy's death had not only left a vacancy in my heart, but in my ability to be around others that I loved.

"But momma, Jeremy is in Florida. I need to go to him. I need to be where I can feel close to him."

"Honey. Please come home. Get off the plane and come talk to us. We can get you help. We can find some way to help you cope with this. Baby..." she paused and I knew she was struggling with what came out of her mouth next.

"Jeremy isn't in Florida. He's gone, baby. I'm so sorry. I know you are still in denial about the whole thing. We all are. I am worried about you."

I hung up on my mother as the flight attendant instructed us to fasten our belts. I didn't want to hear her talk about Jeremy anymore. I knew where he was. Florida was the last place we were together. It was the last place we made love, kissed, and told each other how much we loved one another. I needed to be able to feel that again. I needed to feel the connection to him again. I hated waking up and feeling like one of my limbs was cut off. It made me feel awkward, like I had a limp because my heart and body felt broken without him.

"Going to spend some time in paradise?" The older woman next to me asked just as the plane ascended into the air. Her smile was warm, the tone of her voice soothing, and for a while it was a great distraction to talk to her.

She spoke about going to see her grandkids and spending a few weeks with her newborn grandson.

A different pang of hurt ripped through my chest when the woman spoke about the baby. Jeremy and I always talked about having children. He was an only child, so he wanted to have several. He told me many times about how he wished he had siblings growing up and that he wanted his children to have them.

Now, we'll never have kids. I'll never have the joy of both of our hearts and love coming together to produce something as precious as a child.

"What is in Florida that you are going for?" The old lady asked, breaking through my painful daydream.

I smiled as sweetly as I could so that she couldn't see just how empty I was feeling.

"I'm going to see my husband."

Chapter Five

ANGER

Ellie

THE SAND STUNG the soles of my feet as I paced back and forth on the beach, watching the ocean, something that looked so beautiful, yet held an ugly soul, crash upon the land. The sun was bright, shining on the tiny crystal pieces of sand making it appear to glow. It was something that enticed vacationers, the beautiful contrast of the cerulean blue ocean and the white sand, yet I hated it.

They always say that beauty comes from pain, but there was nothing beautiful about the pain I was feeling. The earth could swallow me whole, scalpels could mar my flesh, disease could overwhelm my body, breaking it down, and it would be less painful than the desperate ache I constantly felt after losing the love of my life.

I hated the sound of laughter, making it feel like an ear piercing squeal that broke through and taunted my subconscious, reminding me of what I lost. My blood boiled. My anger was aimed at inanimate objects, complete strangers, and even my own friends and family. How dare they be happy? How could they say they knew what I was going through when I was the one going through it? I hated the coast guards for not being able to find him. I hated the boat Captain for not recognizing that the storm was so close, and I was even angry with Jeremy for leaving me.

"Will you marry me?" I heard just a few feet from me and then turned in the direction of the voice. A man, probably no older than I was, knelt on one knee holding out what appeared to be a ring box, while the girl in front of him covered her mouth with her hands like she was in shock. I had to bite back the bile that threatened to rise as I witnessed the proposal. The woman nodding her head frantically and the man then standing to scoop her in his arms and kiss her passionately. Needing to get away, I quickened my pace to the point I was almost in a sprint and my legs burned from running in the sand.

Slowing my pace, I bent over to catch my breath, hands on my knees as sweat dripped off the end of my nose. Sinking to the sand, I dropped to my knees as pain tore through me. I hated that I felt so angry. I hated that I hated Jeremy for leaving me. I felt abandoned, lonely, like there wasn't a soul on this planet that knew the torment I experienced everyday.

I crawled on my hands and knees over to the beach edge. Sitting down where the water slid up the sand, yet not touching me, I looked to the horizon trying to find some clarity, and reached out my hand to touch the water as it appeared right in front of me. It felt like it stung my skin and I jerked my hand back. I have never been so afraid of something in my life. Baths were no longer a question and on the occasion when I did feel like bathing, it was always a quick shower. Water was now my enemy. It was something that gave you life. Hell, the body was made up of eighty percent of it, but it was also a killer. A sick, sadistic and twisted murderer that was unrelenting when it wanted something.

"Hello, Miss," a young man said as he appeared at my side. Sunglasses hid his eyes and a ball cap shaded most of his face from me as I glanced up and the sun shined in my eyes.

"Sol-Mate Rentals is having a special on Sea-Doo rentals and sailboat lessons if you are interested."

He reached into a backpack that was strapped across his stupidly muscled, bare chest, and handed me a bright orange flyer that advertised their deals.

"Uh, thank you," I said meekly, accepting the flyer from him. He stared at me for a really uncomfortably long period of time as I pretended to be interested in the sales on the piece of paper.

"Are you okay, Miss?" He asked as he shifted from foot to foot.

"Mrs."

"Huh?"

"Mrs. I'm a Mrs. Not a Miss," I scolded him. He didn't deserve to be on the receiving end of my anger, but nothing and no one was immune to my hate of the world at the moment. There was tightness in my eyes and I felt my face redden from the sun.

"I'm sorry, I was just trying to be polite."

"Well, the answer to your question…" I paused gesturing for his name.

"Sebastian, but my friends call me Baz."

"Well, Sebastian, no. I am not all right. See that out there?" I pointed directly in front of me.

"The ocean?" He asked as he pulled off his sunglasses and revealed whiter skin around his eyes that hinted that he did this job every day.

"Yep," I replied sarcastically. "That is why I'm not okay."

"Can't swim? There are some awesome instructors I know over at Surf Shack, they would be more than happy to help…"

"I know how to swim," I interrupted him. "The ocean killed my husband. Ripped him right away from me without relenting. It was our honeymoon. He wasn't supposed to die."

I looked away from the guy, not wanting him to see the tears in my eyes or the sadness on my face. I didn't want to be sad. I wanted to be angry. Anger was the only thing that I could deal with. Anger is what kept me from thinking about Jeremy's death being my entire fault. If I could put the blame on someone or something else, then maybe I wouldn't hurt so badly. Anger I was good at.

"I—I'm sorry, I didn't…"

"Know? How could you? You don't know me. You didn't know the ocean was Satan in beautiful disguise. You see it for how fun it is or how beautiful it is. I see it for what it really is."

"They don't teach you how to deal with situations like this in orientation," he sighed. If I felt any kind of amusement, I would have laughed, but my smiles and laughter all died the day Jeremy did.

"Just go. Leave me alone," I insisted. Then added, "Thank you for the flyer." He hesitated only briefly then went about his way down the beach talking to other patrons.

When he was out a distance, I looked down to the flyer withering away in my hands from the spray of the ocean. Suddenly a brilliant, yet terrifying idea came to me and I jumped up from the sand, not bothering to brush it off my legs as I began walking down the beach with determination.

Evan

FUCK THE DAMN hospital. Fuck the administration. Fuck everyone and everything I thought as I reached down and threw a seashell out into the ocean. The beach was crowded like it normally always was, but today I wished that there wasn't anyone there so that I could be left to wallow in my own anger and self pity. I felt irritable. I didn't want to listen to anyone or anything. My mind constantly jumped to conclusions and I had a hard time separating what was fantasy and what was real.

Fantasy would have been Lilly holding my hand as we walked along the beach. Fantasy would be us going to our very first doctor's appointment and getting to hear my baby's heartbeat for the first time. Reality was that Lilly was dead, and with her the life of our unborn child. I had been so lost inside of myself since I watched the angry waves sweep my wife off to sea, that I didn't recollect the fact that not only had I lost my wife, but I had also lost my child. An innocent that didn't deserve to have its life ripped away from it before it even began.

How was it even possible to love someone that you had never even met, so much? My muscles jumped under my skin and I begged for any kind of emotional release. Feeling trapped inside the darkest place I've ever been, I was terrified that I may never come up for air again.

Anxiety began to take over me and I could feel my breathing start to escalate. I've never had a panic attack in my life, but I felt like I could have been on the verge of one from having to witness all of the happy couples and families on the beach. I knew it was the last place I needed to come to, but Lilly and I had met on the beach when I was still in medical school. It was the place we always came to when we felt like we needed to re-connect. It held nothing but wonderful memories for both of us, and now it held the darkest memory of my life.

I continued to walk up the beach to get away from the crowd. Walking past some marinas where beautiful large sailboats were waiting as their masts flapped in the wind. A beautiful memory came to mind of the first time that Lilly and I went sailing.

"You look pretty cute in that life jacket, Sailor," Lilly said to me as she sauntered over in her white bikini that accented each one of her beautiful curves. Watching her approach as the sun shone from behind her, casting her in an angelic halo of light, she was the most gorgeous thing I had ever seen. Her long, dark hair was loose as it danced around her face from the wind and sent the tiniest of hints of her floral shampoo into the air. I inhaled deeply, getting a mixture of sea, sand, and air with her sweet scent and quickly closed the distance between us.

"Looking good yourself, wench," I teased as I wrapped her in my arms and pressed a soft kiss to her lips.

"It's so beautiful out here, Evan. Thank you for bringing me."

"It is very beautiful out here, but it is nothing compared to you."

"Now you're just being cheesy," she laughed and it was the most beautiful sound.

"Cheesy or not, it's true."

"Well, you aren't such an ugly duckling yourself."

I smiled and leaned my forehead against hers. I was nervous. I felt restless and my breathing began coming in quicker pants. I could feel my hands go clammy and I hoped she couldn't feel them sweat as I held onto her.

She made me feel things no other person had ever felt. There were different kinds of love. The kind of love you felt when you genuinely cared for someone and their well-being. The warm feeling you got based upon knowing and accepting someone. The kind of maternal/paternal love between a child and its parents. There was infatuation, a feeling of love toward someone mainly based off fantasy or idealization.

There was also puppy love. The kind of love that was new in a relationship. A child-like, innocent and temporary crush for someone you don't know that well. There was romantic love, an abiding love for someone whom you feel attraction, passion, caring and respect.

Then, there was unconditional love. A type of caring and affection so strong, that you felt it constantly.

Unconditional love. That is what I felt for Lilly. She was my soul mate. Someone that I felt like I had spent several lifetimes with before. We just clicked like that. We were two separate people made better by being together.

"Lilly," I breathed as I removed one hand from her and raked it through the side of my windblown hair.

"What's wrong, Evan?" She asked, concern marring her beautiful features. I opened my eyes so that I could get lost in hers, the same gorgeous color of the ocean. Her cheeks had

gone pink from the windburn and her hair matted around her shoulders in a beautiful, tangled mess.

"I—I need to tell you something."

"Just tell me. You are kind of scaring me," She breathed as her fingers found their way under my life jacket to grip the shirt on my back.

"I love you."

She looked at me puzzled, a serious and nearly deadpan look on her face before tilting her head back and erupting in full out laughter.

"Oh my God!" She yelled out as she clutched her belly and tears streamed down her cheeks from the giggle fit.

"Okay, not the reaction I was expecting," I said arching my brows at her and wondering if I had made a fatal mistake in our still relatively new relationship.

"I thought you were going to say the hospital was transferring you, or that you were breaking up with me, or hell you had cancer or something." She walked back up to me and shoved me hard in the chest.

"Don't ever do that to me again, you hear me? You're lucky I love you back or I'd kick you in the nuts!"

I smiled a wide, toothy grin. My face was beaming and my heart rate sped up.

"It's not funny, Taylor!" She said faking being mad and folding her arms across her chest, throwing out her hip and tapping her foot.

"That's not while I'm smiling," I said reaching for her and pulling her into me as I crashed my mouth to hers. She relented, all fake anger long gone as we got lost into the

passion of our kiss.

"You love me too?" I asked, needing the reassurance that what I heard her say was true.

"More than anything."

Fucking sailboats. I thought as I was brought out from one of my best memories of Lilly. If my heart weren't hurting already, it would have exploded in my chest. The pain was almost too much to bear. It felt like I was standing away in the distance, a part of the background of my life while everyone else got to live in the foreground. It probably would have hurt less to have a bullet strike me straight in the heart.

I continued to walk along the beach edge with my hands shoved in my pocket, lost in my own thoughts as the tears flowed down my cheeks. I barely had enough energy to put one foot in front of the other, much less lift my hands to wipe them away.

"Hey! What do you think you are doing?" I heard someone yell a few seconds after the rumble of a small outboard motor hit my ears.

"Lady! Lady! Come back!" I saw a young kid yell toward a woman who was on a Sea-Doo quickly speeding out into open waters. She didn't have on a life jacket and looked like she barely hung on to control as the waves pounded against the tiny watercraft.

Jogging over to where the kid stood at the end of the dock yelling at the woman, I kept my eyes locked onto the woman, who when I squinted my eyes looked eerily familiar.

"What's going on?" I asked, out of breath, as I approached the kid.

"That woman. She was asking about the Jet Ski and I was showing them to her. She asked if she could start one and then next thing I know, she was taking off on it."

"She stole it? Why don't you go after her?"

"Dude, if I leave the marina unattended, my boss will have my ass."

"He's probably going to have your ass anyway. Where's a spare life jacket?" I asked as I pulled my white cotton tee over my head and threw it down on the dock.

"Right here, why?"

"That woman is heading out to open waters without a life jacket on a stolen Jet Ski. I'm going after her. She'll get herself killed. Give me the keys to the other craft."

He looked at me as if I had grown two heads and took a few steps away from me.

"I'm not stealing it. Look," I said as I reached into my wallet and produced my medical ID card. "I'm a surgeon in Miami at the University Hospital. You can trust me, but if I don't get out there to her she could die."

Still hesitant, he finally relented and handed me the keys. I jumped onto the Jet Ski he pointed to and cranked it up before speeding off in the direction the woman went.

The waves were increasingly choppier the further I got out and I struggled to hang on as they tried to toss the Jet Ski around like a ragdoll. I was barely hanging on, so for the life of me I didn't see how the woman was still on hers and not already in the water.

God, don't let her fall off. I thought as I opened the throttle and sped faster. The only good thing about the waves was that they seemed to slow her down, allowing me ample time to catch up with her.

"Hey!" I yelled over and over when I was close enough to her, but with the sound of the motor and the water, there was no way she could hear me. Fighting through the seawater spraying in my eyes, I closed more distance just as a huge wave knocked her right off the Jet Ski. Immediately, I killed the engine and dove straight into the water. Adrenaline fueled me as I fought against both the ocean and flashbacks of the night Lilly was taken from me. It was these same waters that took her from me and I was bound and determined to not let this woman suffer the same fate.

My muscles burned and my chest was tight when I finally reached her below the surface. Clasping onto her wrist, I pulled with all my might until we broke the surface and I sucked in air, thankful to get to breathe again. She coughed loudly and water came spewing out of her nose and mouth.

I froze.

Right there in the middle of the ocean as we floated in between the waves. My stomach lurched and I felt like I was going to throw up. My heart had to have skipped a few hundred beats in the span of only a few seconds as I looked at what or should I say who was responsible for me losing Lilly. It was the woman I tried to save the night I let go of her.

"No! Let me go! Let me go! I have to get to him! I have to get to my husband!" She yelled, frantic as she tried to remove herself from my grasp.

"Are you trying to get yourself killed," I asked as I shook her by the shoulders while still trying to tread water.

"I said let go of me you asshole!" She yelled, but I didn't let her go, instead swimming back to where my jet ski was floating in the water.

"If I would have let you go that night then maybe my wife would be here and not you," I yelled back. She went dead in my hands, no longer fighting against me. I turned around to look at her and her gasp of shock should have surprised me. Her already porcelain skin was even whiter as the blood drained from her face. In the distance I could hear sirens but pulled for her to keep swimming until we finally reached the Jet Ski.

"You're…" she said in the faintest of whispers, her voice meek and barely audible.

"Yeah," was all I could say as I struggled to catch my breath. Not only was I winded from swimming back to the Jet Ski, but also I was winded from the sucker punch to the gut when I saw just who it was I was rescuing. A newfound anger bubbled up inside of me. Coming face to face with the reason why my wife was no longer with me was not something I wanted to do now, or in my entire lifetime.

The sirens were right up on us now, sending an ear piercing shrill echoing off of the back of my already throbbing skull.

"This is the coast guard," a voice echoed through a loudspeaker as a large boat approached us.

"Put your hands up on the motor craft where they can be seen."

I did what was said and then was pulled by one of the officers into the boat. Wrapping a towel around both of us, they placed a set of handcuffs on both of our wrists and instructed us to have a seat while they retrieved both of the jet-skis from the water.

Chapter
Six

BARGAINING

Ellie

If only we hadn't gotten on that boat.

If only we would have chosen another location to go on our honeymoon.

If only I could have convinced him to stay in the hotel room and make love to me all night instead of going on that damn boat.

If only…
If only…
If only…

I SAT ON THE HARD BENCH across from several others thinking about all the things that could have happened if Jeremy and I hadn't gone on the dinner cruise that night. I certainly wouldn't be sitting in this jail cell, feeling the eyes of the man who on the very same night, lost his wife.

All because he let her go to stop me from going back inside after

Jeremy.

My stomach felt sick as I hugged it, my shoulders curving in towards my chest and my posture crumbling. Not only was I responsible for the death of my husband, but for another person losing the love of their life too.

I stared down at the floor where my legs shook beneath me uncontrollably. I couldn't bear looking up to see him stare at me. And he was staring at me. I could feel the hatred of his eyes without actually having to see them aimed at me. There was no doubt in my mind that he held me responsible. He was only a Good Samaritan trying to keep me from killing myself and chose to try and save me. And not only did he do it once, but twice.

Why the hell did I take off on that Sea-Do? What purpose would it have achieved? Some would say that I had lost my mind; others would say that I was desperate.

Maybe it was both.

I just felt like if I could only go back out there, I could find him. I could bring his body home with me and maybe I would feel more secure knowing that he was close to me.

If only…

If only…

"I'm sorry," I spoke out into the cell, aimed at no one in particular. I didn't know if I was saying it to myself, to Jeremy, or to the man who was probably wishing it were me dead instead of his lovely wife.

And lovely she was. I had only spoken to her for a couple of hours while on the boat cruise, but she was beautiful, sweet, and his eyes would light up just from watching her.

"You're sorry?" He growled as he stood up, hands still bound in the front from handcuffs. Saltwater had stiffened the clothes I was wearing to the point they were uncomfortably hard, and I shifted in my seat to try and gain relief.

"Was it your thoughts to try and die twice in the matter of a few weeks? What the fuck were you thinking going out there like that?"

I turned my face away from his, not wanting him to see the tears falling down my face.

"I wanted to find my husband."

His pacing stopped and I risked a glance up at him. His face was hard, his hair a mess of golden brown and blond highlights. About a weeks' worth of scruff graced his jaw and his blue eyes seemed as cold as ice.

"You realize your husband is dead."

It couldn't have hurt anymore if he had shoved a knife into my heart.

I hardened my own gaze as I narrowed my eyes at him while my blood heated to astronomical proportions.

"You don't think I know that? At least they found your wife! Jeremy is still out there somewhere." I said nodding my head towards the tiny square on the wall that didn't qualify as a window.

"Oh, and so you thought you could just hijack a Jet Ski and go out there and find him? Smart, real smart, lady."

"My name is Ellie," I growled.

"I don't care who you are, *Ellie*. All I know is you are here when Lilly isn't. Not only did I have to pull you out of the water once, but twice now. Excuse me if my greeting isn't anything more than hostile," he growled back.

"What's going on in here?" A tall uniformed officer spoke loudly as he approached the cell.

"Nothing officer, just trying to break through someone's logic as to why they have a death wish."

"I wasn't trying to kill myself! I was trying to find my husband!" I yelled as the tears flowed freely down my face.

"Her dead husband."

"Fuck you!" I whispered and then collapsed into my own lap as heavy sobs tore through me. My eyes were swollen and I found it difficult to catch my breath.

"Ease up on the woman will ya?" The officer said to him.

"Ease up on her? Have you not seen the news? I'm Evan Taylor. My wife died right along with her husband. She isn't the only one feeling the aftermath of this fucked up shit. I was just trying to help her, yet again. Why the hell did I get arrested?"

"We'll find out why Mr. Taylor."

"Doctor. It's Doctor."

"Noted, Doctor. Just sit tight. I'll see what's going on."

I sat crying as I listened to the man whose name I now remembered to be Evan, talk to the officer. My stomach twisted in knots and I wished I could be anywhere but here.

God, if you could just get me out of here. If you could just take this pain away, I'll do better. If you could just bring Jeremy back to me, I promise to do everything right. I'll volunteer. I'll give to the poor. I'll go to church more often.

The thoughts circulated through me as I thought of every excuse I could to bargain with God. I had so many *if only's, I wills,* and *if you would justs* that God himself was probably tired of hearing me.

I felt someone come and sit next to me and I didn't bother looking over to see who it was. I kept my face turned, my focus trained on the tiny square that let the only piece of natural light into the dark, dank jail cell.

"Look, I'm sorry. I know you are hurting just as much as I am and I shouldn't take it out on you. I'm still so angry over the whole thing. You don't deserve my wrath. If it were Lilly that was stuck in the cabin of that boat, I would have tried to go back in too."

I was shocked to hear his apology and it only made me cry even harder.

It felt like hours had passed, both of us sitting next to each other not speaking, not looking at one another, but only existing in the same space. It hurt to breath the same air as him, to feel responsible for two lives. I didn't want him to hate me, but I didn't blame him that he did.

"Ellison Morris and Evan Taylor?" A younger female officer said as she approached the gate.

"Yes?" We both said in unison.

"The court is ready for you now. Please follow me," she said as she opened the cell and waited for both of us to pass.

"I thought it was usually a couple of days before we would have a hearing. Our lawyers haven't even arrived."

"Your lawyer, Doctor Taylor, has arrived. He is waiting in the courtroom for you. Mrs. Morris has chosen to represent herself."

"You what?" Evan turned to ask me as we walked down a large white hallway illuminated in old yellow fluorescent lighting.

"Paralegal," was all I said as we followed the officer down several more hallways.

"That doesn't make you a lawyer," he scolded.

"No, but I know enough about the process to know what I am doing."

"What are you going to do? Claim insanity?"

I guess I could claim insanity. A woman who only days after

losing the love of her life, now lost all cognitive thoughts and went off into a fit of madness as she grieved her dead husband.

I didn't reply as we walked down several more corridors before finally reaching the entrance to the courthouse. Even though all of our possessions had been taken from us, including the wedding rings we still wore, we were patted down again before we stepped inside. People were huddled in groups no doubt discussing their options with their lawyers. The lady officer guided Evan toward his lawyer who reached out to shake his handcuffed hands.

"Wait here for instructions," the officer said to me and I nodded as I sat on a bench while she sat behind me. Several minutes, could have been ten or even twenty, went by and I sat picking at my cuticles wondering what the hell I was going to do to get out of this mess.

"All rise for the honorable Judge Lucas," the bailiff announced to the audience and we all stood up while an old man with pepper grey hair took the bench in his dark robe. Banging the mallet against the bench, he called the court to order.

Several cases were called before us. Most of them were young kids caught shoplifting or traffic violations. Evan sat across the aisle from me secretly whispering to his lawyer, every once in a while looking my direction out of the corner of his eye.

"Dr. Evan Taylor," the judge said as he shuffled through some papers in front of him. Evan and his lawyer stood up and made their way to stand in front of the judge.

"Afternoon, Dr. Taylor," the judge said, addressing Evan. "What is a good outstanding citizen like yourself doing in my courtroom accused of felony theft?" He asked, raising his eyebrows expectantly at Evan. Meanwhile, I sat back and watched the whole interaction, trying to plan out what it was I was going to say. Evan probably had it half in his mind to accuse me of everything, which, technically, was true. I was the one who stole the Jet Ski. I was the one who drove out into the middle of the ocean like a woman possessed. All he did was try to save me.

"Your honor, if I may, my client Dr. Taylor, was just trying to prevent Miss Morris from potentially killing herself. He didn't steal the other jet ski, only borrowed it because the employee refused to leave the business in order to retrieve the one stolen."

Mrs. I am a Goddamned Mrs.! I thought to myself. I wanted to leap up from the bench and proclaim that I was still married even though my husband was no longer with me, instead, I chose to keep quiet in order to not get myself into anymore trouble than I was already in.

"Miss Morris, approach the bench please," the Judge said, looking down at me over the top of his thick-framed glasses. Tentatively, I stood up and scooted myself out of the narrowly placed bench and made my way to stand before him.

"Mrs. Your honor," I spoke quietly.

"Beg your pardon?" He asked raising his caterpillar like brows at me. I swallowed hard past the lump in my throat and cleared it before speaking again.

"I am Mrs. Morris, not Miss, Sir."

"Noted Mrs. Morris. Now, care to tell me what happened today?"

Taking a deep breath, I decided to stick with the words I had been practicing over and over in my mind as I had been sitting in the courtroom.

"I wasn't thinking, your honor. See—" I said pausing to take another breath, this time shaky.

"A little over a week ago I was on this very beach celebrating my honeymoon with my husband. He surprised me with this wonderful dinner cruise out on the ocean at sunset."

I paused again, feeling the tears begin to sting my eyes. As much as I have cried, I was surprised that I even had any remaining. Eventually your tear ducts would just give up and dry up, right? I couldn't imagine going on like this anymore.

"You were a victim of the boat accident," he stated rather than questioned. Realization dawned on him as he looked to Evan and then back to me.

"Both of you."

I only nodded and Evan replied with a desolate, "Yes, sir," as the first hot tear trickled down my cheek.

"Please continue, Mrs. Morris."

"Not all of the, um, bodies were recovered from the boat. My husband's was one of them."

I could hear whispers in the courtroom and the judge had to ask everyone to remain quiet.

"I've very sorry for your loss, Mrs. Morris, and yours as well Dr. Taylor, but stealing private property is a felony offense, you know that right?" The judge reprimanded.

Again I nodded my head.

God please. Please let the judge have a heart. Please. I'll do anything. I'll try to adjust to this better.

"I can't imagine what you're both going through. Losing a loved one, especially a spouse as young as yours, has to be incredibly difficult. But, that doesn't give you privilege to think you can go above and beyond the law."

More tears followed and this time, I wiped them by lifting my handcuffed clad hands to my face.

The judged looked down at his paperwork, then removed his glasses and rubbed at his tired looking eyes.

"I'm really struggling with what the right thing to do here would be. I know that your actions were based on the grief you are both feeling right now. The pain has to be unbearable and quite frankly, if it were me, I probably would feel the same way."

Placing his glasses back on the bridge of his nose and looked to both Evan and me. My eyes felt like sandpaper and sweat made my shirt cling to my back and my chin quivered as I tried to gain control over my emotions.

"This is what I'm going to propose. If the facility in which the jet skis were unlawfully taken agrees, all charges pending against you, Dr. Taylor and Mrs. Morris, will be dropped upon the completion of grief counseling."

I looked up at him in surprise, shock apparently written on my features.

"After the loss of a loved one, we experience a wide variety of feelings and emotions. The ever-changing emotions we experience with grief can catch us off guard, causing us to act out of character, like in your case, Mrs. Morris. It can also cause you to act differently than your typical personality or demeanor."

Pausing to look at both of us, he clasped his hands together and continued.

"You need a support system to help you work through your grief. While family and friends are vital, unless they have experienced the personal loss that you both have experienced, they most likely don't fully get what you are going through. Grief support groups will offer you companionship and understanding from others who have experienced a similar loss, and are experiencing the similar challenges. Is this something you two are willing to do? I think it would be beneficial to you both to go through this together seeing as how you both suffered the same tragedy."

I nodded, willing to agree to anything in order to not have a felony on my record from my own stupidity. I had dragged Evan into this situation and would also do anything I could to help him get out of it.

"Yes, your honor," Evan replied as he looked towards the floor.

"Good. Like I said I think this will truly help you. Again I am sorry for your loss. Information will be sent to you in the next few days about dates and times of the meetings. Case dismissed."

The female officer approached both Evan and I and removed our handcuffs before she led us back to the jail to retrieve our belongings. I was thankful to the kid at the marina who had held onto my purse when I took off on the Jet Ski. I owed him a huge apology and prayed that I didn't get him fired and planned to try to talk to the owner of the business as soon as I could.

A man behind a glass window handed me a manila envelope that contained all my belongings. The first thing I did was take out my wedding rings and slip them back onto my finger before I did anything else. I had felt naked without them. Evan retrieved his things and turned around and walked out of the building without saying one word to me.

After I retrieved everything and placed it back into my purse, I walked out of the jail, the harsh sunlight hitting me in the eyes as I did. I was desperate for a shower, my skin being dry from the salt that clung to it from the ocean. Physically and emotionally I was drained, wanting nothing more than to crawl into bed and sleep for a good solid week.

Maybe if I woke up, this would all be a dream.

Shit.

Where was I going to go? I hadn't really thought about where I was going to go or stay when I'd hopped on the plane back to the Keys. I had plenty of cash and credit cards to get me buy for a while, but I needed to find a place to stay, seeing as how I would have to stay in the Keys longer than I expected.

How long had I intended to stay originally? I wasn't sure.

"Hey."

Stunned, I turned around to see Evan sitting on a bench just outside the door.

"I just called a cab. They will be here in a few minutes. Where are you headed? We can share so you don't have to call one too."

I stood there, lifting my hands to my face to try and shield my eyes from the sun.

"I'm not sure. I kind of came back on a whim. I don't live here. Not even close," I laughed sarcastically.

"Where are you from?" He asked as he looked up at me and squinted one of his eyes.

"North Carolina, about an hour away from Wilmington," I replied as I shifted from foot to foot. His sudden shift in mood from angry to being nice had me thrown for a bit of a loop. Don't get me wrong, I was much more receptive to the nicer side, but it was still awkward between us considering the circumstances.

"Do you ever look back on that day and ask 'what if'?" He inhaled before continuing, "Lilly wanted to stay in bed. She begged me to stay in the hotel so that we could just be together and alone. I wanted to go on that damn dinner cruise. I was the one that convinced her to get up. If only I had listened to her."

I walked over to him and sat down on the bench beside him, dropping my purse heavily to the ground between my legs.

"I have asked myself about a thousand *what ifs* over the last few days. There are so many things I wish I had done differently. Mainly, I wish you wouldn't have stopped me from going back into the cab of the boat."

He turned to me, looking at my face in profile as I stared out into the road as cars passed us by. The palm trees swayed with the gentle breeze and seagulls could be seen in the distance fighting each other for something on the ground.

"But then you could have died." I turned to look at him.

"Exactly."

He didn't say anything for a few moments, as we sat stoically staring at each other. He was a very attractive man. His hair was lighter than Jeremy's, more like a golden dark blond with small lighter blond highlights. His shoulders were much broader than Jeremy's and he looked like he exercised regularly, the shirt he wore molded to perfectly sculpted muscles. His nose was shorter than Jeremy's and his jaw more broad. Jeremy had a very boy-ish handsome quality to him, more tall than built. More preppy than rugged. Evan was more like the boy scout type. Not afraid to get his hands dirty. Someone who was probably really big into sports or fitness. Hell, he was a doctor, so he indeed seemed to take his health seriously.

"Why would you say that? We're both lucky to be alive, even though it doesn't seem that way," his face fell even more.

"Because, if I had died along with Jeremy, this wouldn't hurt so much. Existing in a world where he doesn't. Living day after day knowing that my soul mate, the one person who got me, understood me, and loved me unconditionally, would never be a part of my life anymore."

I bit my lip trying to hold back the tears. I watched Evan's hands as he flexed and relaxed them in an even pattern, signaling his own struggle to gain control.

"Then maybe your wife would still be alive, too." I added quietly. He stilled, the sound of his breaths increasing and the audible swallow he made before he responded to my statement.

"I never should have said that Ellison. I'm sorry. I know my anger towards you was unattractive and messy. It was completely unpredictable and out of character for me to act that way towards you."

"Evan, you let go of Lilly to stop me."

A cab suddenly appeared and honked loudly right in front of us like we weren't even sitting there.

"Does this jerk think we didn't see him or something?" Evan said, his tone lightening the solemn mood from before.

"I have no clue, but we should probably get in before he blows our eardrums out."

"One-Eleven Pearl Street, please," Evan told the driver.

"You aren't staying in a hotel?" I asked quizzically.

"My parents own a timeshare here. They made sure that no one was renting it out these last few weeks because Lilly and I..." he paused and he didn't have to finish out the sentence.

Used it for their honeymoon.

"Where are you going to stay?"

"Um, I'm not sure. I guess I'll have him drop me off at a chain of the hotels and I can find something there to rent out for a while."

"You're probably looking at paying a pretty penny to say on the beach during season."

"Well, I can't exactly go home now, not that I want to," I replied as I stared out of the window while the cab rolled down the street. People walked about, laughing, enjoying their summer in paradise, only this was no longer a place that was considered paradise for me. It was my own personal hell.

I felt Evan shift in the seat beside me, even though he was being friendly, I still felt the enormous amount of animosity that was between us, sitting like a heavy smoke from a fire and intoxicating our lungs with each breath.

"There's a spare room, or rooms rather, at the timeshare. Separate entrance. It used to be my dad's man cave when we vacationed here, but my mom converted it to a mini apartment so they could make more profit renting it out. You are welcome to stay if you wish," he offered, trying to sound nonchalant, but I could still hear the hesitation in his voice.

I turned to look at him a little flabbergasted by his generosity. I looked all around the inside of the cab trying to find answers. His offer was more than generous, and he was right. Staying at a hotel would cost me a fortune and would deplete my finances quickly. There was no telling how long it would take for us to finish the grief counseling.

"That is very nice of you. Are you sure it won't be an issue, being me and all?" I asked as my shoulders caved in and I looked at my hands, fidgeting with them in my lap so that I didn't have to see the rejection on his face.

He reached over and placed a hand on mine, stilling them. Something happened the instant we touched and we both found ourselves jerking our hands away from each other.

What the hell just happened? It felt like he had delivered an electric shock through my body, awareness that I should not have felt overwhelmed me. It also made me want to vomit.

"I meant what I said, Ellie. I'm sorry for what I said at the jail earlier."

"Thank you," I replied in a whisper, still fighting to find my voice after he had touched me. Something deep down told me this was a bad idea. Every fiber of my being was telling me to run in the other direction. But if I had any chance to be able to pick up the pieces that were my new fucked up life, then I needed to learn how to move on without Jeremy. Maybe grief counseling wasn't such a bad idea.

"Thank you, Evan. If it's not too much trouble, I accept your offer."

Chapter Seven

Depression

Evan

IT'S BEEN FIVE DAYS. Five lonely, misery-ridden days that I've sat in this bed, mindlessly flipping through the channels on the TV. My only companions have been the few saltine crackers that I had managed to choke down and the fifth of Jack Daniels I had been nursing, trying to numb my pain.

If I didn't already feel vacant and hollow enough, the fact that I couldn't even cry anymore made me feel like the biggest asshole on the earth. I couldn't even mourn my wife properly. I still fought back and forth with the anger and bargaining with God over what I should do. What I should have done. What I could do.

I hadn't seen or spoken to Ellie after getting out of the cab when we were released from jail. I had no clue if she was doing the very same thing I had done for the last five days.

Absolutely nothing.

I could sit in front of anyone, my peers at work, my friends and pretend to be okay. But in the loneliness of this room, I couldn't hide from myself. I was the one who had to look in the mirror every day. I was the one who had to get up everyday and conjure every ounce of strength I could find in order to be able to even walk to the bathroom.

I felt like I was dying myself. Death was trapped inside my body, eager to find its way outward to consume what little of me there was left.

I looked over at the pamphlet that had arrived in the mail yesterday. The information about the grief counseling stared back at me, and I had read it so many times, I could probably quote it verbatim.

- Trying to ignore your pain or keep it from surfacing will only make it worse in the long run. For real healing it is necessary to face your grief and actively deal with it.
- Grieving is a personal and highly individual experience. How you grieve depends on many factors, including your personality and coping style, your life experience, your faith, and the nature of the loss.
- The grieving process is a roller coaster, full of ups and downs, highs and lows. Like many roller coasters, the ride tends to be rougher in the beginning, the lows may be deeper and longer.

Being a medical doctor, I knew most of these things. I have had the not so wonderful privilege to have to inform loved ones of my patients that their child wouldn't be coming home, or that they only had a matter of weeks or months to live. Never, though, had I understood the enormity of loss they felt until now. I never even got to meet my child. Never even knew he or she existed until Lilly told me on the boat that night. My stomach hardened as nausea threatened to take over. There was a weakness in my muscles and my limbs trembled while a painful tightness formed in the back of my throat.

Yet not a tear fell.

Was I some emotionless bastard who couldn't even shed a tear over my wife and unborn child's death? Was I some cold-hearted son-of-a-bitch that wasn't normal?

I turned up the volume on the TV, needing to hear some other voice besides my own. I had to keep my thoughts from spinning, focusing on the inward pain that consumed me.

Looking over at the clock sitting on the nightstand, I noted that it was barely after eleven in the morning.

But it didn't matter what time it was.

I picked up the shot glass and the nearly empty bottle of Jack, needing something to once again numb me against my reality. Instead, I unscrewed the cap and chugged the remaining amber liquid so fast, it burned the back of my already aching throat. I tossed it haphazardly to the floor as I wiped at my mouth with the back of my hand.

Picking up the pamphlet once more, I re-read all of the information listed. Ellie and I were to report to our first meeting in two days. I wasn't sure if they had called to tell Ellie about the information and thought it best to go downstairs and tell her. This also meant that I needed to venture out from the solace of my withdrawal from the world that I had created inside this bedroom.

Pushing the covers aside, I walked into the bathroom and caught a glimpse of myself in the mirror. My normal bright blue eyes had faded, no longer holding a spark for life as they stared back at me. Dark circles decorated my eyes showing my inability to get a good nights rest. My usually tamed hair was a tangled, oily mess and I had began to start looking like one of the guys on *Duck Dynasty* with how long my beard had gotten.

I reached for my travel kit and removed my hair trimmers and began to trim away the hair on my face, letting the whiskers drop into the porcelain sink below me. My desire to escape the overwhelming sadness that was more potent than anything I have felt. I swear a part of me died the day Lilly and our baby did, but I was still alive. I still had to go on without her and I didn't want to spend the rest of my life feeling this miserable.

Determined to get a grip on myself, I jumped in the shower, not only to clean my body, but also hopefully be able to wash away the demons that have been present and begin something new.

The rest of my life.

Ellie

"HEY, BABY."

A strong voice whispered against my ear sending shivers running down my spine. I felt a warmth flood me, eradicating the frigid and cold flow that had been present in my veins for a while now. Hearing his voice stirred me from out of the depth of hell in which I have been inhabited.

"Hey, yourself," I replied smiling for the first time in what seemed like forever. My mouth felt foreign to the emotion and I could feel the protest in my facial muscles as my lips turned

up.

"*I've missed you,*" *he whispered again in my ear, the warmth of his breath feeling more real than if it were the wind blowing against me.*

"*Jeremy, I've missed you more than you could ever know.*"

"*I'm here now, baby.*"

"*Please, please don't leave me.*" *I began to sob. I tried to open my eyes, feeling the bite as sunlight filtered in. I couldn't see Jeremy, only his silhouette that was surrounded by light, a beautiful, illuminating halo that made him appear angelic.*

"*I've never left you, Ellie. I'll always be a part of you, just as you are me.*"

"*Why did you have to go?*" *I asked struggling to try and sit up, but felt like a weight was holding me down.*

"*There were plans for me, Ellie. Plans that I had no idea of. You have plans too. I need you to live, Ellie. I need you to go on and be happy.*"

"*I can't be happy without you, Jeremy. I'm so lost. So, so, lost. My heart hurts constantly. It hurts to breathe. I don't want to go to sleep, and when I do, I don't want to wake up. Every time I close my eyes, I see you. Then when I wake up you are gone and it hurts all over again.*"

I felt the warmth of his hands as he gently brushed back the hair from my face, yet I still couldn't see him. I wanted to see his face. I wanted those blue eyes staring back at me, to give me some sense of hope that this wasn't another dream.

His hands encompassed both of mine as I felt his body lay next to mine, holding our hands between us. My heart was beating erratically in my chest and my throat tightened as tears began to form.

"I need you to listen, Ellie. You have a purpose. You have meaning. You may not think so, but you do. Before long, my memory won't hurt so much. Your heart will heal and you will be able to feel like you can breathe again. I need you to do that for me. I need you to promise me that you will rise above this. Not let the darkness take over you anymore, baby. It kills me to watch you lie here as if your life is over. You have so much left to live for. I want you to fall in love again. I want you to live joyfully and vivaciously until the day we will be together again."

I shook my head violently from side to side. I couldn't. I can't. I won't.

"I—I can't. I can't do it, Jeremy. My life will never be the same without you. You have left a hole so vacant inside me, nothing will ever be big enough to fill it again."

He kissed my hands as he held them between his, the feel of his lips leaving their mark on my body and a yearning so deep, the cut would never heal.

"You can, and you will, baby. Just know that I will always be your biggest supporter. I'll always be watching over you, but I have to go now."

"No! No! Don't you dare leave me again!" I yelled as I felt his grip on my hands loosen and he got up from the bed. I tried with all my might to get up and go after him, but it felt as if all my limbs were shackled to the frame of the bed. Darkness began to invade the light surrounding him. "Jeremy please! Please don't go. I'll do anything! Please!" I begged over and over. I screamed so loud, I felt my voice *would give out as I began thrashing around in the bed trying to escape the monster holding me down.*

"Live, Ellie," was all I heard him say as his silhouette faded into darkness and I could no longer see him. I was hyperventilating to the point that I felt my breathing could seize at any moment. My chin trembled as angry tears coursed down both sides of my temples to land on the bed beneath me.

"Ellie."

I thrashed harder, determined to break the chains that bound me, to defeat the supernatural force keeping me from my husband.

"Ellie."

I screamed with all my might to the point that I coughed violently as the back of my throat burned with angry force.

"Ellie!"

I shot straight up from the bed, sweat trickling down my forehead. I rubbed at my eyes, feeling the reality of my tears.

"Ellie."

I looked up to see Evan sitting on the bed next to me with worry written all across his face. His brows were furrowed together and he had a gentle hand placed on my leg where it was half covered by the duvet. It was what I couldn't get out from under. It is what had me pinned to the bed as I had tried to reach for Jeremy.

"Are you okay? Can I get you a glass of water?" He asked nervously.

I nodded, not able to find my voice, knowing my vocal chords were strained and swollen from my screams.

It was another dream.

The same dream I've been having nearly every night.

Each night, Jeremy would come to me.

And each night he would leave again.

Evan retreated into the tiny kitchen in the other room and returned with a tall glass of water and what looked like a bottle of ibuprofen.

"Here," he said as he handed them to me and sat back down on the bed. I placed the two tablets on my tongue and washed them down with the cool water, thankful for the relief when the liquid hit the back of my throat.

"Are you okay?" He asked as he accepted the empty glass from me when I had finished it.

"Yeah, I think so," I replied meekly.

"Are you having bad dreams about them too?"

His questions stunned me slightly and I nodded.

"I have them too. Sometimes, they seem so real, that I can't decipher if I'm actually sleeping or awake."

"Yeah, I know what you mean."

I looked at him as a solemn look crossed his face. It was then that I noticed that he had shaved, even showered. I began feeling a little self-conscious as a hand lifted to my greasy, matted hair that was stuck to the side of my head.

"Do you think they'll ever stop?" I asked as I pulled the duvet closer to my chest. I watched his shoulders shrug in what? Defeat?

Hope? Desperation?

"Eventually they have to, don't they? Eventually we will wake up one day and this won't hurt so damn bad, will it?"

I knew he was looking to me for reassurance, but I couldn't give it to him and I definitely couldn't give it to myself.

Suddenly, I became very aware of how close we were sitting on the bed and felt uneasy when our eyes met each other's at the same time. His blue eyes didn't hold as much ice and animosity towards me as they had days ago and he seemed softer today, more defeated. I think as the loss of our spouses fully settled in our soul, there is nothing left for us to do but to slip into the seemingly endless, depressive road that we both had began to travel down. At the same time, I felt more connected with him than I had thought about before. The last few days had given me the realization that not only were we connected because we both lost loved ones that day, but connected by the fact that he was the only other person who truly understood what I was going through.

Because he felt the same thing.

We both knew the deprivation of loss and the overwhelming feeling of anguish and sadness. We both had vacancies within our hearts that nothing would be able to replace or fill. I think the biggest connection we had is that we both understood. Understood that our lives would no longer be the same. Understood that we had to go on living, knowing that our spouses were never coming back. And understood the feelings that we were both simultaneously experiencing.

"I'm sorry that you got sentenced to the counseling with me," I said apologizing for the first time since he had rescued me off the jet ski.

He shrugged again.

"Maybe it will be good for us. Maybe being with others who have experienced the same thing will help us pick up the pieces that your husband and Lilly left behind."

"Jeremy."

He looked at me, his blue eyes questioning.

"His name was Jeremy."

"Jeremy," he tested, letting my husband's name roll off his tongue.

"I didn't get to talk to him much because the old man kept my attention most of the night." His lip turned up in the corner with the faintest of smiles.

"Yeah, Jeremy was occupied by his wife. Lilly and I were both laughing about it. We decided not to rescue you two because we were enjoying just sitting back and watching."

I fidgeted with the duvet that I had let fall back down to my lap.

"You wife was lovely. I only got to chat with her very briefly during dinner, but I could tell she was a very sweet person, and that she loved you very much."

My statement earned a slightly bigger smile than the one before as he absorbed the compliment I gave about his wife.

"Thank you. She was very lovely."

His look turned dark again as if the memory of her was too much to take on. Each flashback sending both him and me reminders that the two people who mattered more than anything in our lives, were now gone.

He looked around the room and then reached into his back pocket and pulled out a purple piece of paper.

"This came from the grief center. We start our group session on

Monday. I didn't know if they had called you or not, so I thought I would come down and let you read this," he said as he handed the pamphlet to me. I accepted the pamphlet from him, our fingers making the slightest contact. The same sharp static surge of awareness hit me just like it had when he placed his hand on my leg in the cab a few days ago. It confused me, deeply. I didn't want to feel *any* kind of awareness at all. The only thing I was fully aware of was the absence of my husband. The torment I felt knowing he was gone forever.

"Thank you. The counselor called me yesterday and informed me, but I'll be sure to read over this," I said gesturing to the paper.

He rose from the bed and began walking towards the door as I sat on the bed staring at the purple rectangle in my hands, the words blurring together to form unintelligible dots, lines and dashes on the page.

He paused at the door, turning around to look at me.

"Have you eaten anything? There hasn't been any food down here for a while. You should have told me, Ellie." His voice was stern, yet leavened with concern as he looked at me with knitted brows.

"It's okay. I haven't had an appetite for much anyway."

"Ellie," his voice a warning. "It's been five days. When is the last time you ate anything?"

I ducked my head, tucking my chin to my chest as my cheeks reddened like a child being scolded. I couldn't meet his eyes as I tried to come up with an excuse to tell him that I've maybe only eaten a handful of things in the last week. Not enough to make me full, yet just enough to keep me from passing out in exhaustion.

"I had some peanut butter crackers not too long ago."

"When?" He asked as he folded his arms across his chest and leant against the doorframe, clearly not leaving until he got a straight answer from me.

"The day after Jeremy's funeral," I admitted.

His expression grew angry, lips flattening into a straight line. The tightness was back in his eyes and his face had reddened slightly.

"Get dressed."

"What?" I asked cocking my head to the side and blinked at him rapidly in disbelief.

"Get dressed. Let's get out of here for a while. I need some air. And you need to eat something. It isn't healthy to go that long without eating."

I stared at him openly, not quite sure how to process his demand or his concern.

"Why do you care, Evan? I'm fine."

His posture stiffened and his muscles turned rigid as he pushed off the doorframe and came to stand in front of me. I leant back against the headboard of the bed trying to create distance between us as he stared down at me.

He reached down and picked up my wrist, pressing his middle finger to my pulse point and held it in his hands for a few seconds. He then flipped my hand back over and looked at my fingernails and then pinched the skin on the top of my hand.

"Ouch," I said in mockery. It didn't really hurt, but he didn't need to know that.

"Your pulse is erratic and your skin has lost elasticity. Both signs of lack of nourishment and dehydration. Just appease me and at least attempt to eat something, Ell. We can go find a place away from the beach so it won't be a... distraction."

By distraction, I knew he was talking about how the sight of the ocean seemed to affect us both. It made me wonder if I would ever truly get over my hatred for something so beautiful, or if I would now fear it for the rest of my life.

"Okay," I conceded as I let out a long, low sigh.

"I'll be upstairs. Just come and get me when you're ready."

I nodded and then he was gone. I dropped my head into my hands as I took several deep breaths as my *erratic* heart thudded dully in my chest.

I couldn't tell if my heart was truly erratic and racing because I was indeed in need of nutrition, or from the same current of awareness I felt every time he touched me.

Chapter Eight

WORKING THROUGH THE PAIN

Ellie

WHEN A LOVED ONE dies, there are no visible injuries to be seen. Nothing that marks your flesh to prove that you went through a traumatic incident. There are no physical symptoms that others can see unless they are truly paying attention to their posture or appearance. There are only feelings that mar you from the inside. A person's loss is invisible, difficult to prove the quantity of pain, and damn near incomprehensible to the naked eye. So how will a person who has suffered such a loss be able to communicate the intangible damages to someone else they know? Or worse, a complete stranger?

I thought about all of these things as Evan and I walked into an old gymnasium of the recreation center where our grief counseling was to take place. The smell of old leather and wood hit my nostrils as we walked across the creaking wood floor to where there were about twelve other people seated in a circle. Twenty-four eyes stared back at us from where they sat in old folded chairs placed in a circle that faced a middle-aged woman standing in the center.

Evan and I took two of the three empty seats, sitting quietly as the councilor made her rounds to everyone in greeting. I took the time to take in all the many different faces that were in the group. Some young, some old. A pretty even number of men and women. It made me curious about all of the different stories, all the different kinds of pain that each person had to go through. Were they as traumatic as Evan's and mine? Worse?

"Hi Evan and Ellison. My name is Sandi. Welcome to the group. My deepest condolences for your loss," she said as she shook each of our hands. "We'll do a formal introduction in a few minutes. Most of these guys have been coming for a while, but we always introduce the new members of the circle."

"Thank you," Evan and I both said before we watched her greet the rest of the people.

"So, you nervous about this?" Evan asked, leaning over to where his shoulder brushed mine. His breath was hot against my ear and an involuntary shiver ran under my skin. I wasn't cold by any means, it was just that damn awareness creeping in, making itself known when it had no business being there. What the hell was wrong with me? I felt sick every time the damn awareness was present because his touch affected me, and it shouldn't. I was here mourning my husband, the love of my life. Yet, every time I felt the brush of his skin with mine, I felt comforted. I felt a sudden zap of peace and electricity at the same time.

"Good evening everyone. Thank you for being here tonight. Most of you know me. My name is Doctor Sandi Dawson, but please call me Sandi. We are all here tonight because we have all suffered a loss in some way or form. We have all been through something very traumatic that has affected the way we live our lives from day to day." She paused as she looked around the circle at each one of us.

"The goal of grief counseling is to help achieve acceptance around the loss. We never truly get over the loss we feel in our hearts. Acceptance isn't about feeling okay or fine, and it certainly isn't about feeling happy after what we are grieving is long gone from our lives. It is about acknowledging that there is a piece missing in your life and then taking that fact and trying to weave it into your life. Try not to think of it as moving on and being okay with the loss, but about developing new friendships and relationships with other people, as well as with yourself."

She walked over to the last remaining seat, crossing her legs and allowing her flowing skirt to drape over her legs like a thin layer of curtains. Her blonde hair was knotted at her nape, secured by a tiny white flower. Dark framed glasses sat over her bright green eyes. Even though there was brightness to them, beneath the glass there was a sense of sadness that you wouldn't see if you weren't looking for it.

"I thought we could start the session with sharing some of our stories. I'll go first. I lived in New York City my entire life. I was used to the hustle and bustle of the big city. My parents both worked on Wall Street and my sister and I got to experience so much in our young lives. As we grew older, we didn't move away, but instead stayed because it is what we knew. Fast paced living was for us."

She smiled slightly as if recalling a memory that made her happy, but then her eyes clouded over in pain as she said her next words.

"On September eleventh, two-thousand and one, I lost my best friend. The person I confided in more than any other. She was more than my sister, she was my other half. The better half of me. You see, we were identical twins. She worked in tower one. The plane was a direct hit to one of the floors she worked on."

My hand covered my mouth as I tried to fight back tears. September eleventh was a hard day for everyone, but to actually lose someone in the terrorist attack had to be one of the most horrific experiences ever. I felt her pain as she spoke so freely about her sister. It has been fourteen years since that day, yet Sandi spoke about it like it had happened yesterday. Would I always feel that way? Would I always look back on my short life with Jeremy and let the overwhelming sadness of that day mask the wonderful times we did have when he was alive and with me?

When she was finished with her story, she called on several of the other people in the group to share their stories. One was a young woman, not much older than I was. Her hair was short, laying against her cheeks like a frame for her face. Her skin was light, which showcased a small tattoo on her inner wrist.

"Hi. My name is Jessica. Three years ago my husband and I found out we were having a baby. It was the biggest joy of our lives and we couldn't have been happier. The pregnancy wasn't a difficult one. In fact, if it were any more perfect, it wouldn't have been normal. At seven months pregnant, we found out we were having a baby girl. Phillip and I were both excited. Daisy was always a very active baby. Sometimes she would keep me awake at night from moving around so much."

Jessica paused as she looked down at her belly, now flat and missing the sign of life growing inside of her.

"The week she was due to arrive, I noticed that her movements had decreased significantly. I called the doctor because I was concerned, but they told me it was normal since she was running out of space. Phillip and I went to our last check up on the day she was due. Everything about that day seemed off. Then we found out why when the doctor put the ultrasound probe on my stomach and couldn't find Daisy's heartbeat."

She paused again taking a deep, shaky breath. Sandi leaned over and handed her a tissue from a pile of boxes that sat on the floor beneath her feet. Apparently there was a need to keep them in a stockpile.

"The chord had gotten wrapped around her neck. The doctors predicted she had died right around the time I noticed her not moving as much. I still had to go through the birth. Still had to push and feel the pain of childbirth, but I would gladly do it and feel that pain everyday for the rest of my life if I it meant I didn't have to feel the pain of seeing my daughter not breathe when she was born. I'd gladly take the damage to my body over and over again if it meant that I could have her here with me now."

The only sounds that could be heard were the sniffles that came from Jessica and some of the other women in the circle, myself included.

So much devastation.

So much loss.

My already heavy heart felt even more weighed down as more stories were brought to the surface. A man whose wife had died of cancer only one month after she was diagnosed. A woman whose son drowned in a neighbor's swimming pool. It was hard having to hear about all the pain that each of these people felt. But at the same time, it gave me hope that eventually I would be able to look upon my short life with Jeremy as something beautiful and not remember the agony and distress of the day he died.

"Evan? Ellison? Would either of you like to share your reason that has led you to this group?" Sandi asked as her kind eyes flicked back and forth between Evan and me. I hesitated, not quite feeling strong enough to speak publicly about my loss, but Evan stood up and spoke for both of us.

"Ellie and I were both celebration our honeymoon," he began and was interrupted by Jessica.

"Oh, congratulations," she smiled sweetly at the both of us and my eyes grew wide. She thought we had married each other.

"No, Ellie and I didn't marry each other, we were celebrating our honeymoon separately, with our respective spouses."

"Oh, I'm sorry," she apologized looking at both of us, "You just looked like an adorable couple, that's all."

Her statement couldn't have shocked me more if I had been electrocuted with a Taser gun. A sudden coldness hit me in my core. My husband had barely been gone a few weeks and yet the awareness of Evan wouldn't leave me. Now to have someone suggest that we were a cute couple, put the last layer of guilt on my conscious. I wasn't supposed to be experiencing this type of feeling with a man so soon after my loss, if ever.

"We were on a diner cruise," he continued, seemingly ignoring Jessica's comment about us being a couple. "Everything was great until we got caught in a storm."

"Oh my gosh! You two were on the boat that sank off shore a few weeks ago?" Jessica interrupted yet again as she brought both of her hands to her breastbone in relief. It was the same reaction nearly everyone gave us when we had to tell our story.

"Yes. I lost my wife, Lilly, and Ellie lost her husband, Jeremy."

"Oh my, I'm so sorry," Jessica said quietly as her chin came to her chest and she stared at her hands as if she felt some sort of inkling of the pain we were feeling.

I hated the look of devastation on everyone's face. I didn't want people to feel sorry for me. It wouldn't do any good, and it certainly wouldn't bring Jeremy or Lilly back.

Evan

TRYING TO IGNORE THE young girl's statement regarding Ellie and me was hard. Not allowing my reaction to show, proved to be difficult as I told the group our painful story. Something stirred inside me every time I had to look at Ellie. It was odd that I was looking for certain little things about her that I hadn't ever noticed before. Like the small ring of dark blue fire that surrounded her pupils and contrasted against the lighter blue of her irises. Or how her long dark hair looked almost auburn in the sun, like it had been spray-painted with rays of sunshine to add a subtle low light effect. If the guilt of losing my wife didn't consume me, it was the guilt of feeling this strange cognizance I felt around Ellie.

I sat back down in my chair after finishing our story. Instinctively, I looked over to Ellie who had her hands fisted in her lap, her shoulders slumped in towards her chest and an overall defeated look to her postures and features.

"Thank you, Evan, for confiding in us with your story," Sandi said as she nodded her head at me. "I have a little activity that I want us to do tonight." She stood up and reached beneath her to produce a stack of blank paper and some pencils, instructing us to take one of each and pass it around.

"On the first side of this paper, I want you to draw your face. But not just any face, I want you to draw the mask that you let others see. Regardless of our circumstances, there are only pieces of us that we truly let others see. I'll give you a few minutes."

Sandi walked around the circle, taking in each person's drawing as she looked over our shoulders. I sat staring at my blank white piece of paper for several minutes. I understood what she was asking us to do, but didn't know exactly how I wanted to put my thoughts into a picture of my face.

"Mark," she said grabbing the attention of the man whose wife had passed away from cancer, "Will you show us your mask?"

Mark stood up slowly, his age showing in the shake of his knees and legs as he made his way to his feet. Turning around his piece of paper revealing a picture that showed him smiling, yet the smile looked forced in his drawing.

"The mask I show is a smile, so that people can't see the hurt and pain I still carry inside. It's been nearly a year since I lost my Betty, but it still feels fresh to me, as I wake up everyday expecting to see her cooking breakfast in the kitchen like she had nearly everyday for the forty-two years we were married." He sat back down and looked at his drawing as he adjusted the wire-framed glasses on his face. Lifting his hand, he rubbed at his eye behind the glasses, wanting to pretend like he was okay, yet I saw the glistening wetness that had formed there when he spoke about his wife.

"Thank you, Mark. Like I said in the beginning, acceptance isn't about being okay or fine with our lives after we experience loss, but about finding a way to live through the loss. It doesn't mean we ever have to forget." She looked over to me and I was nervous about having to show mine to the group.

"Evan?"

Slowly, I stood up looking down at my paper then to the group as I turned it around.

"You didn't draw anything?" Sandi asked me with a look of puzzlement on her face.

"I didn't have to. This is my mask. Blank. Stoic. Vacant. This is what I show the world. No emotions. I pretend to go about my life normally, letting my outward appearance seem as if nothing ever happened and I am just fine. But really, there is a storm inside of me. There is anger, resentment, sorrow and a shit ton of regret." I paused swallowing past the lump in my throat and looked down at Ellie who had her face downcast and turned away from me. I knew she had taken my statement of regret to heart. Did I blame her for losing Lilly? Absolutely not, but that didn't mean that she didn't blame herself. I saved her, and in reaction, Lilly was the one I couldn't hang on to.

"Thank you Evan. I understand your picture completely and thank you for explaining that to us. Ellie, how about you, dear?"

The paper in Ellie's hand trembled as she stood and turned her paper around. On the white page, it showed downcast eyes, with cracks on the tops of her cheekbones. I didn't know if they were a strange version of tears, but I wanted to reach out and take her hand. I could feel the fear radiate off her and knew that for her to speak about her feelings and her deceased husband had to be terrifying for her. I had an instinct to want to comfort her, give her some reassurance, even though I couldn't even do it for myself.

"My mask shows how I dry my tears so that no one else can see them. The cracks under my eyes represent dryness. I show this mask to the world because I don't want them to think I am weak. I don't want people to constantly feel like they need to walk on eggshells around me as if I could break any second."

"Is that how you feel, Ellie? You fear that people see you as weak because you mourn your husband?" Sandi asked looking at Ellie with kind eyes.

"Sadness does not mean you are weak. It just shows the depths of your love for the person you lost. Sometimes when people close to us die, the other people that surround us daily feel like they have to be softer towards you. No one wants to upset you more than you already are. They hurt seeing you hurt because they love you."

Ellie nodded at Sandi and in return Sandi smiled sweetly at her.

A few other people shared their mask drawings with us, but my attention was solely focused on Ellie. Her confession had me feeling concern for her. She was anything but weak, in fact, she was probably one of the strongest people I knew. I knew the kind of pain she was going through, because I myself felt that same pain. I knew what the anguish felt like, and the physical and emotional blow that we were both hit with when Lilly and Jeremy died.

"The purpose of this exercise," Sandi said breaking me out of my thoughts, "Was to show you that what you show others, hides what you truly feel on the inside. Yes, I understand that it is your purpose to hide certain things, but by doing that, we also don't give our relationships with other people the chance to understand what it is we really need from them. If we let others know what we need and what we really are, then that builds better and lasting relationships with the people who are still in our lives. It is those relationships that we tend to let slip through our fingers when we experience the loss of someone. The key is to feed those relationships. To nourish them because it is those relationships that will help you ease your devastation. That's all I have for tonight. For those who have one-on-one time scheduled with me, I'll be ready in a few minutes. Have a good night."

The group disbursed as they grabbed their belongings. I waited for Ellie since we rode together, when Sandi approached us.

"Thank you for being here tonight and for your cooperation. I know that these sessions are court ordered for you two, but I truly believe that this group will be beneficial in helping you learn to deal and work through the heaviness in both of your hearts. I know what you two went through was traumatic. Your spouses were both very young. You both recently married. Saying that, I also think that the biggest support you can find, is in each other. Your pain and anguish is similar. It may not seem like it, but you two share a bond. Even though that bond was brought from grief, it is important that you two confide in each other."

Sandi shook both of our hands before we walked out of the rec building towards the rental car that I had gotten for us since we would be staying in the Keys for an unknown amount of time. The warm night air hit my face and I felt relief being away from all of the people inside. It was one thing to have to deal with the pain myself, but I had felt a little uncomfortable talking to strangers about what I was going through. Even if it did seem to help.

I helped Ellie into the passenger seat before rounding the car to take us home.

"Can we roll down the windows?" Ellie asked as I eased the car out into traffic.

"Sure. I could use the air."

Hitting the button on the automatic windows, I took a deep

breath as the salty air hit my nostrils. Ellie eased back into the seat and I couldn't help but notice how the wind made her hair whip gently around her face. It reminded me of the day on the sailboat with Lilly and I briefly closed my eyes tightly at the now painful memory and focused my eyes back on the road.

"Think this will really help us?" I asked her as we sat in a line of traffic on our way back to the house.

"I don't know. If feels like an invasion of privacy having to personally tell people I don't even know about what I went through. What we went through," she admitted. "At the same time though, it felt nice to let it out. Holding everything in hasn't helped." She looked down to the knotted hands in her lap.

"I was thinking the same thing. I just hope Sandi is right."

"Right about what?" She asked me as she gathered her hair over one shoulder to keep it under control as the warm breeze floated through the car.

"I hope that we can help each other."

TIME

Ellie

TWO WEEKS HAD passed since the day Evan and I were arrested for what we now call "jet-skigate". Before, I had always wished that time would slow down. I wished that I could savor the warm and sweet moments that I had with Jeremy, time I would gladly take back if I could. Now that time crept by painstakingly slow, I wanted it to speed up so that with it, time could take away my pain.

Evan and I had settled into a comfortable camaraderie. We generally kept to ourselves most of the time, but occasionally we would go and get dinner or sit outside on the back porch sharing stories about Lilly and Jeremy.

Still, time went by slowly. Like I was frozen in a few seconds of time, that never seemed to progress. It felt like the day that Jeremy died, my life paused. Stilled in time and there was nothing and no one that could give it the jumpstart I needed, in order to move past it and manage to live the rest of my life.

"Hello, baby," my mother's voice said on the other end of the phone. It had become a ritual for her to call me everyday. I knew she worried about me, often wondering if my mind was in a good place or if I got lost so deeply in my own anguish, that I wasn't able to function in life successfully.

"Hey, mom."

"I really wish you would come home. We miss you. Want you here with us."

"I know, but you know I can't. I have to finish the counseling in order to make sure that my Jet Ski theft doesn't go on my record. The owner of the property had agreed not to press charges if I followed through. Besides, how good would it look if a paralegal had a record? No one would want to hire me."

A knock sounded at my door just as I finished running a brush through the ends of my hair. Evan and I had counseling homework that we had to do and thought we would do it together.

"Oh, hey, Mom? I gotta go. Evan is here and we are heading to the beach today."

I heard her sigh on the other end of the phone and knew she was still reluctant about me staying with Evan.

"Baby, I know that you both went through something horrific together, but we don't know him. Our offer still stands for us to get you a place while you are there."

"I appreciate that mom, but I'm good here."

And I really was.

At first I was apprehensive about staying with Evan, but the last few weeks with him have been a lot more comforting than if I had to be completely on my own.

"Okay, dear. Just call if you need anything. I'll talk to you tomorrow. I love you, sweetie."

"Love you too, mom."

I hung up the phone and slipped it into my purse before going to answer the door. Even though this was Evan's house, he still respected my privacy and I was grateful for it. I tried to put on a brave face for what we were both about to have to do. Neither one of us had returned to the beach since the jet ski incident. If I had been thinking rationally that day, I probably wouldn't have even gone then.

Opening the door, I expected to see the quiet and composed demeanor that Evan always portrayed, but instead was met with a man whose eyes were bloodshot read and tears that dripped off the end of his nose to land on the concrete beneath our feet.

"Evan? What's wrong?' I asked as I placed my hand on his forearm. I watching his shoulders move up and down as he took in a long, shaky breath trying to gain his composure. Without even thinking, I pulled him into the apartment and led him over to the couch and sat down with him. I had seen him teary-eyed over Lilly many times, but this pain was something else entirely.

"Evan?" I prodded when he sat there silently, his hands fisted tightly in his lap, a hard line to his lips like he was on the verge of letting out a painful cry, yet tried to keep it in.

"I just got a call from the hospital," he began, his voice shaky with anguish. "The little girl that I had been caring for passed away his morning."

My hands flew to cover my mouth. I had remembered Lilly briefly telling me about a child that was Evan's patient whose health was not in good condition. That was the reason they had stayed so close to Miami on their honeymoon. Evan didn't want to be too far away from her in case she took a turn for the worse.

"Oh, Evan. I'm so, so sorry." I said, knowing that my words would be little comfort, yet it hurt me to see him like this. He was a doctor, a man who obviously cared deeply for his patients. Then to add the pain of losing this little girl, who meant a great deal to him on top of losing his wife, had to be his breaking point.

"I called her mother. Apologized for not being there for her. I—I didn't even get to say goodbye to Kellie. I didn't get to say goodbye to Lilly. I didn't even get to meet my child to say goodbye to it."

I froze, ridged on the spot as if my muscles couldn't move.

"What?" I whispered not knowing if I had heard him correctly or not.

His red eyes looked up towards me as my eyes widened to the point of nearly bulging from their sockets.

"Lilly had only told me a few hours before the accident that she was pregnant."

No.

No.

No.

I began shaking my head back and forth as hot, raging tears extruded from my eyes. I couldn't stop them and my face grew hot to the point I felt like I could pass out.

"No, Evan, no." I kept saying over and over.

He sobered, almost instantly when he began to register my reaction to the information that he had just revealed to me.

"Ellie, no. Don't. Don't you dare go blaming yourself for that! Don't you fucking do it." He said sternly and he reached over to me, placing both hands on my shoulders.

"If it weren't for me…" I began, barely able to hang on to my control. I was distraught, to the point that my only thoughts that I had were of Lilly and the child she was carrying. The color red, the same color of the dress she wore as the waves took her and swept her out to sea to disappear from sight, disappear from Evan's life.

"Ellie, it wasn't your fault. Please. Please don't."

He gathered me in his arms, holding me to him. It was the first time we had ever embraced. The first time that I had allowed anyone to show me that much affection since the accident. I sobbed into his chest as my stomach twisted in painful, agonizing knots to the point of nearly stealing my breath. He was going to be a father, and I had taken that away from him. Now, he lost a little girl whom he had grown to love while caring for her and it made my pain even worse.

He continued to hold me as he gently stroked my hair. His own staggered breaths proving that his own tears continued to fall. I didn't know how long we stayed that way, needing something that we found in each other.

Comfort.

Reassurance.

Time. Time passed and as he held me, it felt a little bit easier. Like each second of that time that passed, tiny chips of ice that had formed around my heart, began to break off. Maybe with more time, the warmth and security I had begun to feel with him would eventually melt everything away and the heart that I had known before Jeremy's death would once again make it's appearance in my life.

Evan

I WASN'T PREPARED FOR the sensations I would feel as I held Ellie in my arms. It felt like only seconds, but minutes had passed as she offered me comfort, stroking my back with her hands, nuzzling her nose into my chest. She made me feel something that I hadn't had since I lost my wife.

Comfort.

Comfort that seemed to help ease the ache in my chest only momentarily. Comfort that seemed to seep into me and warm me from the outside in. Her softness to my hardness. Both of us having darkness in us, yet coming together to try and light a pathway to continue on with our lives.

Finally lifting her head from my chest, she looked at me with swollen eyes and tearstained cheeks. Involuntarily, I reached up to wipe a tear that had fallen from her eyes and she squeezed them shut, as if my touch seemed to soothe the ache inside of her.

"I'm sorry, Evan. I —dammit, why does life have to be so hard? Why is it that death, one of the most predictable outcomes in life, is also the most tragic? It is a certainty that we will have to deal eventually, but that doesn't make it easy. I'm so sorry about the baby. About the little girl, about Lilly."

My heart constricted in my chest because I knew she blamed herself for most of those outcomes. My devastation only made hers worse and it killed me to know that she thought that about herself. I reached for her chin, tilting it so that she had to look me in the eyes. I pinned her with a gaze, my eyes flickering back and forth between her eyes, which were as blue as the ocean I hated. Nearly the exact same color the love of my life's were.

Call me crazy. A madman not thinking rationally. My own logical thought completely slipping away as I lowered my head towards hers. I overlooked the widening of her eyes or the fact that she froze beneath my touch. I was compelled by a force greater than the two of us, as my lips gently touched hers. At first her mouth was hard, not quite understanding what was happening, but in the next instant, softened as her body and mind seemed to relent and give in to the moment. Not taking it any further, I just enjoyed the feel of her flesh on mine, seeping in the comfort that her presence brought to me before reasonable thoughts began to filter back in and I pulled away from her.

"Ellie…" I said trying to apologize for my actions, yet not able to get the words past my lips.

She sat there for several seconds, not moving and not saying anything. Internally I was kicking the shit out of myself for doing what I just did. I felt guilty and tormented by my actions. Tormented because I had no clue what the fuck I was thinking when I kissed her. Guilty because she was the first person in nearly five years that I had kissed that wasn't my wife. Guilty that only a few weeks had passed since my wife had died, yet here I was making the moves on someone else.

My mind swam with every degrading thought that I could think of. Every rotten and vile thing I could call or think about myself as I searched her eyes for some kind of reaction. She looked like she was on the verge of something, and I couldn't tell if it was a freak out or what. All I knew was if my actions had done something to jeopardize our fragile, new friendship, I wouldn't be able to forgive myself.

"Ellie, I'm sorry, I don't know what I was thinking." She closed her eyes and I feared she was going to slap me, run, or maybe a combination of the two. But when she opened them, there was a softness, resignation, as she stared back at me with forgiveness in her features.

"It's okay, Evan. You were upset. I understand. We both haven't been thinking clearly. We are comfortable with each other. You have brought me so much comfort by just being here with me through all of this. I don't want to ruin that. I need this. I need us. I need your support."

I nodded my head in understanding as I finally let my hands fall from her face, already feeling the loss of her warm skin as I placed my palms flat on my jeans.

"I need this too, Ellie. I don't think I would have even made it this far if it hadn't been for you."

She wiped the tears from under her face and sat up straighter.

"Well, we still have a challenge ahead of us today," she said changing the subject and relieving some of the awkwardness that had developed between us.

That's right. Sandi's homework.

Our last session ended with Sandi telling us to go back to where the accident happened. She insisted that if we went to the beach and confronted the thing that took Lilly and Jeremy from us, it would be one step closer towards acceptance. Ellie stood up and reached out for me and I placed my hand in hers. The warmth of her palm invaded my thoughts as our fingers laced together. A look of determination was forcefully written on her face and I knew she needed this. We needed this.

It just didn't make it easy.

As we walked out of her apartment hand in hand towards the car, silent guilt consumed me. I couldn't stop reliving the kiss over and over, still feeling the taste of her lips on mine as I flicked my tongue out to savor it. Not only was I guilty for kissing her, but guilty because I liked it.

Too much.

What did that mean? Was it because I was distraught and not thinking clearly? Or, was I actually lurking through semi-muddy water still able to see my feet on the ground through the surface, yet clouded by what my thoughts *should* be and what they *wanted* to be?

Only time would tell.

⁓

THE SUN BEAMED UP in the sky like a giant heating lamp. The rays bounced off our shoulders as we walked through the sand to the water's edge. To the right was nothing but open sea as far as the eyes could see. But on our left, was the twin of the vessel that tore our loved ones away from us. I felt Ellie's steps stumble when she saw the boat and I reached for her hand, looping her arm through mine. I wanted to offer her support so that we could confront a place that we both loathed. I hated how my heart rate sped up and the sweat that had began to form on my brow, became more prominent. And it wasn't from the heat of the sun. I have talked to patients in my earlier years of practice, before I decided to specialize in pediatrics, about PTSD. Post Traumatic Stress Disorder. Not something that I ever imagined myself having to deal with, but the closer we got to the boat, the more my anxiety ripened.

Ellie's nails dug into the flesh of my arm, and I doubt she even realized she was doing it. I watched her in profile, managing to tear my eyes away from the boat so that I didn't lose it. I needed to try and stay strong for the both of us. From the expression on her face, I could tell she was on the verge of breaking down. I watched her chew on her bottom lip, worrying the flesh between her teeth. The soft blue of her eyes was dominated by wide pupils, even in the harsh light of the sun.

"Are you okay?" I asked, reaching over to place my hand on her forearm.

"I'm not sure," she spoke quietly, fear and pain evident in the sound of her voice. I wanted to take her away from here. *Anywhere but here.*

We both stopped in front of the boat peering up at it as its shadow casted upon us. The coolness from stepping into the shade matched the coldness in my heart as we both looked at the huge vessel with hatred, but, it wasn't the boat that Jeremy and Lilly were on because that boat was ripped to shreds. Splintered by the angry vengeance of Mother Nature.

I hated being here. Hated having to look at an exact replica of the thing that caused us so much trauma. Beside me, I could feel the tremble in Ellie's touch and I rubbed my hand up and down her forearm to try and soothe her.

"What is it we were supposed to do?" Ellie asked me as she continued to stare at the boat with wide eyes.

I reached into my back pocket, only letting go of Ellie's arm so that I could unfold the piece of paper that Sandi had given us.

"It says here that we are to practice grounding techniques. Describe things we see in the present, not focus on what our memories see as we recall the trauma of the incident."

"Okay, what do you see then?" She asked turning to me. Her eyes held the sadness I felt in my heart and I wanted to gather her in my arms to comfort her. Being with her and offering her support helped me take the focus off my own pain. It helped me to harness my energy into helping her cope with her loss, so that I didn't have to constantly be reminded of my own.

"Well, I see the sand. It's kind of sparkly today," I said looking around at our surroundings.

"Sparkly? That's the first thing you noticed?" She smiled, nothing like I'm sure she used to, but her lips tipped up at the corners and gave me a glimpse of her pearly white teeth. It didn't quite meet her eyes, but just the fact that I was able to spark even the tiniest bit of humor into our dark thoughts made me feel better.

"What do you see?" I asked as I nudged her shoulder and returning her small smile. Her eyes left mine and for a moment, I could read the pain as it tried to make it's way back into her thoughts. Her low ponytail, secured at her nape, left her face open to me, giving me a clear view of her expressions. She was one of those people who, no matter how hard they tried to hide things from the outside world, still have their feelings written all over their face. Her eyes would lighten or darken with mood, switching back and forth between a bright vivid blue when she was happy or amused, and a darker, cloudier blue when the pain consumed her. More often than not, the dark was what I saw, but there were those rare instances when I was rewarded with the happier, vibrancy of her cerulean blues.

"Remember, Ellie, shift your focus and your attention onto the present. Concentrate on something else. Not the memories," I reminded her. She took a few steps away from me and stared out at the ocean for a long time, lifting her hands to shield the harsh sunlight from her eyes. I stood behind her, basking in the beauty of watching her stare out into open water. The gentle breeze wrapping her loose fitting blouse around her small frame. Her ponytail dancing in the wind as it hung down her back. The way her skin sparkled in the sun, casting a bronze tint onto her sleeveless shoulders. My gaze traveled down her body to where her toes dug into the sand. Hints of pink from her toenails disappearing and reappearing as they burrowed in and out of the sand.

"Look! Dolphins!" She exclaimed and brought me out of my trance. I shook my head trying to clear my thoughts as I looked out to where she was pointing. Sure enough, a small pod of dolphins danced playfully in the distance, the bright blue sky and the crystal water creating a perfect backdrop behind them.

"I hear they come pretty close to the beach sometimes," I said as I walked up to where she was standing.

"We don't get to see them off the coast of North Carolina often. I think they like the warmer waters here better."

We stood there for several minutes before we made our way back towards the car. When we first came out here, I thought our councilor was crazy for making us return to a place that held so much devastation for both of us. Trying to create new memories from ones that were clouded in darkness when we returned to the beach, seemed damn near impossible. But somehow, standing there, I was able to complete the exercise without even realizing that I had. As Ellie had tried to find something to concentrate on other than the memory of Jeremy, I was able to find something almost instantly. I was able to focus on a different kind of beauty other than the view of the beach or even the dolphins that had created the beautiful grin on Ellie's face.

Because it was Ellie I wasn't able to take my eyes away from.

Chapter
Ten

ANNIVERSARY OF A DIFFERENT KIND

Ellie

"I STILL FEEL SO LOST *without you, Jeremy.*" *I said as we sat on the dock that we had gone to so many times before when we were dating.*

"*I know sweetheart, but I promise you, as each day goes by, it will get easier.*" *His soft, dirty blond hair danced in the wind as the last remnants of the sun began to sink below the horizon. It cast an orange/red glow against our skin, illuminating us in the beauty of the sunset.*

"*Each day I wake up determined to put one foot in front of the other. I try to focus on the good things I still have in my life instead of what I don't have with me anymore. Mom keeps begging me to come home, but I can't. I still have to complete the counseling. And...*" *I said pausing to look at him,* "*I'm not entirely sure I want to leave just yet.*"

"*Evan has been helping you. I'm grateful for him, you*

know," he said as he nudged my shoulder.

"I'm grateful for him too, Jer. If I had to do this alone, if I had to try and pick up the pieces of losing you by myself, I'm not sure I would be able to. Evan has kept me from being lost in my own thoughts. He has held my hand this entire journey even though he feels some of the same devastation that I do.

Jeremy nodded his head and smiled as he looked down at me.

"You may not realize it, but helping you, helps him."

"How's that?" I asked curious as to why he would think that.

"Well, by being there for you and offering support, it helps take his mind off Lilly."

"But he can't always do that. By focusing on me and helping me, it doesn't give him time to heal from his own wounds."

Jeremy nodded again.

"True, but that is where you need to help him. You both help each other. Your friendship has been developed out of tragedy, and you two share a bond that is greater than most people could build in a lifetime, Ellie. Maybe focus on that. Build that relationship instead of focusing on the past. Work towards a new future."

I looked at Jeremy as my head flinched back slightly and my mouth opened and closed without a word or sound coming out of it.

"Are you suggesting that I develop a relationship with Evan?" I was finally able to ask as my eyes blinked rapidly and my tone uncertain.

Jeremy shrugged, his shoulders coming up to brush the bottom of his ears as he stared out at the horizon. The sun was just beginning to go down, the sky lit up with purple and orange hues.

"Remember when Toby Martin and Kattie Storm had started dating?" He asked me and I only became more confused by the question, but decided to humor him.

"Yes. It was right around the time you and I started dating."

Toby and Kattie were both friends of Jeremy and me. They married about a year ago and already had their first child.

"Well," he continued, "Toby had just gotten out of a bad relationship with the one girl he dated that went to Carolina State. Kattie was the one who helped him get through all of that and look how well it turned out with them."

"Yeah, but Jer, Kattie and Toby were friends long before they ever started dating," I said matter of factly like he didn't already know.

"Exactly," he said as he reached for my hand, gently running the tips of his fingers over the center of my palm. Chill bumps formed on my arm from his touch. I missed him so very much and my heart literally felt like it had been on the outside of my body since the day he died.

"Toby and Kattie were able to make it work because they were friends first. Love came later and it was stronger than anyone could ever imagine possible, even for Toby and Kattie themselves."

I tried to consider what it was that Jeremy was trying to

tell me, but if I had any inkling, I didn't like the direction in which his thoughts led, but I didn't get a chance to protest because he turned completely to face me. Stretching his legs out, he reached for me, turning me around to settle between his legs as I leant my back into his chest. He wrapped his arms around me and for a few moments, I enjoyed their warmth. Their comfort, and all the love I knew he was capable of giving to someone.

"Ellie, no one knows exactly what God has in store for them. I didn't ever imagine that I wouldn't get to live the rest of my life out with you. In fact, it was the one thing I was absolutely certain about. But what if I was only in your life as a pathway to something bigger? What if God brought us together because he had a bigger plan than you and me? Maybe it was fate that we got on that boat. Maybe it was the plan all along."

Hot tears cascaded down my cheeks as I sniffled and slid my fingers in between Jeremy's, holding onto him securely, because I had no clue how much time we had left together.

"You were my fate, Jeremy. You were my life. My everything. I can't move on from this. I don't want to. I'm afraid that if I move on, it means that I will forget you. It means I'll no longer get to look back and remember you. I've already lost you in my physical world, I can't lose the memory of you also."

He wrapped his arms around me tighter, cocooning me to him. He felt so alive to me even though I knew he wasn't really there. I could feel his warm breath across the back of my neck and ear. I could feel the perfect rhythm of his heart beating against my back, and it only made me cry harder.

"You will never lose the memory of me, or us, Ellie. I'll always be a part of you, baby. But I need you to live. I want you to fall in love again. I want you to open your heart up again. It kills me to see you like this."

I was crying so hard, I could barely catch my breath. Jeremy rested his chin on my shoulder, and placed a gentle kiss right below my ear.

"Jer," I managed to say through tangled sobs, "You consumed every piece of my heart. There isn't any part of it left for me to give to someone else. It belongs to you. You stole it from me years ago, and I never want it back."

"Your heart is bigger than any person I know, Ellie. It may feel like you had given it all away, and I am the luckiest man to be on the receiving end of it, but there is so much more of you left to give. Don't lock it away."

He paused and took a deep, hesitant breath.

"I have to go, baby. I love you. I'll always love you. You will always love me. A love like ours is not easily forgotten, but each day, it will get better. Each day the pain will fade a little more and you will find that space in your heart to give to someone again. Promise me, you'll do it, Ellie. Promise me that you will be willing to let yourself open up again."

He placed a kiss on my cheek. The warmth of his mouth more real than anything I've ever felt in my entire life.

"Promise," he whispered again.

"I —pr—promise," I managed to choke out, the tightness in the back of my throat making it difficult to speak.

"Love, Ellie." He whispered once more and just as quickly

as he appeared, he was gone.

I WOKE TO HARSH light invading my eyes as it filtered in through the window and landed in beams upon my face. I reached up to wipe away the sleep to find the remnants of my tears. Tears that I had shed as I sat on the dock with Jeremy while my subconscious granted me the blessing to get to see him. Over the last month, I had gotten to spend several times a week just talking to him, being in his presence. Somehow, it made my heart feel better, even if it were all a dream. As I sat up though, I felt like this last time was different. My heart shattered again for the millionth time since his death thinking that this last dream was goodbye.

"Promise me, you'll do it, Ellie. Promise me that you will be willing to let yourself open up again."

I kept hearing his whispered words over and over.

"I —pr—promise." My whispered reply echoed his words.

I had stayed up late last night hoping that I would be able to sleep most of today away. I didn't want to be conscious and have to come to terms with the fact that the love of my life died one month ago today. Or the fact that yesterday was my one-month wedding anniversary.

One day.

I got to spend one day as his wife.

I wiped away the tears that had begun to fall. I couldn't take the pain. I wanted something, anything to numb it. Some days were easier than others. Some days were horrible, and some days I was distracted enough not to fall into my own thoughts.

What was the distraction that helped me?

Evan.

Two broken souls that had been brought together and ended up helping each other through the most difficult time of our lives. Two strangers, who had a horrible memory in common, and worked together in order to cope with our grief.

I was thankful for Evan. Sure, I had my mom, dad, and friends back home who had offered me support, but I don't think they really understood the depths of my despair the way Evan did.

Slowly, I made my way into the bathroom as I robotically brushed my teeth. Risking a glance in the mirror, I noticed that my normally vibrant skin had lost its luster. My hair looked dull and thin, the fullness no longer remaining. My cheeks were more hollowed out than ever, due to the amount of weight I had lost from my already small frame.

I looked sick.

I looked run down.

I looked broken.

Faded.

Lifeless.

Reaching for the brush, I ran it through my long strands, breaking through the obstacle of tangles that resisted along the way.

"I need you to live."

Jeremy's words making a presence in my thoughts again. I closed my eyes, feeling his presence with me. Like somehow, he was still with me. Through our talks in my dreams, I felt us grow closer. Not that we weren't close in life, but his death had created a different element to our relationship.

I reached over to my makeup case, and removed all the products that I hadn't touched in a long time. I had no purpose before to use them. Had no reason why I wanted to make myself feel beautiful and like a woman again.

Until Jeremy's request.

"I need you to live."

And as I picked up my facial brush, I was determined to do so.

I HATE THIS FUCKING day. I hate the thought of an anniversary that wasn't about celebration or happiness, but instead one that was nothing but pain. The gut wrenching devastation that comes with losing a loved one.

I sat at the island in the kitchen nursing my second cup of coffee as I stared out of the back window of the house. I scowled at the brightness of the day. How the sun shone through the palm trees in the back yard giving off the fake impression that it was supposed to be a beautiful day.

It was anything but.

The lightness was a stark contradiction to the inner turmoil that was swirling through me. Taking a drink of my coffee, it singed my tongue and burnt the back of my throat as it went down, but I didn't care. If I could forget everything about this day, I would. I would let my heart feel happy if I knew a way to do it without missing Lilly so desperately.

Tearing my gaze away from the window, I reached for the newspaper trying to find something else to occupy my mind. I skimmed over articles, business reports and even classified ads before my eyes zeroed in on a small headline about a small carnival that was in town.

I sat staring at the picture of a lit up Ferris wheel, and the smile that was on the girl's face in the picture. I took in the lines of her face and her wide grin as she pointed to something on the ground. Her eyes were wide with wonder and amazement while she seemed to be on the ride of her life.

A sudden thought came to me and quickly I downed the coffee, not stopping long enough to taste the bold flavor before I stood up and rinsed it out in the sink. I searched for my car keys finding them on the counter before I raced out of the door.

I RETURNED TO THE house after being gone all afternoon. I ripped the tags off the new clothes I had purchased and slipped into a comfortable pair of cargo shorts and neon pink tank top. Heading into the bathroom, I shaved away the scruff that had developed on my face and even managed to tame my rapidly growing hair with a little product. A few splashes of my cologne and I was done. Heading back to where I had left a box on the counter in the kitchen, I grabbed it before walking out of the door and went downstairs to Ellie's apartment.

I hated to admit that I was a little nervous and excited to present this idea to her, but I hoped like hell that it would be just what we needed in order to forget and be able, for just one day, to let go of the pain and embrace the fact that we were both still very much alive.

"Evan?" Ellie said as she opened the door. I was hit with a sucker punch to the gut when I saw her standing barefoot before me in a tank top and athletic shorts. But it wasn't her attire that had grabbed my attention. Her long brown hair that was normally secured in a ponytail hung loosely around her shoulders in soft, romantic waves. Her face seemed to glow as I took in the faintest amount of blush upon her cheeks that added a hint of color she had been missing. Here eyes were exquisitely framed by a set of dark lashes and the slight brown hue of her eye shadow made her already blue eyes seem bluer. Her lips were painted with a soft pink, shiny gloss, brightening her face even more.

There was no telling how long I stood there staring at her like some crazed madman. I mean, she was a very beautiful girl without a lick of makeup on, but with the few small touches she made, wow. It was like being star struck by someone you idolized. I couldn't find my voice or what I even wanted to say to her. My voice lodged in my throat as I stood there looking at her with unabashed shame.

"Evan?" She repeated again, this time ducking down to gain my attention.

"Hi," I said finally breaking my trance and offering her a small smile.

"Um, hi?" She said, more like a question than a statement.

"Can I come in?" I asked nodding my head inside the apartment.

"Of course."

She stepped back allowing me to enter. The already normally small space seemed even smaller, and I couldn't help but notice the sudden rush of anxiety that had taken over me. I was nervous around her for some reason, not able to enjoy our usual easy camaraderie.

"What's going on?" She asked as she looked at the box in my hands. I turned my gaze down to where I was holding it in my hands at my side.

"Oh, uh, this is for you," I replied tentatively as I extended the box out to her. She walked over to the couch and sat down, playing with the small purple bow that I had placed on top.

"What is it for?" She asked, blue eyes peering back up at me, cheeks rosy with what? Curiosity?

Embarrassment?

I rounded the couch and came to sit beside her, praying that I wasn't making a mistake. Praying that she would accept.

"This," I said pointing to the box, "Is for you to wear to the carnival tonight."

"Carnival?

I ran a hand through the side of my hair.

"There is a small carnival in town that has rides, junk food, a crowd. You know, the works. I hear that there may even be funnel cake involved."

She bit her lip, teeth sinking into the shiny softness of her flesh. I couldn't read the expression on her face, but my heart rate sped up a few notches as I sat on pins and needles waiting for her answer.

Sliding the top of the box off, she removed some of the tissue paper to reveal the sundress I had bought her. When I saw it in the store, I knew it would be perfect for her. It wasn't anything special, just classic white with a touch of lace embroidery on the trim.

"Wow, this is beautiful," she said as she fingered the light fabric.

"The sales lady said it was an empire waist and that you would probably like it. I had to guess your size."

Which meant I had to picture your body. I thought to myself.

"It's perfect. Thank you. But why are we going to a carnival?"

"I thought we could go do something fun. I know how hard today has been on you because it has burned me from the inside out since I woke up this morning. Sandi said last week in group that we needed to try and start doing things that we used to do prior to…"

I paused, taking a deep breath trying not to let my emotions get the best of me. As I looked away from her, Ellie placed her small hand on top of mine and I turned back to look at her. A beautiful smile was on her face and her eyes were tender, not filled with grief like I had seen them everyday for a month, but instead they looked almost...*alive*.

"I think the carnival sounds like a great idea. Besides, you had me at *funnel cake*. Wait for me to change?"

"Of course," I said chuckling and returned her smile, one that wasn't forced. Wasn't conjured up from the mask I showed others, but felt real. Felt almost...happy. And it was all because of her.

Chapter Eleven

COTTON CANDY, CORN DOGS, and a KISS

Ellie

THE BRIGHT LIGHTS from all the rides shone back at us as we bought our bracelets from the ticket counter. I couldn't remember the last time I went to a carnival or fair that had rides. A new, fresher feeling came over me as we walked through the grass taking in all of the noise, excitement and laughter all around us. The surroundings made it painfully hard not to have a smile on our faces, or for one night, just enjoy time. Enjoy the feeling of being alive.

"So, what first? Food or rides?" Evan asked as he looked at me with a bright smile. I could tell his excitement level was just as high as mine. I tapped a single finger against my lips contemplating a game plan.

"How about we do the crazy rides first, then take a break to eat? That way we don't get sick on the *Zipper* or the *Tilt-a-Whirl*."

"I think that sounds like a brilliant idea," He answered and reached for my hand tugging me towards the *Gravitron*. We stood in line waiting our turn as we watched the giant spaceship travel around in a circle at breakneck speed. The colors mixed together in a long line of blended greens, blues, yellows and reds.

"I don't think I've ever been on this ride before," I admitted.

"What?" He asked as he placed his hand over his heart and feigned hurt. "You've never been on the awesomeness that is the *Gravitron*? I don't even know you anymore," he laughed and shook his head at me as the ride slowed and eventually came to a stop allowing the passengers to get off before we showed our bracelets to the operator and went inside.

Red padded walls surrounded the inside with what looked like thin strap belts hanging from each one.

"What do we do?" I asked not knowing where to go.

He took my hand again, something that was beginning to feel really...nice, and leant me up against the red pads.

"You just lean against it. Put the belt over you and wait for the fun to begin."

"Seriously? That's it? No metal bar? No secure straps?" I said looking at him with wide eyed shock. Suddenly, I didn't think it was a great idea to go on this ride.

"Yes, just trust me, okay?" He asked. I stood back with my arms crossed over my chest as he buckled himself in and looked at me as if saying "See?" I studied his features. The normal worry lines that were between his eyes were smooth now. The dark circles that had graced both of our eyes appeared lighter, giving his eyes almost a youthful look. Couple that with the fact that he looked as giddy as a twelve year old, and I couldn't help but relent.

"Fine, but if I throw up, I'm aiming in your direction," I said as I took the pad next to him and secured the belt across my midsection.

The operator came around to each person testing that the belts were secure and then loud music began to play as the ride began to move.

Okay. So far, so good. Nothing major happening.

"Who is ready to rock?" The operator's voice beamed through the hidden speakers in the man-made space craft. Hoots and cat whistles scatter sporadically throughout the ride as everyone gets psyched up. The craft starts to spin faster and I notice how my backside starts to be forcefully glued to the padding at my back. I turn my head to see Evan's gorgeous smile beaming back at me as one of his eyebrows lifts higher.

"Having fun yet?" He yelled, trying to carry his voice over the sound of the music. The ride spins faster.

And faster.

And faster.

Until the point I am now completely plastered to the wall of the ride. My face suddenly feels like I have had a facelift as the skin peels back. I smile and laugh as the feeling of almost being weightless overcomes me.

"Oh my God! This is amazing!" I yell and I can faintly hear the sound of Evan's reply. I turned my head to the side again, this time it was harder due to the gravity pulling against me and met Evan's eyes that are once more, starting straight at me. Reaching over, I grab his hand and entwine my fingers with his.

I can't say exactly what it was that passed between us. Some strange, but intense feeling that materialized out of both of our grief. It was because of him, that I was able to add a few rays of sunshine back into the darkness that had become my life. His smile soothed me, comforted me, and made me feel the faintest hint of butterflies in my stomach. His eyes sparkled with delight, and with the feelings that he created in me, I have no doubt that my expression matched his own.

The ride began to slow, bringing us both back down to earth where we had ascended to a new height.

And not just from the ride.

I kept repeating Jeremy's words over and over in my mind.

"I need you to live."

The ride came to a final stop and we unbuckled our belts and made our way off the space ship, laughing and smiling all the way. I had to wipe at my eyes, praying that the tears were forced from them as my head clung to the wall of the *Gravitron*.

"So thoughts about your first trip to outer space?" Evan asked me as he still noticeably held onto my hand as we began walking around towards the other rides.

"Space is nice, but I feel like my makeup is smeared across my face," I chuckled as I wiped again at my eyes with my free hand.

"Nah, you still look as beautiful as ever," he said nonchalantly like he said things like that to me all the time. My steps faltered and if it hadn't been for his hold on my hand, I probably would have kissed the ground beneath my feet.

"Where to now, miss?" He asked playfully as he bowed in my direction in a fake chivalrous move. I thought about it for a moment as I let go of his hand and did a full three hundred and sixty degree turn around the park.

"The *Zipper*," I stated matter of factly.

His face fell and an ashen look crossed his face.

"What? What's wrong? Don't you like the *Zipper*?"

Swallowing, he walked over to me and leaned in to whisper in my ear, the warmth of his breath sending an involuntary shiver through my body. My body felt like it was buzzing, a dull hum that could be felt from my fingers all the way to my toes.

"When I was fourteen," He whispered as if it were one of the best kept secrets in the world, "I rode the *Zipper* with Nancy Farmer. It was all fun and games until I got sick and threw up all over her. Needless to say, she never called me after that."

He tried to act like he was embarrassed as he pulled away from me, but I saw the tug at the corner of his mouth when he tried to hide his smile.

"Well," I said as I laid a hand upon his chest and gave him a playful shove, "You haven't eaten, I'm not Nancy Farmer, and instead of not calling you, I'll just kick your ass if you get sick on me."

I folded my arms across my chest trying to act stern, trying to keep the laughter that was building within me as he looked at me with a playfully shocked expression. I couldn't contain it and the dam broke, expelling my laughter out into the crowd and throwing my head back. My abs began to hurt as I felt him approach me, large hands circling around my waist and I snapped my head back up to look at him. He looked at me seriously for a moment and I couldn't tell by his features what he was thinking. The laughter died within me as I stared into his blue eyes, feeling consumed by the pools of blue ink before me.

Suddenly, a massive, heartbreaking grin crossed his gorgeous face and the large hands that had settled on my waist moved up my ribcage and he proceeded to tickle me. Barking laughter escaped me as my body submitted to the punishment of his fingers.

"Think it's funny do ya?" He asked as he continued to wiggle his fingers into my ribcage.

"What if I really liked Nancy Farmer?"

"Evan! Stop! I swear I'll pee my pants!" I said through fits of laughter. He had pulled me all the way into his arms as he wrapped them over my shoulders, pinning my arms to my sides. The feeling of his skin against my arms sent a lightning bolt of electricity through me and I sucked in a breath from the surprise of it. My laughter began to subside as he stopped the torture and we stayed in that position for several minutes. My back to his chest. His arms wrapped around me. His breath against my neck and shoulder. The way his newly shaved jaw felt smooth against my shoulder as he rested his chin in the curvature of my neck and shoulder.

"Ellie?" He asked, his voice sounding hopeful and pained at the same time. I swallowed, both enjoying the feeling of him wrapped around me and confused by it at the exact same time.

"Nothing. Let's go and ride the *Zipper*. I'd really love to witness the ass-kicking you plan to give me if I relive being fourteen again."

The moment that had passed between us was gone and he reluctantly let me go as if he had to force his body to do so. I felt just as confused as he did about what seemed to be happening between us. But at the same time my body was telling me to go for it, my mind was telling me something completely different.

Evan pulled me toward the ride as it flipped around and screams bellowed from within the cages of the metal beast.

"You sure?" I said arching my brow and smirking at him.

"Bring it on. In fact, let's make a wager. If I lose my stomach, I buy you dinner. If I come out unscathed, you buy."

"Deal." I stuck out my hand and he placed his in mine sealing our deal. The ride came to a stop, letting people out and the operator ushered us into the newly vacated cage. After he made sure we were securely placed inside, he shut the gate and we ascended into the air.

We stopped a few more times allowing the transition of riders before we began to fully move. Our cage rocked back and forth a few times and as we crested the top where we met nothing but the dark sky above us, we catapulted forward and rounded the other side.

I squealed in delight and laughter and could swear I heard a scream come from Evan when we began to make our second circle in the loop.

"Are you okay?" I asked as I reached over and patted his hand that was gripped tightly on the bar securing us in our seats.

"Never better," he replied as his face looked a little pale, but pretended to be brave as he fronted a 'I'm not scared at all' face.

Several more loops around, a few more screams from Evan and a ton of giggles from me and the ride began to slow, stopping us at the bottom to get off.

"You screamed like a girl," I said nudging him with my hip as we walked away from the ride and towards the food venders.

"I did not! I think it was your own voice you were hearing," he teased. "And I do believe that you owe me dinner. I didn't even come close to throwing up on you." His smile beamed at me and I couldn't help but return his easy humor.

"Pick your poison," I said waving my arm in the direction of the food trucks that were lined up side by side just a little way down from the rides. The smell of fried foods, salty sea, and dusk filled the air, instantly making my mouth water and my stomach protest from my lack of food.

"Corn dogs. Definitely corn dogs."

"Corn dogs it is then."

This time I reached for his hand, like it was something that I did in instinct all the time. The familiarity of his palm as it touch mine was slowly becoming a soothing balm to my suffering soul. The energy that radiated from skin to skin made it hard for me to ignore the awareness of him. It made it hard not to concentrate on the way it made me feel, which in return also made me feel guilty. Here I was, a widow. My husband only passing away just one short month ago, yet my heart jumped every time this man touched me.

It felt so right and so wrong at the same time.

"Hey," Evan said as he walked in stride next to me, noticing the furrow of my brows as I contemplated in my mind the feelings he seemed to so easily evoke from me. When I didn't answer, he stopped, tugging on my hand in the process until I was forced to turn around and look at him.

"What's wrong?" He asked as he reached the hand I wasn't holding onto and rubbed the pad of his thumb between my brows, smoothing out the crease that was placed there from my worry.

"It's nothing. I'm starving. How about those corn dogs?"

"Ellie," he said in warning, not in a harsh tone, but one that hinted at his genuine concern for where my thoughts were.

I risked a glance up at him, his blue eyes sparkling at me with questions, worries, concern. What I also saw there was the same conflict that I was internally battling within myself.

"I—I'm just confused I guess."

"Confused about what?" He asked ducking his head down so that he could meet my eyes better. The pad of his thumb smoothed over my eyebrow before he traced the tips of his fingers down my temple and across the side of my cheek.

"This," I replied softly as I indicated the two of us by waving my hand back and forth between us.

Leaning in, he placed his forehead against mine, practically sharing the same breath with me, our lips were so close.

"I don't know what is happening either, Ellie. All I do know is that whenever I'm with you, the pain seems to subside a little more each day. When I'm with you, it's like I can let go of the guilt, the anger, and the hurt, even if only for a brief moment. I don't care if it is two seconds of relief or if it is longer, but you, you make it better."

"I know what you mean," I reiterated, placing my hands on the narrow part of his waist just where his shorts met the seam of his shirt.

We stayed like that for several moments while the world around us seemed to pass us by. I inhaled the wonderfully masculine scent of him thinking he was going to kiss me at any moment, yet he didn't. Lifting his forehead from mine, he then broke the moment by leading me to one of the food trucks.

"Two corn dogs please, oh and a bag of cotton candy," he said to the lady inside while he reached for his wallet.

"I thought I had to buy?" I asked, placing my hand on his wallet and pushing it away.

"My mom would skin me alive if I let a woman pay for her dinner. Trust me. No one wants to see Momma angry," he feigned a shiver like the thought was scary and atrocious at the same time, but the smile on his face gave him away.

After paying for our corn dogs, we walked over to find the shade of several palm trees and sat on the grass facing each other. Though the sun had already fallen below the horizon, it was still relatively hot, the mugginess of the air making my dress cling to me like a second skin.

We sat Indian style waiting for the corn dogs to cool and I thought it would be a good opportunity to ask him some questions about him.

"So, your mom is old fashioned, huh?" I asked as I placed my hands behind me and leaned back.

"I guess you could say that. She was born and raised in Texas, but when my dad got offered a job at a hospital here in Florida, they moved here. I was probably about four or five. They wanted to do it sooner rather than when I went off to kindergarten. My mom was afraid that pulling me from a school that I just started would probably confuse me."

"So your dad is a surgeon too?"

"Yeah," he said dipping his corndog into the massive pile of yellow mustard on the paper tray it was in. "He's cardiac though."

"That's gross."

"What? That my dad works on hearts?"

I shook my head.

"No. That huge pile of yellow crap you just put on your corndog. Everyone knows you put ketchup on a corndog."

He raised his eyebrow at me and the look on his face said disgust, but his smile told me he was playing with me.

"I beg to differ."

"Ewww."

"Don't knock it till you try it, sweetheart."

He scooted in closer to me and dipped his corndog again into the mustard before extending it out to me.

"No way. I'll stick with my ketchup, thank you."

He moved even closer.

"Just one, teeny, tiny bite?" He said and this time put the corndog up to my mouth. I made the mistake of turning my head at the last minute and was rewarded with a cool, bright yellow smear of mustard across my cheek all the way to my hairline.

I looked at him, my mouth hung open, my eyes wide in shock. His expression, too, matched mine as he looked at me and my now tart smelling makeup job.

"Oh shit! I didn't mean to do that," he laughed. "But you are the cutest girl I've ever seen to wear mustard as blush."

"Ha, ha, ha. Pass me the napkins." I tried to sound wounded, but I couldn't stop the rise of laughter that lit me up from the inside out and suddenly, threw my head back and couldn't help myself. Tears peeked out of the corners of my eyes due to laughing so hard and it wasn't too long before Evan had joined me.

It felt good.

To laugh.

To have a good time.

If only for a few hours, I was able to allow the ice that had formed around my heart to thaw. I welcomed the warmth that Evan created in me. I prayed that I could depend on him to keep my insides from freezing up again. He had taken a day that would have been shrouded in pain and caused me to tune out the rest of the world only to fall victim to my own thoughts again.

Evan

ELLIE'S LAUGHTER WAS beautiful. Soothing. Unfiltered. The thing I liked about her the most was that she was very easy to read. One of those girls that truly had her heart on her sleeve for everyone to see. Even though the memory of our loved ones still haunted both of us, she let me see what others didn't.

Reaching for the pile of napkins, I cupped the side of her head as she continued to laugh hysterically and began wiping away the mustard. Her laughter dies the minute I pulled her into me and wiped the side of her face. Her breathing hitched and then a long, content sigh came from her and it did something to me. Call it crazy, call me the most insensitive, insane person on the planet, I needed to know. I needed to know if her soft lips felt as good as they looked. I had already kissed her once, but it really was a no big deal kind of thing, but for some reason, I *wanted* to kiss her. I wanted to memorize the contours of her mouth. I wanted to taste her tongue on mine so I went for it.

Tilting her head to the side, I lean in carefully as I threaded both of my hands through her hair. She didn't hesitate, didn't pull away, but instead leant into me to where our chests faintly touched when our lips finally came into contact. All background noise fell away, the familiar sounds of rides, laughing and screaming people, melted away only to reveal the heavy thudding of my heart in my chest.

I've kissed a few girls in my life, but it was Lilly that I was with for so long that I wasn't what you would call a kissing expert in my eyes. I was nervous, probably more nervous than I had ever been. I concentrated on how just the barest touch of our lips made most of my senses come alive. The ferocious beating of my heart coupled with how she smelled like sunshine and sweet roses, had my thoughts going into overdrive.

Testing, I brushed the tip of my tongue along the seam of her lips and on a sigh she opened to me, all hesitation gone as if it were the very thing she was seeking. My skin was on fire as her hands held onto my forearms. Her lips were soft, providing a sweet cushion for my own as our tongues began to leisurely entwine together. It wasn't hurried. Wasn't rushed. We teased, tasted and relished in each other as if time were on our side. As if we had slowed it down enough that nothing else mattered, besides what was happening between us right at that moment.

Reluctantly, I felt her begin to pull away, yet I wanted to hold her to me. It hurt to have to let her go, not having nearly enough time to relish in the taste of her. We sat there staring at each other for a matter of moments, taking in what was no doubt our first experience with something new.

Someone new.

That's when her expression changed, as if the thought had suddenly hit her.

Then it hit me.

The guilt.

The remorse.

The pain in knowing that I had just kissed, really kissed, someone who wasn't my wife.

"Ellie," I breathed not knowing if it was a plea for forgiveness, or to beg her to return her lips to mine so that I could lose myself in them again.

"I—I have to go," she stuttered and quickly rose to her feet, knocking over her corndog in the process and sent it rolling into the dirt.

Before I had even had the chance to get up, she was already quickly walking in the other direction. I felt my stomach drop and my heart leap from my chest, but thought it was a better idea to let her have the time she seemed to desperately need. Through the remorse and guilt I felt about kissing her, I also felt that it was the right thing to do. It was a need that was aroused in me, a compulsion that wouldn't go away until it was exercised.

"Fuck," I thought to myself as I continued to watch her retreating form, never once seeing her face again because she never turned around to look back at me. I picked up our trash from the ground and discarded it in a nearby trashcan before I took off in the same direction in which she headed. I didn't bother trying to catch up with her, but instead shoved my hands in the pockets of my shorts and headed home.

Chapter Twelve

GUILT AND PROGRESS

Ellie

Evan: Please tell me that you have made it home okay.

THAT WAS THE LAST words I heard from Evan when I ran away from him at the carnival almost a week ago. I had only replied with a curt yes and then nothing more afterwards. In the heat of the moment, the kiss was…amazing, passionate, enticing and both completely right and completely wrong at the same time. His feelings had to have been all over the place when I ran away, but the guilt and the pain that consumed me when I thought about Jeremy immediately after, was almost too much for me to take. I didn't want Evan to see me fall apart in front of him. I made it out of the carnival, into a cab, and all the way back to the apartment before I locked myself in my room and let the tears fall. The conflicting emotions were like a giant wave that were crashing on my soul. I felt horrible for the fact that I enjoyed the kiss. I felt despair for taking in the joy and elation I felt when Evan's mouth touched mine.

It also felt like a betrayal.

Betrayal to the person who I had pledged my life to. The person who I told I could remain faithful and true to for the rest of my life. It didn't matter that Jeremy wasn't with me here in the physical sense anymore. We were connected by the soul, and that was more powerful than any physicality could create.

Night after night I prayed Jeremy would return to me when I let my exhausted and achy eyes succumb to sleep, and night after night I was left heartbroken and disappointed. Other than Jeremy, Evan was the only one I felt comfortable talking to about everything that has happened with Jeremy's death and everything since then, yet he was now the source of my torment, effectively ripping that resource away from me.

I had stayed holed up in the apartment for the better part of a week. Only leaving when I needed to go to the store, or to get a few minutes of fresh air. The risk of running into Evan and the confrontation that I knew was bubbling on the surface between us wasn't something I was prepared to deal with.

I had no choice but to see him today though. In a few minutes, we would both have to leave to go to counseling and would be forced to come face to face with one another. Sit next to each other in the confines of a small car. Breathe the same air. Live the kiss over and over again as the heat from his body radiated over to me.

Taking a deep breath, I grabbed my purse and tentatively walked out of my apartment only to slam into a brick wall.

A brick wall of Evan.

His arms encompassed me as he tried to hold onto me to keep me from propelling to the ground.

"You okay?" His deep voice vibrated through me as he hugged me to his chest. Somehow the tone in his voice was asking more than if I were okay from nearly kissing the pavement. I righted myself, brushing off imaginary dust from my clothes like I had fallen on the beach and I was covered in sand.

"I'm okay," I replied, dismissively.

"Are you ready to go?"

"Um, yeah. I'm ready."

We walked to the car in uncomfortable silence. My nerves had me on edge and when I climbed into the car, I immediately wanted to get out. Being in the confined space with Evan was only making me feel worse.

Evan tapped his fingers on the steering wheel as we drove through town to get to the rec center. His eyes never left the road, his expression looking pained as if it were taking everything he had not to look at me.

I know. Because I kept risking glances at him.

"Are you going to talk to me, Ellie? Or are you just going to keep looking at me and not say a word?" He finally said breaking the ice-cold tension between us.

"What do you want me to say, Evan? We kissed. Can't we just move past that and go back to how things were? I'm not ready to even think about another relationship right now. Jeremy and Lilly have only been gone a little over a month, yet we made out like teenagers. Doesn't that concern you a little?"

My breathing escalated as my anger reared its ugly head. How could he seriously not be affected by our actions while our spouses lay in the cold ground?

"You don't have to remind me that my wife is dead, Ellie. I wake up ever single day of my life since then with that reminder. Every time I open my eyes, I'm reminded that she is gone. I don't need your vocalization of it," he bit out. The anger was present in his voice and he didn't even try to hide it. I felt a little guilty for evoking such an emotion from him, but dammit, it was eating me up inside.

"I'm sorry, I didn't mean to upset you. I like you, Evan. I really do. I would be completely lost if I hadn't had you all this time, and I don't want to jeopardize that."

He nodded his head as if he understood what I was saying and some of the anger began to melt away from his features.

We drove the rest of the way to the rec center in silence, neither one of us wanting to fracture the fragile state that our relationship was in. I felt guilty for what had happened between us and was scared to death that I could lose the one person helping me get over the grief that was just there on the surface, threatening to consume me. In a short period of time, he had become my best friend, my only friend, and the one person on this earth that knew *exactly* what I was going through.

Almost everyone was already seated by the time we arrived. I noticed that our usual places were occupied by some of the others and the only seats left were directly opposite from each other. Evan took one and I reluctantly took the other, feeling a little nervous that I wasn't seated next to him. His presence comforted me. I needed him by my side to coach, guide, and protect me, not only from the outside world, but from myself.

"Hello everyone," Sandi said in greeting as the session began. "Tonight we are going to talk about self-forgiveness. With grief, we are so easy to blame ourselves for what has happened. We feel guilt and so many other emotions that lead us to believe that we were either the cause of the devastation or a catalyst. We find ourselves thinking about what we should or shouldn't have done, what we can do to take it all back. These feelings of guilt are very much normal. Some of you may even feel guilt just for being alive. That is called survivor's guilt. You hold on to that feeling of 'damned if we do, damned if we don't'. This exercise is to help you look past those feelings so that you can continue your road towards acceptance."

Sandi's words hit me square in the chest and I placed my hand above my heart as if someone had actually struck me there. She was right. So, so right. Everything she just described was exactly how I had felt and still did. I looked up to find Evan blatantly staring at me, his expression carved with worry and concern. I looked back at him silently trying to convince him that I was okay, even though it felt like I could implode with the slightest provoking.

"A majority of the time, it is helpful to share our feelings of regret and guilt with others who have lost loved ones so that we better understand that we aren't the only ones having these feelings. Now, I know that at this point in time, you may not be ready to let go of those feelings and that is okay, but expressing hopes for self-forgiveness can be a great beginning."

Sandi looked at us all expectantly and a new concern began to grow within me. I couldn't confess to this group that I had kissed Evan. I couldn't confide in them and tell them that although it felt so incredibly good, it also felt tremendously wrong at the same time. How would these people see me? Would they think I was a selfish and emotionless asshole who instead of grieving her husband was sticking her tongue down another man's throat? Would they even understand? Would I be some whore in their eyes because my husband had only died just a short time ago?

I looked at Evan and my concern grew even more. What if Sandi asked him first before me and he told the group about our debauchery?

"I'll go first," Sandi said breaking through my troublesome thoughts.

"In the beginning when I lost my sister, the days after nine-eleven, I couldn't cry, rather, I *wouldn't*. I was afraid I would look stupid, foolish, and weak even. I wanted to be strong and to help my mom and dad deal with their pain. I wanted to be the shoulder they could lean on. The one person that they could hold on to for support. I had to forgive myself for not crying. I had to tell myself it was okay to. I had to tell myself that it was okay that I was alive while she died, no matter how much it hurt my heart to do so."

Sandi paused, clearing her throat, evidence that her own words had her choked up.

"Who's next? Jessica?"

Jessica rose to stand and looked around the circle at all of us.

"The guilt I feel is that maybe I over did it. Maybe if I would have taken it easy those last few weeks and not worked so hard or worry so much about what I needed to get done before Daisy's birth, that maybe the chord wouldn't have ever wrapped around her neck. Maybe I shifted wrong. Maybe I should have slept on my side like the doctor's suggested instead of on my back where it was more comfortable for my hips." She looked down, twiddling her thumbs in front of her and I watched a tear escape from her eye and land upon the floor.

"Would anyone like to respond to Jessica's thoughts?" Sandi asked the group. I didn't even give anyone else a chance to respond and spoke up immediately.

"Jessica, there is no way of knowing why things happened with Daisy the way they did. Just from these last few weeks of getting to know you, I can tell you that you would have been an amazing mother to her. Circumstances were out of your control and sometimes those things happen, but you can't blame yourself for her death. It wasn't in your hands, or by your hands. You did everything right with the pregnancy."

Her eyes filled with fresh tears and she looked at me with kind eyes. My heart broke for her. I've never had the luxury of being pregnant. Jeremy and I had talked about having kids, but we also both wanted to enjoy each other for just a little while before we started a family. I couldn't imagine having to carry a child for an entire pregnancy, only to lose it before it was even born.

I then immediately looked at Evan who wore a distraught expression on his face. There were two other people in the group who had lost children and every time they spoke or told their story, it really hurt Evan. He also lost a child. One that he had only known about for a matter of hours, but it didn't matter how long he knew about it. It could have been seconds or years he had with his child and it wouldn't hurt any less. The pain of losing a child never goes away.

"Thank you, Jessica. Next? Ellie?'

I froze like a statue in my seat not expecting for her to call on me so quickly. I tried to think of something to say. Anything other than what it was I needed to say. She said that sharing our guilt would help us and the only way I would be able to move on after Jeremy was if I told the truth. Lies wouldn't help me, only hinder me. I took a deep breath and rose to stand.

"Losing Jeremy was the most unexpected and life altering

experience of my life. I, like you Sandi, couldn't cry in the beginning. I felt that if I put on a brave face, people wouldn't see just how broken I really was. But even more unexpected is the fact that I have grown to depend on someone to help me get through this. I feel guilty that I have confided in this person. I feel guilty that I have grown to really like this person. And most of all I feel guilty for the feelings that I have developed for this person because it is too soon. It's way to early to even imagine trying to move on right now."

I sat back down, hanging my head so that I didn't have to look at Evan.

There.

I said it.

I put my feelings out there hoping that he would understand, yet kept it vague enough that I wouldn't be judged by the group for my thoughts and actions.

"Thoughts?" Sandi asked the group. I prayed, no, begged in silence that Evan wouldn't be the one to respond. I didn't want the group to think we were involved or having some salacious affair. Despite what people say, opinions of others matter, no matter how much we try to convince ourselves otherwise.

One of the older gentlemen in the group spoke up.

"Ellie, I met my fiancé just three weeks after I laid my Violet to rest. I felt guilty because there was this instant connection with her. I wasn't looking for a relationship. I wasn't seeking comfort or companionship in anyone else. She just happened. It was platonic for a very long time, until one day I realized I was in love with her. She helped me through the darkest part of my life. I knew that we would be able to handle anything together after all of that. It was almost as if Violet sent her to me." His smile was sweet as he reflected back on his late wife. "I still miss my Violet, but having my fiancée makes it easier."

I took his thoughts into consideration as I sat silently and pondered what the man had said. There was something that he said that specifically caught my attention.

It was almost as if Violet sent her to me.

Was it Jeremy's intention for me to return to Florida just so that Evan and I would cross paths again? Was it a weird and sick twist of fate that he was the one who saved me from the Jet Ski incident, or was it merely coincidence?

Several other people took turns admitting what they felt guilty for or what seemed to be holding them back regarding their lost loved ones, until it was Evan's turn. I was on pins and needles waiting to hear what he had to say. Was he experiencing the same type of guilt I was, regarding our kiss? Was he regretting it even now in his mind?

"I've felt guilty for many things since I lost Lilly. I felt guilty for letting her go that night. I've felt guilty for being angry at God for taking her from me, and for surviving when she didn't. I've felt the pain every time someone mentions their child because I barely even got to acknowledge that I was going to have one. But most of all, right now, I feel guilty for not feeling guilty about certain feelings I am having. There's this incredible person that I have met that, when we are together, my pain is subsided. It is subdued to the point where I actually feel as if I could possibly live again. I feel guilty for the regret I don't feel."

He sat back down, but not without pinning his blue eyes on mine briefly. I had to fight back the tears that threatened to form. I had to take long, deep breaths to keep from falling apart in front of the whole group.

"Anyone have any feedback for Evan?" Sandi asked the group and when no one responded, Sandi spoke again.

"Evan, I am so very glad to hear that you found comfort in a new relationship with someone. That is what getting through our grief is about—how to form relationships with the people that remain in our lives instead of focusing on what we no longer have. You know," she said pausing to look around at the circle. "Life is a gamble, but we are still in the game. Only, we control who wins or loses. It is life's illusions that will bring us to our knees, but what we have in plain site in front of us that keep us on our feet."

Wow. I thought as my heart nearly stopped from her words. I looked to Evan whose lips were set in a hard line as he looked out of the window of the rec center as if he were pondering the same thing I was.

"Our final exercise tonight is for each of us to take one of these," Sandi said as she handed everyone a small strip of paper.

"I want you to write your name on it and then put it in this basket. I'll then let everyone choose a piece of paper and I want you to write one good thing about that person and then share it with them before you leave. I hope you all have a good night."

Sandi walked around and gathered all of our names and placed them in a basket before she walked around the circle again to have us choose one. I reached in and pulled a piece out when Sandi made her way back over to me and I nearly laughed out loud when I saw the name on the piece of paper.

Evan.

Fate had a wicked sense of humor.

I didn't even have to think about what I was going to say, but instead quickly wrote something down on the paper and then made my way over to him.

Evan

WHEN ELLIE APPROACHED me as soon as she had written her message on the piece of paper in her hands, I thought she was going to tell me she was ready to go. Instead, she handed me the piece of paper in her hand. Curious, I opened it up to reveal that she had drawn my name.

I'll be damned.

But what was more shocking than the fact that she drew my name, was what she had written beneath it.

I don't regret it either.

"SHE'S GOOD FOR YOU, you know?"

I nodded my head while I sat with my wife on the back porch swing, glancing out towards the horizon, watching the sunlight dance across the water.

"I still feel guilty for kissing her. Guilty because it felt like a betrayal to you. Guilty because she felt so guilty. And guilty because I enjoyed it. But also mad as hell because it has seemed to put up a wall between us."

"Evan, the guilt you feel is brought on by yourself. We

discussed this several years ago if you recall."

I squinted my eyes as if the conversation she was referring to would easily come to mind, then shook my head when I couldn't think of anything.

"It was while you were doing your residency. One of your patients had...passed on. You came home upset because you had to be the one to tell the family. We talked about how if one of us were to die before the other, what we wanted for the person who still remained."

I chuckled, but it wasn't out of amusement, but instead with sarcasm and resentment.

"What a great conversation that was. Look at us now," I bit out, not sure where my anger was focused on.

"Sweetheart, we had no way of knowing what was going to happen. But if you remember, we both said that we wanted each other to move on and be happy. Do you remember?"

"Yeah. But I didn't plan on having to move on, Lil. My plan was to spend everyday for the rest of my life with you next to me."

"You are a kind, loving, sexy man, Evan. You have so much to offer others around you. I know you feel closed off and secluded in your own anguish, but for some reason you aren't like that with Ellie. I knew that I liked her the very first time we talked on the boat that night. I could tell right away that she was warm and caring. If I can't be the one to get to experience life with you, my wish is for you to have someone like her to spend your days with."

"You've only been gone for two months, Lilly. Isn't there some time frame I'm supposed to follow, or procedure that

I need to exercise when it comes to moving on? People will think that I have no heart, running after someone so soon after the death of my wife."

I faltered trying to get those last few words out. Even though I got the luxury of seeing Lilly on occasion in my unconscious state, it was nothing compared to having her with me physically.

"There are no timeframes when it comes to the heart, Evan. The heart wants what it wants. You feel a connection with her. I've seen her. I've watched the way she looks at you when you aren't paying attention. I've seen the sorrow in her eyes from the loss of Jeremy, but when she looks at you, it softens, sometimes even vanishes momentarily. Even though the bond you and her have developed was initially from grief, it has grown into so much more."

Hearing my wife take notice and be aware of feelings I haven't quite acknowledged in myself was an uneasy feeling. I knew that I cared for Ellie, but did those feeling go beyond kinship? Was my need to kiss her the proof that my feelings went beyond friendship?

"You don't have to say it if you don't want to, Evan. But if you do, it won't hurt my feelings. I want you to be happy. All I've ever wanted was for you to be happy."

"I know that, but it doesn't make it easier to admit that to you or myself."

"Give her some time. She is still grieving as much as you are. Just help each other. Be there. If it is meant to happen it will. And baby, you have my full blessing. Be happy so that I can rest happy knowing that you are."

Her beautiful smile lit up her face, the one she always showed me when she was passionate about something. Slowly, she got up from the swing and began walking through the back yard and towards the water. When she had only gotten a few steps away from me, she turned and smiled at me over her shoulder.

"Make her your famous pancakes. No girl can resist those. You reeled me in with them," she winked and just like morning dew when the sun rises, she vanished, fading off into the view before me.

Chapter Thirteen

BUILDING A FOUNDATION

Evan

TWO AND A HALF months goes by slowly when you miss someone. Time slows. Taunting you with a snails pace as you are constantly reminded through your surroundings of what you lost. I have had to tell myself a ton of times over the last seventy-five days that if I could just have one more day, one more moment to share with Lilly, that I would be satisfied. The bad things about that is that it would leave me wanting just one more day with her everyday.

The only thing keeping me going was Ellie. We had fallen into a comfortable place with each other since that counseling session where she said she didn't regret kissing me. I don't know what I should have felt from her admission, but elation was probably not what it was supposed to be.

I've found myself thinking about her constantly, lately. Thinking about Lilly's words in my dreams and how she wanted me to be happy. I had no doubt in my mind that Lilly was completely truthful about that, but it still didn't help diminish the guilt I felt for my growing feelings for Ellie. She had become the reason to help me begin to release my chains of pain, worry, and depression. Some would see her as a filler, someone who I had in my life in order to replace the loss I had endured, but she was anything but. She was a companion. Someone who had grown to compliment my forward path in life. She gave me a sense of renewal, replacing the toxic thoughts and feelings I had harbored since Lilly's death.

The ringing of my cell phone broke me from my revere. I had grown to enjoy my morning sitting at the island in the kitchen as I watched the world outside the window pass by. It was the only place of comfort that I felt like I had, where I could just sit and think about anything and everything.

Especially Ellie.

"Hello?" I said as I held the phone up to my ear, trying to answer before it went to voicemail.

"Hello sweetheart," my mother's voice rang through the other end. I was too busy trying to answer the phone that I didn't glance at the screen before answering.

"Hey, mom," I replied with polite fondness for the person who birthed me.

"What are you doing at the house on such a pretty day. The weatherman says the weather is perfect down there."

"Well, currently I'm sitting at the island nursing a cup of coffee. Don't tell dad that I broke into his secret Colombian stash," I teased. She chuckled and it warmed my heart to hear the comforts of home. I heard her sigh audibly on the other end of the phone and knew that something was on her mind.

"The reason I'm calling, love, is to tell you that your father and I have decided that we want to come down for the weekend. Maybe go to dinner with you and just spend some time with you. You've been holed up down there for two months now. You need interaction with people. People who love you, Evan."

Shit.

For the last few months, my parents have thought that I have just been down in the Keys trying to get my thoughts clear while I have been on sabbatical from work. They know nothing of the Jet Ski incident, nor about the fact that I have been going to grief counseling. Not that my parents would reject that idea, in fact, my mom will probably be very pleased with that aspect. But they also knew nothing about Ellie. Not her name, the fact that she had been living with me for these last couple of months, nor the fact in which we were so deeply connected. I needed to try and deflect their efforts until I found a way to break the news to them.

"Mom, really. I'm fine. I've been doing much better. I just want to stay a little while longer. There is no need for you to come down here. I could always come home for a few days."

"Nonsense, honey. Besides, I think your father needs a break from the hospital. He's been working long shifts and could use a rest. He isn't getting any younger, you know."

My mother. Always the wise cracker.

I stumbled around trying to think of anything I could tell them. Anything that would prepare them for what they would find when they arrived.

"Mom, so I haven't uh—exactly been here alone."

"Oh?" My mother's hopeful voice rang back at me. I could feel her curiosity and interest practically radiating through the receiver.

"Well, I've been letting someone stay in the basement apartment since I've been here."

"What? Evan. Do you know this person? Did you do a background check? Are they legal?"

She spat out questions as quickly as she could.

"Mom, trust me, everything is okay. She just needed a place to stay because she would be in town for a while. I couldn't very well make her pay the money to stay in a hotel long term. Especially with it being peak season."

"She?"

Somehow, I knew that one tiny detail wouldn't slip past my mother. My friends called her bionic when I was younger. They claimed she had the superpower to hear and see all because she somehow knew if we were up to no good long before we ever executed one of our hair-brained schemes.

"Yes, *she*, mom. She is a nice and sweet woman. She is clean and isn't into anything illegal or immoral. You can trust my judgment."

"How in the world did you meet her, Evan? You told me you haven't gone out much."

"I just happened to run into her on the beach one day and we got to talking." *Rather ran after her*, I thought to myself.

"Huh," she huffed. "Have you been spending time with this girl?" She asked inquisitively.

"A little, but not in the way you are thinkin—"

"Oh well, I can't wait to meet her. Listen, baby, the girls are starting to arrive for book club. We'll see you in a few days. I love you."

Then she hung up.

I just got brushed off by my own mother. And I knew she did it on purpose.

Shit.

How was I going to explain to Ellie that my parents would be here in a few days? How was I going to explain to my parents Ellie's reason for being here?

Double shit.

The coffee in front of me no longer had its appeal and the sanctuary of my morning routine was disturbed, so I got up and rinsed out my coffee mug in the sink. I guess it would be better to warn Ellie ahead of time instead springing the news on her last minute, so I walked out the back and down the stairs to her apartment.

I hadn't been down here since the night I took her to the carnival, wanting to give her the space she needed, so needless to say, my nerves were heightened. I knocked softly on the door, praying that she either wasn't home, or that she was still asleep so that I wouldn't have to break the news of my parent's impending arrival upon her.

No such luck.

She answered almost immediately and goddammit if it weren't a sucker punch in the ribs when she stood there in the same dress I had bought her. Paired with her bare feet and the one single braid that laid gently over her shoulder, she looked damn near breathtaking.

"Hi," she replied sweetly and curiously.

"Hi," I replied still awestruck by the beauty of her. I've noticed it before. Any man in his right mind would see how completely gorgeous she was, but for some reason, this time, it was different.

"You aren't busy are you?"

"No, I was just reading," she said and that is when I noticed the large hardback novel in her hands.

"I don't want to disturb you."

"You aren't. Would you like to come in?"

I nodded, following her into the apartment and praying to God to stop me from looking at her ass. Or the way that the dress flowed over it. Nor the way that it sashayed slightly with each step she took. And I definitely didn't want to look at the tanned and toned skin of her shoulders.

Dammit. Dammit all to hell.

She looked up at me and instantly I peeled my eyes away from her and then sat down next to her on the couch. Setting the book down on the coffee table she then tugged her legs underneath her adjusting the dress so that it covered her smooth thighs that had begun to peek out from under the softness of the fabric.

"Is something wrong, Evan?" She asked as she tilted her head to the side and took in my expression.

"Um—well, yes—and no. I just got a phone call from my mom."

"That's not very surprising, Evan. My mother calls me at least twice a day I think. Sometimes more," she teased.

I took in a deep breath and thought it better that I just laid it all out instead of dancing around the subject.

"My mom and dad are coming down to visit."

"Really?" Her eyebrows perked up and she had a small smile on her lips.

"Yeah, well, I haven't exactly been truthful with them. They know nothing about the counseling or the Jet Ski situation or the fact that you are even staying with me."

"Oh," she replied, her tone hinting that she could possibly feel a little hurt about me not telling my parents she was here.

"Ell, it isn't you, it's just that my mother tends to…how do I put this gently? She still thinks I'm sixteen and wants to help control my life. She means well, but she tends to try and stick her nose in my personal business and doesn't quite know when to back off. If I'd told her a month ago you were here, she would have been down here in a heartbeat asking all kinds of questions about our relationship and why you are here. I didn't want to have to deal with that. I didn't want you to have to deal with that either."

"I understand. My mom is the same way. My dad however? He's just a big teddy bear who only wants his daughter to be happy."

"Wow," I chuckled. I think that our parents were cloned from the same cloth." We both laughed, and it felt really great to just be casual with her, even with the underlying feelings bubbling on the surface.

"I can always go and stay in a hotel or something while they are here. I don't want to give you any unnecessary stress or anything. I mean, you're a doctor and all, but I doubt if you're allowed to write your own blood pressure medicine." She was teasing and it was cute.

Really fucking cute.

"One, no, I'm not allowed to do that, though I can probably safely say my blood pressure will be a few points higher than normal with my mom here. And two, you aren't going to stay in a hotel. We'll just tell them the truth. We have nothing to hide."

"They're going to blame me for getting their son in trouble!" She gasped her hands flying up to meet her mouth.

"I can't meet them? What if they think I'm some hardened criminal?"

I laughed deeply, the effects of her words tickling all the way into my ribcage until my abs hurt from the force.

"Sweetheart, I would bet my medical license on no one ever thinking you are a hardened criminal. There isn't a mean bone is this sweet little body of yours," I said reaching out to tickle her ribs. I watched as her face flushed about twenty shades of crimson as she giggled and it was then that I realized what I said.

"I meant that you are sweet. No one would think you are capable of organized crime, not that your body is sweet. I mean it is sweet, I just—oh hell. I'm going to quit talking now."

This time it was my turn to blush as heat crept up my neck and my ears burned.

"It's okay. I knew what you meant," she said and reached out her hand, planting it on top of mine. The awareness, the feelings came rearing out full force the moment her skin touched mine. Instinctively, I turned my palm over allowing her fingers to thread through mine. It was amazing how just one simple touch from this woman made every dark cloud that hovered over me, melt away, leaving me to bask in her light that shone over me.

"Evan," she breathed, but I noticed that she didn't pull away from me, instead giving my hand a tight squeeze.

"Ellie, I don't know what this is," I said gesturing between us, "I don't know how to keep the thoughts and feelings I have towards you under control without scaring you or myself into running in the other direction. I can't deny that there isn't something there. I can't say that my mind doesn't race and that I don't feel the tiny flutters in my stomach every time I am near you. You make things better for me. Easier. And it scares me."

Removing her legs from beneath her, she slid over to where our thighs were touching and placed her other hand over where ours were still connected.

"I know, Evan. I feel something too. It is both liberating and terrifying at the same time. I feel free of the pain of losing Jeremy when I'm with you. You are the only reason I think I have been able to keep sane. Your strength guides me everyday. I watch you and wish that I could have more courage. But at the same time, it feels like a betrayal. I feel like it is wrong of me to have these feelings. But my resistance is weakening by the day."

I brought my free hand up to the side of her cheek, the smoothness of her skin feeling luxurious beneath my palm. Ellie closed the distance between us to where our lips were mere inches apart. I wanted to just give into my thoughts and feelings and capture her mouth with my own, but after what happened at the carnival, I held back, wanting her to be the one to make the decision.

Her blue eyes flicked back and forth between mine as if seeking permission, and it wasn't me she was seeking it from. It was like she was silently asking herself if it were okay to give in to her feelings, her wants. I saw it the moment the storm clouds in her eyes opened up and the rain began pouring down as she let the dam break. Leaning in she softly pressed her lips to mine, clinging to where she had grasped my shirt in the hand I wasn't holding on to. My heart thundered in my chest, matching the storm that was brewing inside of her. But it was the lightening that was the most noticeable. The electrical current composed from the static of our bodies as we slowly began to deepen the kiss. Her sigh of contentment gave me the courage to urge her on as I slowly traced the seam of her lips with my tongue, instantly getting her to open for me.

That was it.

All it took.

I accepted her invitation and released her hand to cup the back of her head to hold her closer to me, not wanting to give her the opportunity to run away. Shock and full blown awareness coursed through me as she climbed onto my lap and kissed me back, matching my fervor. I closed my eyes thinking that it was all a dream. A wonderful dream that I didn't want to wake up from. Because right then, in this moment, was when I truly believed what Lilly told me. It also made me believe that maybe there was a reason that she and I were on that boat that night. As much as my heart ached from my beloved wife, the ache I felt now was anything but grief. It was a longing of the likes I had never felt before. I felt my body stir naturally from the position she was in on my lap, hoping that she didn't feel the erection that was growing beneath her thighs.

Breaking my lips away from hers, I kissed her jaw and down the curve of her neck, marveling at the smoothness of her skin, the fluent map of her flesh, teasing me, taunting me through my lips as I trailed kisses along her clavicle.

"Oh, God," she whispered, pleasure evident in her voice as she ran her fingers through my hair and tilted her head back, granting me greater access.

"You are so beautiful, Ellie. Both inside and out," I admitted as lifted my head to whisper in her ear. She shuddered as a ripple of ecstasy invaded her system and she sighed contently. Slowly, sleepily, relaxed, I captured her lips again, this time taking the opportunity to savor the unique taste. The way her mouth tasted of fresh coffee mingled with a flavor that could only be completely Ellie. I was trapped in a haze of sensual bliss luxuriated by the possessiveness she seemed to have over me.

Wrapping one arm around her back and my other under her knees, I eased her down onto the couch coming to rest beside her. Gently, I stroked her hair behind her ear trying to gage her thoughts.

"Evan?" She asked, a small shake in her voice.

"Hmmm?" I replied as I continued to play with her hair.

"Kiss me again?" Her voice sounded so small, yet livened with a desire that was never present before. I didn't even respond, instead, taking her lips once more enjoying the gratifyingly enticing way they felt against my own. I stroked her cheek with the pad of my thumb, needing—wanting to touch her more, but also not wanting to take it any further than what she felt like she could handle.

As if she couldn't surprise me anymore, she grabbed my hand and trailed it down her throat and across the top of her chest until it came to rest on the plump pillow that was her breast.

"Touch me, Evan. I want you to touch me."

Flicking my thumb across the tips of her hardened nipple under the fabric of her dress, she arched her back, causing her breast to press further into my hand. I continued to taste her as I cupped her breast, gently kneading and earning an appreciable murmur of pleasure from her.

"Ellie, God you feel so good. I need this. Need you," I said as I pressed kisses along the line of her jaw.

"But God, we need to stop if this isn't what you want. Please tell me, tell me that you don't want this so I will stop."

It was small, but I saw her shake her head back and forth, her blue eyes sparkling with desire.

"I—I want this. Want you, Evan. God I want you so bad," she admitted. Another dam somewhere broke within me and the next thing I knew, I was lying on top of her as my knees nudged her legs apart allowing me to settle between them. My erection pressed into the softness of her as I devoured her lips. Her arms circled me as she clung to my back as if anchoring herself to me.

"Are you sure about this?" I asked, kissing the corner of her mouth.

"Yes. Yes, please," she admitted, her pelvic bone rising to add pressure on the spot that was aching for her.

I snaked my hand under her dress, delight filling me as my fingertips trailed up her inner thigh until I was met with the barrier of her underwear.

Lace. Sexiest thing on the planet.

Without thinking, I removed her panties, allowing my fingertips to trace down the smooth skin of her thighs. Once they were removed, I inserted a finger inside of her, slowly, capturing her lips once more, not feeling like I could ever get enough of them.

I stroked her sensitive flesh to the point she nearly came undone, backing off just before she crested over the edge. I enjoyed watching the pleasure build on her face, the way she bit her lip between kisses, seeking more from me and breathing out a protest when my rhythm slowed.

"Evan, please," she panted, her throaty voice filled with desire. Slowly, I reached for the hem of her dress and began to slide it up her body, allowing my fingertips to trace against her skin with my ascent. I felt the bumps on her skin form from my touch coupled with the small shiver of passion her body released from the contact. I paused only long enough for her to sit up and lift the dress over her head. Laying beneath me in nothing but her underwear, I marveled with awe as I openly gawked at her beautiful body. I allowed my palms to connect with the flat plain of her stomach, feeling her abs flex beneath my hand. As if I had all the time in the world, I allowed my palms to glide further up until I was palming one of her plump breasts. Arching into my hand, she squeezed her eyes shut and let her mouth hang open as she pressed her breast further into my hand.

"You are so damn beautiful," I admitted as I leant in to kiss the hollow space of her throat. I felt her arms slip between us and her fingers begin to mess with the button of my jeans. I reached behind my head, pulling my shirt over it before tossing it to the floor. I watched Ellie's eyes open wide as she bit her lip in appreciation for my body.

I closed my eyes briefly and knew it was probably something I shouldn't have done. Why? Because that brief pause allowed rationality to filter into my thoughts trying to replace the impulsivity that had consumed me when Ellie was beneath me practically begging me to take her. The only thing that made me think twice about what we were doing was knowing that it was wrong. I felt like I was taking advantage of her vulnerability and both of our deep need to get lost in something or someone other than our grief. I have always prided myself on being a passionate man. Someone who had a high sense of what was right and wrong, and made my decisions based on those values.

Then why did something that seemed so wrong, feel so incredibly right?

"What's wrong?" Ellie's soft voice said breaking me from my inner thoughts.

"I don't know. I—I don't think I can do this," I admitted in defeat as I leant down and placed my forehead on her belly, feeling the rapid rise and fall of her chest.

She sighed long and hard while several minutes passed and neither of us said a word. I knew she was contemplating the consequences over in her mind of what the outcome of us making love would mean.

"Evan, I know you probably think that I wanted this in the heat of the moment, or that I'm trying to use what is happening between us as some sort of cover up for the true feelings inside of me. I want to be honest with you. I'm scared to death. I also don't want to feel this, yet at the same time I do. I wouldn't just offer myself up to anyone in order to free myself from the pain. You have been here for me these last few months when I needed someone. You have reached me on a level that I don't feel anyone else could. Our whole world has been shaken, but in the midst of it, you are the only thing that has kept me steady. Kept me grounded."

She peered up at me, never breaking eye contact. I took the moment to study her face, her features that made her so beautiful. There was a seriousness to her gaze, yet it had undertones of vulnerability. After suffering such great loss like the two of us have, I knew how terrifying it was for her to put herself on the line.

"Ellie, there isn't a doubt in my mind about the truthfulness of your words. I know that you offering yourself to me isn't laced with hidden agendas or with a subliminal message. That is what makes you unique. Your honesty and your kindness, your ability to put yourself out on a limb is one of the best things about you."

I stroked the tender flesh of her cheek and watched as she closed her eyes and leant into my touch.

"I want you, Ellie. God, I want you. I just don't want us to both rush into something that we will regret later. I don't think I could handle it if I became a disappointment or a remorse you feel after we, well, you know."

Her eyes opened, the crystal blue staring directly into mine reminded me of the color of the ocean that I once loved. Even though my love for its beauty had faded in the shadow of what happened, looking into Ellie's eyes, made me feel like I wanted to forgive it for taking away the beauty that I once saw in it.

"I could never regret you. I could never look upon our time together as something that I wish didn't happen. I think the only reason my heart still beats is because of you."

Any anguish or hesitation that I was feeling was instantly washed away as soon as she said those words to me. I captured her lips with mine, relishing once again in the taste of her. Her softness pressed beneath my hardness. I shivered as both of her hands wrapped around my shoulders and she threaded her fingers through my hair. Tiny tingles of delight spread throughout my scalp until they filtered down to my backside. Her taste was unique, but the way we kissed was like we had known each other forever. The way our mouths formed and molded to each other's in such a perfect way, couldn't really be described.

With the pad of my thumbs I traced lazy circles on her ribcage just beneath the globes of her breasts. Pressure began building within me and my chest pounded with a carnal need to be inside of her. When I slid my hands higher, I gently took her nipple between my thumb and forefinger, rubbing in a circular motion. Her back arched from the couch pressing her body further into my groin.

Friction. I needed the friction. I needed the sweet release of being inside of her, of staking my claim over something I had no right to want to own, but desperately wanted to. She began to try and slide my jeans down my hips, and this time, I let her as I rid my body of the only barrier left between us. Lying on top of her, we finally became flesh to flesh. No barriers. No walls to come between us. I could feel the heat radiating from her body melding with the smolder of my own. The warmth although physical, was nothing compared to the heat in which our souls slowly began to mold together. It was an out of body experience. A magical, spiritual connection that made everything about the intimacy between us seem so much more.

"Evan," she whispered as she leant up ever so slightly, placing her lips directly next to my ear. The flesh of her mouth tracing the shell of my ear with her words.

"Make love to me."

Without hesitation, I aligned myself with her and in what seemed like one of the most perfect and sublime moments to ever happen to me, we became one. I paused as I allowed her body to adjust to me.

Welcoming me.

Accepting me.

Wrapping around me.

"Evan."

Her gasp of my name upon her lips sent a soul shattering feeling to encompass me. Clinging tightly to each other, we began to move. Each thrust synchronized with each other to the point where we were nothing short of perfect unison.

And when the pressure began to build and a white light began to invade my sight, blinding me with passion, pleasure and an emotional high like no other, we both crested the hill together. Tumbling over the edge and freefalling into each other until the climax subsided and we were left with the lethargic after effects of being with each other. To describe the feeling would be like trying to describe the beauty of a sunset to someone who was born blind. There was no true way to describe how it made me feel inside, but I do know that I had never felt more complete.

Chapter Fourteen

MEET THE PARENTS

Evan

"THERE'S MY BABY," my mother said as she came towards me with arms wide open while my father retrieved their bags from the rental car. I stepped off the front porch to meet her half way, enveloping her tiny frame and hugging her. She smelled like cherries as I inhaled the scent of her hair while resting my cheek on the top of her head. My dad soon approached, placing the bags on the ground long enough to extend a handshake to me as I released my mom, looking at him funny as I placed my hand in his. A goofy smile crossed his features as he pulled me in and hugged me, clapping his other hand on my back. In the history of parents, I had to say that mine were the best. Always supportive, always there for me and they built a good foundation of morals, love, and mutual respect for one another as I grew up.

Eleanor and Rusty Taylor made the perfect couple. They were so much alike that I swear they knew each other in a past life. Even though their physicality's sharply contrasted each other, my mom being five foot two and my dad well over six feet, their personalities and souls were the same. My mother's long blonde hair had gotten shorter over the years and was now speckled with a gray that showed her age, but didn't take away from her beauty. My father, having lost most of the hair on the crown of his head at a young age, kept what was left closely clipped or sometimes shaved.

"How are you son?" My dad asked as he leant down to grab the bags once more. I beat him to the punch, taking both bags by the handle and lifted them before he could. I chuckled and shook my head as I felt how heavy my mom's bag was compared to my dad's.

"Good, dad. How was the trip?"

"Oh pretty good. My hand survived as you can see," he said holding it up for me to see. "Your mom managed to not completely crush it on the short flight down here."

I chuckled again.

"Mom, how many years have you been flying down here now? Ten? Twenty? You still get nervous?" I asked as we all turned to enter the house.

"Planes still go down all the time son," my mom said with a shiver.

We entered the house and my mom took off her sunglasses as my father took the bags from me and headed down the hallway to the bedrooms.

"Huh." My mom said as she looked all around and a few 'mercies' came from her.

"What?" I asked her as I watched her look all the way around the living room with her mouth half open.

"Oh well I guess I just expected something different I suppose."

"What exactly is it you were expecting?" I asked as I arched my brow in curiosity.

"It's so…clean. Did you clean up before we came sweetheart?" She asked looking around again as if trash and debris would materialize out of thin air at any moment.

"Mom, I'm perfectly capable of keeping things clean. I was raised well." A flash of pride graced her face at my words.

"I don't know. I just half expected empty beer bottles and pizza boxes to be littered around. Do you keep it clean for *her*?" A slow smile began to build up on her face as she tilted her head to the side, observing my reaction.

"Who is *her*?" I prodded.

"Your young woman you told us about downstairs."

Ellie.

"No, mom. I don't keep it clean for her. I just like stuff organized and tidy. I wouldn't want my hospital to be a mess, why would I want my home to be?"

"Good point sweetheart."

My father joined us in the living room and took a seat on the couch, extending his arm along the back.

"So, how are things going, son? Has the hospital given you any timeframe for when you can return to work?"

Yeah. My chief of staff informed me real quick that I wasn't to return until I completed grief counseling. But they didn't know about any of that yet.

"They just said that I shouldn't come back until I was completely and competently ready." I replied, deciding to hold the truth from them a little while longer.

"Well, they have your best interest as well as all of your patient's at heart. I'm sure once you are ready, you'll know."

Suddenly, the front door opened startling all of us.

"Evan, do you have a copy of the assignment we were to do this week—oh…" Ellie stopped mid stride when she looked around the room and found three pairs of eyes staring back at her. Shock and surprise crossed her features causing her cheeks to burn a bright shade of crimson. It was cute. It was kind of sexy, really.

It has been two days since that day on the couch when we made love. We haven't done anything since then, not even kiss. But that didn't mean that my body wasn't screaming too. I figured a little space between us would give us both time to think about what had happened and whether or not there was going to be anything else developing between us.

"I'm sorry. I didn't know you had company," she said as she raised both of her hands to her cheeks and shuffled back a step or two to retreat back through the door.

I couldn't help but admire her beauty in that moment and felt the corners of my lips turn up at the thought. The memory of the way she felt beneath me as we made love, still very fresh in my mind. I tore my gaze from her as she began to turn and leave the room and caught my mother staring at me. Her eyes inquisitive, her curiosity peaked, and a small smile of mischief upon her lips.

Jumping up quicker than any sixty-two year old woman probably should, she was at Ellie's side in a matter of seconds.

"Oh sweetheart, do come in. I've heard so much about you from our Evan. Come. Have a seat with us." She said to Ellie as she cupped her elbow and tried to practically drag her back into the room.

"I'm sure you would love to visit with your son. I don't want to intrude," Ellie said as her eyes locked with mine searching for help, a small amount of fear piercing through her blue orbs.

"Don't be ridiculous! I can see my son any old time. You just come on back in here."

Something you have to learn about my mom. She doesn't take no for an answer. Once Eleanor has her sights set on something, she usually doesn't stop until she gets what she wants. Just ask my father.

My mom guided Ellie over to sit next to me on the loveseat before joining my father on the couch. Several long, awkward seconds passed between as we sat there. Ellie and I risked sideways glances between each other, her smile in place to hide the anxiety she was feeling. I thought it would be good of me to try and rescue her.

"Mom, Dad, this is Ellison Morris. Ellie, these are my parents, Eleanor and Russell Taylor." Ellie stood slightly and reached over to extend a hand to both of them.

"It's a pleasure to meet both of you."

"Pleasure, Ellison," my father replied smiling warmly at her.

"Oh, please call me Ellie."

"As long as you call me Rusty. My dad was Russell, and he was an old fart."

Ellie giggled and like that, it seemed some of the ease was lifted from her shoulders.

"So are the two of you taking classes or something?" My mom asked glancing at both of us. Her hands poised in her lap as her eyes flicked back and forth between Ellie and me.

Ellie stiffened by my side from my mom's question and I stuttered in response.

"What do you mean?"

"Oh, it's just that when Ellie came into the room, she was asking about an assignment."

Shit.

"Where are you from, Ellie?" My father chimed in. I silently thanked him even though I knew we were only delaying the inevitable. One thing about my father is that his years of being a doctor gave him the uncanny ability to read people. He could always tell if they were lying, sad, or hiding things. Luckily, he hadn't seemed to catch on to the fact of why or how Ellie and I knew each other in the first place.

"I'm from North Carolina," she replied sweetly.

"I went deep sea fishing near Wilmington once. Beautiful area."

"Yes, it is."

A look of sadness briefly washed across Ellie's face and I knew she was missing home. It's been two months that she has been in the Keys with me, not having gone home at all yet. That may be something that I should do something about.

"So what brings you all the way down here, sweetie?" My mom asked.

Ellie tucked her hair behind her ear, but I noticed the small tremble of her hand as she did so. Her knee bounced slightly as she cleared her throat. I reached over and grabbed her hand, entwining our fingers without thinking. I felt desperate to offer the comfort that came so easy for me to give to her. My mom's eyes grew wide and she smiled once what I just did registered with her.

I blew out a sigh of resignation.

"Ellie is here because well, shit…" I said trying to find the words to tell them the truth.

"Evan, language. There is a lady present," my mom scolded.

"Oh trust me, mom. She's heard a lot worse from me."

My mother just shook her head at me and I knew that if it weren't for Ellie being right next to me, I would get a thorough scolding from her about manners and how a gentleman should act.

"Ellie and I know each other," I began again, "Because she lost her husband in the accident."

Everyone was silent for several long seconds. My father sat up straighter and my mother lifted her hands to her mouth to cover the tremble of her lips as tears swam in her eyes.

"Oh my goodness, Ellie. I'm so sorry. We had no idea."

My mom stood up and came over and wrapped her arms around Ellie. Peering over her shoulder, my mom looked at me, sympathy glaring at me through her unshed tears. My parents loved Lilly just as much as I did. Just as much as I do. They didn't take the news well about her death and it still seems to have an effect on them. Especially my mom. I am an only child, so when Lilly and I began dating, my mother gained the daughter she never had and they bonded instantly. Ellie sniffled next to me as my mother reluctantly released her, and I rubbed her back offering my own comfort.

"Honestly, Mrs. Taylor, if it weren't for Evan these last few months, I'm not sure I would even be here right now." Ellie turned to look at me and the tears in her eye showed her grief, but they also held something more for me.

Longing.

I could feel the tension radiate between us. It wasn't a bad tension, but instead something completely welcome and profound. I wanted to kiss her. Take away the hurt and fill her with promises that everything was going to be okay. That as long as we had each other, we could get through anything. Shock registered through me as I realized that my feelings for her seemed to run deeper than I ever thought that they did.

"That's not the whole story," Ellie said wiping at her eyes.

"I'm afraid that I have gotten Evan and myself into some trouble and that is why we are both still down here."

"What do you mean?" My mother asked her looking puzzled.

"I kind of stole a Jet Ski and Evan and I were both arrested when he took one to come after me because I took off out into the middle of the ocean."

"What?" My father said, his voice raising several levels.

"You were arrested? Does the hospital know about this?"

"Dad, calm down. No. The hospital doesn't know, yet." I reassured him.

"But it is a matter of public record, Evan. How could you be so careless? You realize that there is potential damage to your career?"

"Rusty," my mom scolded.

"Eleanor. We have watched him bust his ass in medical school to get to where he is today. What would happen if his arrest reflected badly on him and all because he stole a Jet Ski?"

"Mr. Morris, in all fairness, Evan was just trying to help me. His intentions were nothing but well intended. I was the one who actually committed the theft," Ellie admitted, defeat and embarrassment written on her face.

"Why in the world would you want to do that, dear?" My mother asked in a calm voice, although I could tell she was affected by the news.

"Well," Ellie began as she swallowed audibly. I reached for her hand again, desperate to have that connection with her. Even if it were just our palms touching. "Most of the bodies were recovered from the ocean, but my Jeremy's wasn't. I was completely distraught by the fact that I had to lay an empty casket in the ground because my husband's body was still lost at sea. I guess I just snapped. I had just lost my husband and reality and I weren't on a first name basis at that moment. I was thinking irrationally and thought that I could go and find him myself. I'm sorry. I'm so, so, sorry. I never wanted Evan to get into trouble. I didn't even know he was even here. I promise."

"Oh you poor thing!" My mom exclaimed as she pulled Ellie in for another hug, effectively breaking our hands apart.

"The judge was quite lenient with us. He said that the owner of the place we took the Jet Skis from agreed to drop all charges if we got counseling. I guess he was informed about how Ellie and I both lost our spouses in the accident. The judge agreed and that is what we were sentenced to. Grief counseling." I said jumping in to Ellie's defense. I saw the silent thank you and relief in her eyes when she turned to look at me after removing herself from my mother's embrace.

"So you two have been going through counseling the entire time you have been here?" My mother questioned. Ellie and I both nodded our heads in unison.

"Well, I guess some good has come out of all of this then. Even though it was forced on you, I think counseling is the best thing that you two could participate in," my father admitted.

"Ellie, dear, have you eaten yet? Rusty and I decided to forego the dinner on the short plane ride so that we would be hungry to dine with Evan. I'm famished. Would you like to join us for dinner? We could all go out so that we don't have to make a mess of the kitchen. What do you say?"

"That sounds really lovely, but I'm sure you would much rather catch up with your son. I just planned on making it a quiet night in," Ellie replied. I felt disappointed that she didn't want to come. I wanted to spend more time with her. The last few days I have been walking around feeling only half full. Now that I have had a taste of her, my desire was only magnified that much more. It no longer felt like a betrayal to Lilly, but instead I felt like she was right there with me, cheering me on, and guiding me. She was always my biggest supporter and I had no doubt in my mind that she was doing so in the afterlife. For some weird, sardonic reason, fate had brought Ellie and I back together, so it was fate I was going to allow to lead me.

"Nonsense, of course you're coming. You can't leave me with two boys. All they will talk about is boy stuff. I need a female companion. Please?" My mom batted her eyelashes playfully at Ellie and I saw the moment she gave in. My mother, always able to talk anyone into anything. Maybe it was her sweetness, or just the way she interacted with people, but again, she hardly ever heard the word no. I was even more thankful for that at that very moment.

Ellie

EVAN'S PARENTS INSISTED on going to this tiny, hole-in-the-wall bar that sat right on the edge of the ocean. The sound of music coming from the local dive all but drowned out the roar of the waves as they crashed upon the shore. Inside, it was crazy busy. Waitresses fluttered around the small space as if it were a modern day Icecapades performance on hardwood.

"Best place in town to get seafood," Rusty said over his shoulder, trying to carry his voice above the music. I glanced all around the restaurant taking in the flashing neon signs, faded seashell wallpaper and a chalkboard menu so large it took up an entire wall. The smell of sizzling shrimp and hushpuppies filled the air and my stomach growled in protest from how hungry I truly was.

"I'll be damned, if it isn't Rusty Morris," a long-haired older man said as he approached Rusty and pulled him into a huge bear hug. He then proceeded to pick up Eleanor and spin her around in a large circle before placing her back on her feet. His shoulder-length, silver hair shone beneath the fluorescent lights. His overly tanned skin gave away the amount of years he had probably lived on the island. But it was the deep wrinkles around his bright green eyes that did me in when he looked at me with kindness and winked.

"Tommy Barnes. Hell, you still running this place?" Rusty said playfully punching his friend on the arm.

"Nah, I signed this shit hole over to Lil' Tommy a few years ago. I just help out on the busy nights. Follow me I'll clear you out a table."

We followed Tommy towards the back of the room, passing a group of people that were crowded around the stage witnessing two college girls belting out horrible lyrics to *I Will Survive*. I smiled when a warm memory of when Jeremy dragged me to a karaoke bar on Costal North Carolina and much to my surprise dragged me on stage to sing Sonny and Cher's *I Got You Babe*.

I held tightly to Evan's hand as he led us through the throws of people and couldn't help but feel comfortable with his touch. It had been several days since we made love. I was afraid that things would be weird between us, or that worse, I wouldn't want to be around him because I had gone back on what I said I wouldn't do and regret the moment we shared.

Tommy stopped in front of a table that had about four people sitting nursing on beers and fruity drinks.

"You all ordering any food?" He asked looking at the group that barely looked as if they were old enough to be in the bar in the first place.

Several of them shook their head.

"Then get on up. This here table is for food buying patrons. If you want to squat, go do it over there," He said hooking his thumb over his shoulder towards the bar where the bartender was working furiously to fill drink orders. We each sat down, Evan's parents on one side and Evan and I on the other. Evan let go of my hand to pull out my chair for me and immediately I missed the warmth of his palm on mine.

Tommy reached over to the table behind him and pulled a chair up to the end of the table, spinning it around so that he straddled it and rested his arms on the back.

"So what brings you to my neck of the woods, Rus? Usually you two don't come down here until Fall."

Dark expressions crossed our faces as the reminder set in as to why it was we were all in the Keys.

"Evan has been here for a while and so we decided to come visit him," my mom chimed in helping to break the sudden wave of anxious tension between us.

"Oh shit man, I didn't even think. I heard all about the accident. Such a tragedy. I'm very sorry about Lilly. She was a great woman," Tommy said as he cupped Evan on the shoulder.

"Thanks. She was."

Tommy leant to the side and caught me with his green eyes.

"And who are you sweetheart?" He asked as he offered a sweet smile. It worked to suppress some of the nervous and uneasy feeling that had suddenly appeared in my stomach.

"My name is Ellie. I'm friends with Evan. Actually, I lost my husband in the accident."

I figured it was probably worth it to just come right out with the information about Jeremy. I didn't want any questions about the relationship between Evan and me. I didn't want to have to define what we were or weren't, and honestly, I didn't even know myself.

Tommy's smile relaxed slightly but he still kept it there to liven the mood.

"Well, you are amongst good people darlin'. I've known this ole chap since we was pulling off his diapers and running on the beach buck naked," he said playfully nudging Evan's shoulder and I watched his face blush a beautiful shade of red that made me giggle.

"Oh good Lord. I couldn't keep pants on him when he was a toddler. Every chance he got, he stripped down to his birthday suit and ran around free-balling it," Eleanor said as she looked longingly at Evan with a huge grin on her face.

"Mom!" Evan scolded and we all erupted in laughter.

"Shelly will be along in a few to take your order," Tommy said winking at us and stood to place the chair he was sitting in back over with the other table.

"Oh, I don't have a menu," I said looking and then noticing that neither did Evan or his parents.

"No need for one, little lady. It's all up there," Tommy said pointing at the large chalkboard covered wall.

"Rus, you better not leave without joining me in a round of pool on the ole table before you leave. You too Evan." Tommy winked once more at me and walked towards the bar.

"So, what's good here?" I asked Evan nudging him with my elbow while I scanned the menu, trying to read the words between all the heads that bobbed around in front of it.

"Just about everything is Tommy's recipe. But if I had to choose my favorite thing up there, it would be the crab cake sandwich and onion rings."

"Sounds good to me. I can't really see what is at the bottom of the menu anyway."

A girl named Shelly came and took our orders before disappearing into the crowd again.

"It's crazy busy here tonight. I bet Tommy's son was glad for the extra help from his dad," I said looking around the room.

"Tommy was being modest, Ellie. This place looks like this almost *every* night."

My eyes widened as I scanned the crowd again.

"Only place on the island that has karaoke," Evan explained.

"This place still looks the same it did twenty years ago. Don't you think Eleanor?"

She chuckled.

"Tommy never was one for change. So yeah, it does."

A set of girls walked up on stage and took the mics from their stands as a familiar set of guitar rips began to play through the speaker. The glassed-over look in their eyes coupled with the slight pink tinge to each of their cheeks told me they were probably already several drinks into their night. Bright colored bikini tops shone through their thin cotton shirts and tank tops, while the shorts they wore were so short, the pockets hung from beneath the hem at their thighs. Seriously. Someone should tell them that your girly bits should never hang lower than your shorts. I shook my head.

"What are you laughing about?" Evan asked, leaning in to whisper in my ear since the volume of the music had risen several octaves. I felt a small shiver of tingly awareness race down my spine from his brush of breath alone.

"Just that my mom would have killed me if I wore clothes like that out in public. They have to barely even be twenty-one."

"Oh, and like you are old? You're what twenty-five? That makes you an expert on fashion, right?" He teased.

I puffed in mock insult while placing my hands on my hips.

"I'm twenty-eight, thank you very much. And I may be no expert, but at least I wear something that doesn't risk suffocating my vagina."

Instantly, my cheeks heated and my hands flew to my mouth when I realized what I had just said. Evan was chuckling at me while I risked a glance toward his parents who were luckily, engaged in their own conversation.

Evan reached up and tucked a strand of hair behind my ear, taking the opportunity to graze the side of my cheek as he did.

Leaning in closer he said, "You are incredibly cute when you are embarrassed."

His smile was beaming and I couldn't help but get lost in a sweet moment that passed between us as I returned his smile.

"Well, I also bet your momma wouldn't let you butcher such a great song like those three are doing. I think one of my ear drums ruptured," he said covering his ear with one hand and wincing. It was my turn to laugh and I did so with liberation. It felt really nice to get out and hang out with people. For so long it had been just me and Evan, and even though I was extremely nervous about meeting his parents, they were really great and accepting of me.

Our moment was broken as a well underserved round of applause thundered the bar when the girls on stage finally finished their song.

Sally delivered our meals to us with precision and I was practically salivating over my plate as the aromas filtered through my nose.

We all made small talk and dove into our meals as several more people went on stage and tried to sing. Tried being the key word.

Evan's dad was hilariously funny when he interacted with Tommy, who came to join us at the table once again when we finished eating. Eleanor also watched her husband lovingly as he and Tommy laughed about times when they were younger. Apparently, Rusty's parents also vacationed in the Keys every year when he was a child and that is how he knew Tommy who was what he referred to as a "lifer" in the Keys, meaning he had lived here his whole life.

"I'll be right back," Evan said as he scooted his chair back and stood up. Without thinking, I unabashedly watched him walk away, marveling at the glorious view of his backside. When he was out of eyesight, I reached for my water in order to soothe my mouth that had suddenly gone dry. That is when I looked up and locked eyes with Eleanor.

Shit.

I just got caught blatantly admiring her son's ass. If I thought my face turned red when I said *vagina* earlier, then now I was crimson. No, more like the deep red of garnet. The corners of her mouth tipped up with a small smile before she joined back in on Tommy and Rusty's conversation.

"Alright, alright, ladies and gents, gonna have a special treat for you. I've been promised one hell of a duet, so please give a warm welcome to Ellie and Evan!" The DJ announced through the speakers.

"What?" I squeaked as I looked all around for Evan and found him staring sheepishly at me from the stage.

I violently began shaking my head back and forth.

"No! No way Morris!" I yelled above the crowd that was now chanting my name over and over, Evan's parents included.

"Come on, Ellie. The crowd wants you up here! Get your cute little ass on this stage or I'll bring you myself."

Forget Garnet. I was probably now a shade of red so deep, it didn't even have a name.

Reluctantly, forcefully, and completely against my will, I stood up, my legs shaking beneath me and walked through the people to the stage. I shot a death glare at Evan who only beamed a radiant, completely sexy, and completely unfair smile at me.

"And here they are folks! Ellie and Evan," The DJ announced again. Stepping behind his computer, he pressed play on a song all the while I was boring holes into Evan with the promise to kick his ass when this was all said and done.

A cold so chilling, it settled instantly into my bones as the intro to the song began to play. I could feel all the heat and redness that only moments before crossed my features completely drain from my face. All the background noise around me faded into the distance and the only thing I could hear was the song. I felt dizzy, teetering on the edge between passing out and holding myself together. Tears stung the back of my eyes and my lips trembled to the point it probably looked like I was freezing. Evan, feeding off the energy of the crowd didn't notice as he began to sing and only looked at me when I didn't join him. Instantly, his voice quieted and he pulled the mic away from his mouth.

"Ellie? Ellie, what's wrong?" He said, his voice dripping with concern. I continued to stand there, barely, as memories flooded in as if the Hoover Dam had just burst, spilling water everywhere.

The mic in my hand slipped to the floor from my hand sending a horrible squealing sound to pierce through the music playing through the speakers. People quickly covered their ears and Evan tossed the mic in his hand to the DJ and came up to place his hands on my shoulders.

"Ellie, are you okay? Your face is really white. Baby, talk to me. Tell me what it is."

I could hear the fear in his voice, yet it still didn't prompt a reaction from me for several more minutes.

"I'm sorry," I whispered as tears now cascaded down my cheeks and I turned from him and ran out of the bar.

Chapter Fifteen

WILL IT EVER GO AWAY?

Ellie

"ELLIE?" I HEARD FROM behind me as I sat in the sand mindlessly letting it sift through my fingers while staring blankly at the ocean.

"I'm sorry, I just needed a minute. I'll be back inside in a few moments."

The soft sound of crunching sand could be heard behind me as footsteps approached where I was perched in the sand. The salty breeze coming off the ocean mingled with my tears. Eleanor sat beside me, not saying anything for a few minutes. It was her silence that was comforting, yet at the same time I felt that if I didn't talk about it, I would combust.

"Your husband?"

I nodded. Eleanor placed one arm around me and hugged me to her side, allowing my head to rest gently on her shoulder.

"It was the song, wasn't it?"

I nodded again, this time my cheek rubbing on her shoulder. I recognized the song almost immediately. Not because it was a very popular one, but because I just so happened to be the same exact song that Jeremy had chosen the night he dragged me to the karaoke.

I Got You Babe.

"I'm sorry, sweetheart," she said hugging me harder. "I'm pretty sure that Evan didn't know, nor did he do it maliciously."

"Oh, I know that. I trust Evan completely. It's just—"

"It's just what?"

"It was a song that Jeremy and I had sung together one night when he dragged me on stage to sing with him."

"Oh, honey, I'm so sorry," She repeated, hugging me closer. We sat like that for several minutes not saying anything. The only sounds were the waves as they beat upon the shore.

"I can't pretend to know what you and Evan are going through. I've never lost a spouse."

She paused, taking a deep breath as her chest rose and fell with the need for courage with her next words.

"When Evan was three, Rusty and I found out we were expecting. We were so excited when we found out because Evan himself was a miracle. Genetically, I am predisposed with infertility. The doctors never knew why."

"I thought Evan was an only child?" I asked sniffling and brushing my hair back from my face to look at her.

"He is. I miscarried her at twenty-three weeks. The ultrasound showed there was a hole in her heart and she wouldn't have lived very long even if I were to carry her full term."

"Oh Eleanor, I'm so sorry."

"I never met her, but I loved her more than anything. It was hard to have to explain to Evan that his baby sister wasn't coming home. I think it could be a big reason why he became a doctor. That and a little influence from his father." She chuckled.

Eleanor turned fully so that she was sitting facing me. Her expression was serious, yet completely kind and warming.

"When Lilly died, Evan just wasn't himself. He had issues at work that caused him to be placed on sabbatical. He took off down here and wouldn't talk to us for several days. I was so worried. I wanted to come down here immediately, but Rusty insisted that we give him time.

"I was worried about what his state of mind would be like when we got here. He and Lilly were best friends. Partners. They loved each other wholeheartedly."

I nodded.

"I know how he feels. It was like that with me and Jeremy."

She returned my nod in understanding.

"We had no idea that you were here with him until our phone call a few days ago. I know what happened was completely devastating, but you cannot understand how thankful I am for you being here for Evan."

"He has helped me more than you could ever know, Eleanor. I honestly probably would have lost my mind if it weren't for him."

"Hmmm," she hummed, agreeing with me.

"Evan loved Lilly. He really did. They were great together. Even though there is still a small amount of sadness reflecting in his eyes, they absolutely shine whenever he looks at you. I loved Lilly like my own daughter, but the way Evan looks at you...it's different. I've never seen his face light up the way it has tonight. He couldn't contain his smile. And the way he just watched you even when you weren't looking has me wondering…"

"Wondering what?"

"Is there anything going on between you two?"

My breath stopped short in my throat and my chest seized briefly from her inquiry. Emotionally, yes I felt like there was something going on between us. Then there was the fact that we had made love only several days ago.

"I, uh, we're friends," I said, stuttering over my own words. It wasn't an outright lie, but it wasn't the complete truth either.

"Well," she replied patting my hand. "My son would be a complete idiot if he remained just friends with you. I've only met you tonight, dear, but I've always had good intuition when it comes to people and I feel in my heart you are a wonderful person. I know it is really soon. I know that both of you are heartbroken, but I also feel something from you two that is unexplainable."

"You don't hate me for getting him in trouble?"

"Ha, no. Honestly, it's probably the best thing to happen to both of you. My husband was worried about Evan's career at first, but it won't have an effect on it. Especially if you two finish the therapy."

She looked out at the ocean, the warm breeze catching her hair and pulling it back from her face.

"I know your heart may not be at peace, Ellie. But it also isn't hardened forever. You and Evan are still both young. You may feel like you lost your heart the day they died, but you both have so much room left in them, that you will find a way to fill it up again."

I laughed, a full on belly laugh as I leaned back and braced myself on my forearms. Eleanor looked at me with question.

"Oh, I'm not laughing at you," I admitted, instantly sobering my laugh. "It's just that Jeremy said the same thing to me."

She arched her brows at me in curiosity and confusion.

"In a dream. I had a dream that I was talking to him and he said those same words to me. That I had so much of my heart left to give, that I shouldn't give up. At first I thought he was crazy. I thought I was crazy. I mean, I was having a conversation with my dead husband. He felt more real to me that night than anything."

"So maybe he really did come to you. If your Jeremy is anything like our Lilly, he wouldn't want to see you suffer for the rest of your life. That also doesn't mean that the pain will ever completely go away. You just find a way to move on and live despite the pain."

"That's what our counselor has told us."

We sat there looking out at the ocean and I let the breeze dry the tear stains on my cheeks. I took in her words as well as Jeremy's. Two completely different people, telling me the exact same thing. It wasn't just coincidence.

"Thank you, Eleanor. I'm sorry I ran out like that. I hope I didn't embarrass Evan."

"You didn't."

I nearly jumped up from the sand at the sound of Evan's voice behind me. I was too lost in my own thoughts sitting there with Eleanor that I didn't even hear him approach.

"Well, I'll let you two talk. I'm going to go see if I can pull your father away from Tommy so we can go to the house and rest. Take your time guys. Us old farts are just going to go to bed."

I watched her hug Evan and whisper something in his ear before she walked back up the beach toward the bar.

"You okay?" Evan asked as he came to sit beside me.

"Yeah, I'm sorry. It's just when that song came on, I couldn't battle the sadness and it kind of took over."

"You sang that song with Jeremy, didn't you?" He asked, but it sounded more like a statement than a question.

I nodded.

"It just feels like taking one step forward and two steps back. When I feel like I come close to accepting his death, something happens to remind me vividly that he isn't here anymore."

Evan reached for my hand and threaded his fingers through mine. It wasn't done in intimacy or to try and seduce me, but out of complete support. Total comfort, and I let him, welcoming the peace that it made me feel just from the small connection.

"I never should have tried to get you on stage."

"Evan, you had no way of knowing. It's not like you knew that one specific memory I had with Jeremy would come rising to the surface. You were only doing what you have been doing for the last few months. Trying to bring joy back into my life. I wouldn't smile if it weren't for you. I wouldn't laugh if you weren't in my life."

"I don't want to be the reason for the memories of the past coming back to haunt you."

I looked at him, awestruck by the fact that even though his wife died the same time as Jeremy, he was still very concerned with my happiness. Maybe it was his way of coping, by helping me cope. But I also wanted to do the same for him. I wanted to watch him smile more and to help the pain subside so that he would be able to move on and live.

"You aren't Evan. You have been every reason for my new, happy memories."

Leaning in, Evan instantly pressed his lips to mine. I could taste the bitterness of the hops on his tongue as he slipped it inside when my lips parted. His hands fisted in my hair pulling me close like I was the air he needed to breathe. In that moment I knew that the pain of losing Jeremy would never go away, but Evan was the one person who could help ease the hurt.

"I can't stop thinking about the other night, Ellie. Every time I close my eyes, I see the look on your face when you were beneath me. It's you that has helped heal me from the inside out. I know that I will never be able to replace the void that Jeremy has left in your heart, but I want to be able to fill up what is remaining."

Fresh hot tears pricked my eyes from his words and my own became lodged in my throat. The feelings that I have developed for Evan in such a short amount of time were nearly overwhelming. To say that the connection between us was instant would be close to accurate.

"I want that too, Evan. I want to do the same for you. I want to see you happy. I want to be the reason that you smile. Lilly was no doubt a very wonderful person. I know she would want the same for you."

We sat there on the beach as we traded slow, leisurely kisses as if we were not replacing the memories of our past, but creating new ones together. The ocean before us is what took away our life, but it also created this alternate one in which we were both able to find happiness from despair.

We made promises to each other on the beach, but I also knew that our time was limited. Once we completed the counseling, Evan would go back to Miami and I would go back to North Carolina. There was no escaping the fact that we were from two different places. All I wanted to do was enjoy the here and now. Relish in the time we did have together instead of focusing on what was to come.

If anything, Jeremy's death has taught me to live in the present. To be able to enjoy each moment as they come. I was so tired of focusing on what could have been and what was going to be, that all I wanted to worry about was now.

⌇

EVAN'S PARENTS STAYED until Sunday. Rusty and Eleanor Taylor where two of the kindest, and most wholehearted people I think I have ever met. They welcomed me with open arms, accepting me as the new person in Evan's life even though there was no definition tagged onto our relationship. I guess you could say we were non-denominational. Like a church would claim to be Baptist, or Catholic, even Protestant, we were simply Evan and Ellie. No titles attached, no clear statement of what we were exactly. It was easy. Simple. Uncomplicated.

The minute Evan was sure that his parents were on the plane back to Miami, he pulled me straight into his arms and carried me down the hallway to his room. In the few months that I have been living under his roof, never once had I been to his room. As he stood me on my feet, I took in the huge four-poster bed that was covered with quite possibly the biggest and fluffiest duvet I had ever seen.

I walked over, running my hands down the smooth wood of the posts, marveling in the beautiful design and texture of the carved wood.

"My dad made it. It is a hobby of his, actually. He has a huge shop at home with all kinds of equipment and tools to do this kind of stuff," Evan said coming up behind me and wrapping his arms around my waist, pulling me back into his chest.

"It's beautiful," I sighed.

"Not as beautiful as you."

"Now you're just being cheesy," I giggled. He pulled my hair to the side, pressing a kiss in the hollow space where my neck and shoulder met. I could feel the tiny bumps rise on my skin and my skin flushed with arousal.

"I love my parents, but I am so glad they're gone," he admitted as he drew lazy circles on my hipbones.

"If you don't want this, Ellie. Tell me now. Because I don't think I can stop once I start."

I spun around in his arms, folding my own over his shoulders and gripping his head in my hand to pull him in for a kiss.

"Mmmm," he moaned against my lips and the vibration sent a furor to my veins, the blood pumping through them to match the fluttering of my heartbeat. My breathing quickened to the point of lightheadedness and I had to break the kiss so that I could draw in a deep breath.

"I take that as a yes?" Evan groaned huskily as his eyes shone with lust, glazed over with want, and softened with need.

"Yes," was all I was able to reply as the tension in my muscles relaxed and my body became flooded with warmth.

In one swift move, Evan scooped me up in his arms, carried me around and placed me on the bed. The down feathered duvet molded to my back, surrounding me in softness and comfort. The first time I was with Evan, I was completely terrified. I'd never been with another man besides Jeremy. Although it was foreign, I enjoyed every minute of it. Noticing how we came together perfectly, like we were designed to be together.

Evan removed his shirt, once again rewarding me with the

mouth-watering muscles of his abs and chest. I bit my lip as I watched his biceps flex as he pulled the shirt over his head. His blue eyes connected with mine once he was free of the fabric and the small smile on his face made him look devastatingly handsome. I wanted that smile on his face every day. I wanted to see the joy in his eyes that only I could bring him. I made a promise to myself to achieve that goal for every day that I remained here with him.

"You have way too many clothes on," he said as he walked over and slowly began unbuttoning my blouse, the tips of his fingers making the smallest touch against the skin of my chest and stomach.

"That is so much better," he admired as he took in the achy swell of my breasts that threatened to burst from the cups of my bra.

Lying down beside me, he caressed the skin of my cheeks with his thumb before he devoured my lips in a painfully slow and seductive kiss.

Slowness turned to swiftness.

Swiftness turned to frantic.

Frantic turned into desperate need.

When we finally came together and Evan filled me, all pain, all hurt and anxiety melted away. He was a soothing balm to my soul. A medication that only he had the prescription to. My heart would never heal completely, but with Evan, it could damn near come close.

Chapter Sixteen

LETTERS

Evan

"TAKE ONE OF THE notebooks from the stack over by the chair please. Each person should have one," Sandi said pointing next to where Ellie was sitting. Another month had passed since we began therapy a few months ago. In the beginning, I thought it was the stupidest thing that anyone should have to go through. Now, I'm eating my thoughts because if it weren't for Ellie and this group, I don't think I could be coping as well as I was with Lilly's death.

One of the biggest reasons was currently sitting across from me. I smiled as I took in her long green sundress that made her eyes look extremely blue. We've been taking things slowly, enjoying the leisure of getting to know one another more on a personal basis. There have been many nights that we have sat together and talked while eating dinner or watching television. I learned all about her family, North

Carolina, and the Ellie I never knew growing up. I would watch as she animatedly told me about her cousins and their crazy antics while she was in high school. She told me about her job as a paralegal and how she worked for a brilliant small town lawyer who treated her well. Knowing that upon completion of the counseling, she wouldn't have a theft on her records was reassuring.

"I want you to all start keeping a journal," Sandi said breaking through my thoughts. "Over the next four weeks, each day, you will answer the same questions.

How do you feel about yourself today?

Have you internally punished yourself today?

What did you do today to make you feel good?

At the end of the week, I want you to see if you find a pattern of behavior. Are you good, or are you hard on yourself, and what was the most constant feeling you had all week. At the end of the four weeks, we'll meet with you one on one, and we'll see how your path is going toward acceptance with your grief."

I looked at the journal in my hands, taking in the faux leather binding as I flipped if from front to back. Writing down my thoughts wasn't something that I felt completely comfortable with, but yet neither had going to counseling in the first place. I thought that being optimistic about it would be better than hanging onto the dread of it.

"I want you to think about your journal as being your 'silent listening partner'. When you write, it helps keep the grieving process to continue from the inside out and a majority of the time helps us get rid of our thoughts when we aren't ready to talk. Constructively, it also helps us put our anxiety or anger toward an inanimate object instead of taking it out of our families or other loved ones. Most importantly, it could help you diminish any feelings of guilt you may be harboring."

My head snapped to Sandi's as soon as she had said the word guilt. Throughout the last few months, my feelings for Ellie had grown steadily to the point that thoughts of her began to overpower my thoughts of Lilly. That is when the guilt would hit me. If someone were to tell me that in only a few short months after the death of my wife, I would find solitude and feelings for another woman, I would have punched them in the throat for being so ridiculous.

"Open your journals to the first page. On this page, I want you to write a letter to your loved one. Start off by telling them when you miss them most. Work your way towards telling them what you learned from them. I know most of you didn't get to say goodbye to your loved ones. If you could, what would you say? Put it all on the page."

Everyone flipped open their journals and began writing. I lifted my eye gaze to find Ellie looking at me. Her cheeks blushed, as if embarrassed that she got caught. I smiled at her trying to offer reassurance. When her eyes flicked from me to the journal in her hands and back again, I offered her a nod. She was probably feeling the same thing I was feeling when Sandi announced the letter. If one kind of guilt wasn't enough, we had another. Even though it was understood between us about our love for our deceased spouses, we felt guilty for thinking about all the great memories we had with them. That in turn seemed to try and tarnish the new memories that Ellie and I worked to create.

One longer glance at me, then Ellie went to work on her letter. Clicking the pen, I too, began writing.

Lilly,

I miss you most when I am lying in bed at night. I miss the comfort our your warmth and the steady rhythm of your heart as you slept. It was my own personal lullaby that always drew me into the most peaceful rest nearly every night. Now, I toss and turn most nights, barely finding comfort in closing my eyes, yet deeply wanting to because sometimes you come to me then.

I think the greatest thing I learned from you was the ability to love unconditionally. To offer my heart and soul to someone and never ask for anything in return and getting my satisfaction from seeing someone so blissfully happy. You would have given me your ability to hear if I were deaf. Your capability to talk if I were mute. In the end, I also know you would have given me the beat of your heart if it meant that I lived while you died. You never asked me to love you because you made it so incredibly easy to do so. So thank you my love, for showing me what it really meant to sacrifice yourself for someone you loved more than your own life.

If I had the chance to say anything to you before I knew I would never see you again, it would be to tell you over and over how much I love you. I would repeat the words until my voice gave out in order to fill your mind and your heart with those words to last you forever. I would imprint the sound of my voice saying them, so that every time you have a vacant thought, or even had any doubt of my feelings for you, you would know. You would know that you were the most precious gift that God had ever given me.

I have no doubt in my mind that you are just as loving in death as you were in life. I know that coming to me in my dreams and telling me that I need to move on was your way of telling me that I have the strength to go on without you. You knew me better than I ever could have known myself. I also know that you would want me to be happy, but the guilt I feel keeps me from doing that.

You see, there's this girl. You know her. She was on the boat the night I lost you. You both chatted, you've spoke to me about her in my dreams. I don't know how to explain it to you, but in a weird and sick twist of fate, I feel as if she was there that night for a purpose. A greater purpose than any of us could ever try to understand. If it weren't for her, I don't think I would be here today. Yes, I know you don't want to hear it, but in the beginning, I thought that if you were dead, then I might as well be too. My purpose for waking in the morning was gone. The breath that I had breathed for four years had left me gasping for oxygen and nothing to replenish it with.

If I thought it was strange that she was on the boat that night, it was even more bizarre that she just happened to be the one on the Jet Ski that day. I took off out into the ocean to save the crazed mad woman who had a death wish of her own.

Talking to you about feelings for another woman is incredibly difficult for me, Lilly. In fact there is a stabbing pain in my chest as I write these words. But I feel as if she was somehow sent to me by either you, or God, or some other power to fill the empty void left in my soul. She has brought sunshine to the darkness that has consumed me. Provided me with the air I needed in order to breathe again.

But there is also the fear I am hanging onto that she will be leaving soon. We both have separate lives, families, jobs. What will become of me then? Dealing with the loss of you was hard enough, but eventually I will have to deal with the loss of her too.

I wish you were here. I wish you would guide me and tell me what I need to do. But I guess if you were here, I wouldn't have a need to be writing this letter.

I love you Lilly. I'll love you forever and a day and will keep you in my heart where you have always been, until the day we are reunited.

Yours forever,
Evan

Ellie

I WATCHED AS EVAN furiously wrote in his journal. It bothered me that his words could flow so easily when I kept staring at the only word I had written down.

Jeremy.

What was I supposed to say to him? How could I consciously pour my heart out to him when I couldn't keep my thoughts from gravitating to the other side of the room towards Evan? Taking a deep breath, I finally stared at the page, before closing my eyes. The truth. That was what I needed to say.

Jeremy,

Miss wouldn't be the right word. It is such a small word in the English language, yet is probably one of the most emotional words that there is. Sure, it has a definition, but you never truly understand it's meaning until you have lost someone you loved very deeply. So I can't tell you how much I miss you because there is no word nor definition that could even begin to explain that to you.

I learned so much from you in the time we were together. Most importantly, I learned how to laugh. I learned how to look at each day differently, embrace each moment like it would be my last. Little did I know that your time would be so short. You lived every day with passion, with drive, with the ability to make everyone around you fall instantly and completely in love with you. Everything you did, you did with your heart and soul, especially when it came to loving me. I never had to sacrifice one ounce of happiness when it came to you because my happiness was your happiness.

I hate that some days I can't remember your face, or what your voice sounded like. I deleted the voicemails months ago because the more I listened to them, the more I had to come to terms with the fact that you weren't coming home. I had to realize that the hopes and dreams we had with each other were no longer going to be. I've had to survive with only the memory of your love, and as great and wonderful as it was, I feel you fade away a little more everyday.

The only thing, or person I should rather say, that has been the comfort that I needed, is in this room. When I'm with Evan, the tightness in my chest eases and the pain that comes from losing you gets a little easier. It doesn't go away, and I know it never will, but he gives me hope that someday, maybe someday, I will get to experience what I felt with you once again. I have felt lost ever since the day you died, but Evan has been the navigation that has kept me on a path to keeping my sanity. He has guided me, offered comfort and opened my heart to new possibilities no matter how scary they may be.

I know you would want me to be happy, and honestly if I saw myself being able to move on, it would be with Evan. God, I hate talking to you about this, but when we have made love, it was the only time that I truly felt relief. Like complete and total relief from the loss and pain.

I want you to know that no one could ever replace you. No one could ever fill the spot within me that you own. But as you said, there is so much more left of me to give, but I'm scared. Jeremy, I don't think I could ever deal with losing someone again like I did with you. The only thing in common Evan and I have is this place and our grief. Even though my feelings for him seem to grow stronger every day, I can't help but feel like I am setting myself up for devastation all over again when we eventually have to return to real life. We have been living in an alternate life for several months now. A universe where you and Lilly are no longer here, but yet we are a soothing comfort to one another. What happens when we find out that the two of you are the only reason why he and I are together? What then? I couldn't survive another heartbreak.

I wish I could talk to you. Hold you. Lose myself in your encouraging words and seek the comfort you have always brought me.

I know you are with me everywhere I go. You are in everything I see, everything I feel and everything I want to do. I love you. And I will always love you until the day I take my last breath.

Forever,
Ellie

Chapter
Seventeen

Journal Week One
MONDAY

Ellie

How do you feel about yourself today?

Today was a rough day. Having to write a letter of goodbye to Jeremy and confess my feelings for Evan was probably one of the hardest things I have had to do other than bury my husband.

Have you internally punished yourself today?

I did. I have beaten myself up most of the night after the guilt consumed me for the letter. I degraded myself over and over to the point my stomach was in knots and I felt nauseous.

What did you do today to make you feel good?

I sought comfort in the only person who could make me feel better.

"I HAVE PLANS FOR us tomorrow," Evan confessed as we reclined on the sofa, my back to his front, while he drew lazy circles on my forearm with his fingertips.

"Oh yeah? And just what plans do you have?"

"Every year there is this craft festival in town. Lots of homemade stuff. Food. Jewelry, you name it. I want to take you. But it is down on the beach."

I stiffened briefly in his arms. I hadn't been to the beach since the night I ran out of the karaoke bar. Even then, I didn't think it registered how close I was to it due to the overwhelming memory of the song that was chosen.

"It will be okay. We'll be together. I'll look after you and you look after me. Sandi told us to get out and do things, remember? There are going to be things that bring us close to where we lost Lilly and Jeremy, but in order for us to move on and accept it, we have to confront those things and show that they have no power over us."

I turned onto my side to face him and smiled when I saw his blue eyes twinkling back at me.

"When did you get so philosophical?" I teased, patting his chest with the palm of my hand.

"What do you mean 'get'? I've always been this smart," he teased back, a devilishly boyish smile on his lips, just before he leaned in and pressed his lips to mine.

~

THE BEACHFRONT WAS filled with tons of vendors. The smell of popcorn, homemade bagels and other deliciously bad for you foods, filtered through the air. My stomach rumbled with hunger, reminding me that I could quite possibly eat one of everything on the entire one mile stretch.

Evan and I walked side by side eyeing all of the homemade trinkets, clothes, and other goodies. I tried to keep my anxiety at bay by resisting the urge to look out at the open water every opportunity I had.

"These are neat. What are they?" I asked one of the vendors as I eyed a strand of beads with a large hole on one end and a smaller loop on the other. In the center was a turquoise bird that was surrounded by two small sterling silver hearts.

"They are called barefoot sandals," the older lady said as she stood up from her chair and walked over to where Evan and I were standing, looking at the display case.

"What is a barefoot sandal?" Evan asked, interrupting before I even had the chance to ask the question myself.

"Traditionally, they originate from South Asia. They were worn in celebration or for ceremonies like weddings. They can be worn by themselves, or they can be worn with open top sandals or flip flops."

Flipping open the case, the older woman reached for the exact pair that I was looking at.

"Did you make these by hand?"

"I did," she said as she removed them from the case and with shaky fingers placed them in my hands.

"This pair is very special," she said as I eyed the beautiful beads of alternating colors. It was the tiny bird that drew my eye.

"I made these for someone. I don't know who. They day I sat down, I just had a feeling that they belonged to a specific person. The bird you see has two hearts. They are of equal size and one no more important than the other. The bird in the middle is surrounded by the hearts because the bird needs those two hearts in order to fly. They are her foundation, provide her the air she needs in order to get off the ground."

Tears sprang to the back of my eyes as I looked at the beautiful work that this woman put her heart into. She had no idea just how close to home her story was hitting.

"We'll take them," Evan said reaching into his back pocket for his wallet. I was still completely awestruck, until the woman reached a hand out to lift my chin so that our gazes met. A lone tear crested from my eyes and fell down my cheek.

"I think they found who they belong to. The moment I saw you walk in here, I knew it was you. Call it an old woman's intuition. Take them. Enjoy them. I don't know your story my dear, but those beads do. Find comfort in them."

Evan tried to give the woman money but she refused. It was the strangest, weirdest and kindest gesture that anyone has ever done for me. I didn't know the woman from any of the other strangers on the beach that day, yet I felt as if she knew more about me than I even knew.

Walking over to a bench, I clutched the beads in my hands, feeling the warmth and heartfelt words she spoke about them.

"Here," Evan said as he knelt down in front of me as I sat on the bench. Taking the beads from my hands, he then slipped the flip flops from my feet and went to work placing the barefoot sandals on my feet.

His fingertips brushed my ankle, creating a shiver that ran up both of my limbs and hitting me in all the right places. He looked up at me, his blue eyes matching the brilliant cerulean hue of the sky as he completed his task and then placed my flip flops on my feet.

Helping me up from the bench, Evan helped me to my feet and gently kissed me on my mouth before taking me by the hand and continuing our adventure through the craft fair.

It was one of the greatest days I've had in a long time.

—

Journal Week Two
FRIDAY

Evan

How do you feel about yourself today?
Today was one of my better days. I surprised Ellie with something she didn't see coming and the smile on her face was all I needed.

Have you internally punished yourself today?
At first I did. I thought I was stupid for not discussing my plans with Ellie first and acting on impulse.

What did you do today to make you feel good?
Getting to see the excitement on Ellie's face was the only thing I needed to feel good today.

"WHAT IS THIS?" Ellie asked as I extended an envelope to her, trying to hide the shake of my hands with how nervous I was.

"Open it and find out."

We sat opposite each other at the dinner table, having just finished a phenomenal meal that Ellie had cooked for both of us. We had decided we would go to the farmer's market every day to get fresh ingredients and then cook a new recipe every night.

I watched as her finger slid beneath the flap of the envelope before her eyes grew wide in disbelief when she pulled out the contents.

"Evan, these are plane tickets."

"They are," I replied, reaching for the coconut cream pie in the center of the table that Ellie and I had baked together. She still had some remnants of the flour on her cheek from when we made the crust.

"There are two."

"Yep," was all I said as I sliced through the creamy meringue and put a piece on two saucers and extended one to her. Her focus was on the tickets in her hand instead of the desert in mine. When her gaze finally lifted to look at me, I offered her a warm smile.

"You bought me a ticket home? For how long?"

"Well," I said setting the pie down in front of her, "It's only for the weekend, but I wanted you to go home and see your family. We have to be back on Monday for therapy, but I figured that two days was better than none at all."

"Why are there two?" She asked, eyes batting at me quizzically.

"Yep."

"You're going with me? Home?"

"If you don't mind."

She shot out of her chair so fast, it nearly tipped over backwards. Running towards me with the tickets still fisted in her hands, she threw herself into my lap and pressed her lips to mine, barely giving me time to swallow the pie in my mouth. Looping her arms around my neck, she deepened the kiss, slipping her tongue into my mouth. Her taste was sweeter than any pie could ever taste. Her body more comfort than any food could provide.

"Thank you," she said between kisses and my resolve was lost and the food in front of us forgotten as I carried her off to my bedroom. I took the tickets from her hand and sat them on the dresser before I took her to bed and made slow, sweet love to her.

———

Ellie

THE TURBULENCE ON the plane made my stomach nauseous. Even though Jeremy was taken from me in a boating accident, somehow any kind of commercial transportation made me increasingly nervous. I could feel the blood drain from my face every time the plane dropped or rolled slightly. My only comfort was the fingers that Evan had threaded through my own as he tried to soothe my anxiety.

I called my parents to let them know that I would be coming home for a few days and that I was bringing a friend with me. I explained to mom on the phone about Evan and how we knew each other. She was apprehensive at first, not sure how to react to the fact that I had been with, what she considered, a complete stranger for the last three months. But when she got a look at Evan, all of her anxiety seemed to melt away. My father even seemed to be enamored with Evan as well.

"Oh my God, baby, I'm so glad you are home," my mother said as she gathered me into a bear hug for about the tenth time since we arrived.

"It's good to see you too mom." I replied pulling away slightly to look at her.

"Baby, are you okay? You look kind of pale," she asked cupping my cheek with her hand and gazing at me with concern.

"I'm fine, momma. I've felt a little tired these last few days. I have trouble sleeping at night sometimes," I answered, risking a quick glance to Evan who was chatting with my father about fishing in the Keys.

"Besides, the turbulence on the plane made me really nervous. I'm glad I had Evan to hold my hand, although he said I almost broke it," I added, chuckling.

"I just worry about you baby. How much longer do you have until you finish counseling?"

"Sandi, my counselor, said it could be as little as three more weeks. It all depends on if she thinks we are the road to acceptance."

"And are you?" She asked looking at me for the truth. I looked over at Evan who was smiling and laughing with my dad. It felt so incredibly normal for him to be here, even if he complained about the giant summer bugs and the fact that the humidity of Coastal Carolina threatened to choke him. The heat in Florida was a little different than in North Carolina and some people had trouble adjusting at first.

"I think so," I replied with honesty, never taking my eyes off Evan as a small smile formed on my mouth. My mom followed my eyes to where Evan and dad were now going into intricate detail about different types of fishing lures.

"You like him," my mom said breaking me from the daydream I was having of Evan lying on top of me. His warmth being absorbed by my body and the fire that he ignites within me.

"Huh?" I asked turning to her as if I didn't hear her. I heard every single word she said, I just wasn't sure if I was ready to admit it to my family yet.

"You heard me, Ellie. You like him. It's easy to see why. He seems very nice and doting of you. But I also don't want you to rush into something so soon. I don't want you to feel like you have to replace Jeremy with someone new just so that you don't feel the pain anymore."

Her words stung me slightly, making me stumble backwards as if she had slapped me across the face.

"Jeremy could never be replaced. I would never do that. Evan just understands me. He lost the love of his life too. We are kindred souls. We get along well with each other because we both know exactly what the other person feels. He makes me feel," I paused as if trying to find the right words I wanted to say, "He makes me feel happy when otherwise I would still be in darkness. He is the only reason I didn't join Jeremy at the bottom of the ocean. Not only did he save my life once, but twice."

"Sweetheart, I didn't mean it that way. I promise. Of course Jeremy can never be replaced. I think Evan is great and if you feel something for him, then we are completely okay with that. I just want you to move forward with no regrets."

She hugged me, and I wrapped my arms around her seeking the comfort that only a mother can provide.

"They've been asking about you, you know."

"What? Who?" I asked pulling away from her.

"Bob and Linda. They call often actually. They loved their son, but they also love you very much as well. I told them you were still taking a break. I didn't tell them about the whole counseling thing."

"Thank you. I should go see them while I am here."

"I think they'd love that."

———

I STOOD ON THE porch of the house that I had gone to many, many times over the past four years. This was the first time that I had come here and Jeremy wasn't either here or with me. With a shaky hand, I lifted my hand to ring the doorbell.

"Are you okay?" Evan asked nudging my shoulder. I was so stiff, he could have knocked me completely over with a gentle push. I swallowed over and over trying to keep my emotions at bay. I thought that having Evan here with me would give me the strength to see Jeremy's parents for the first time since the funeral, but then I also started to think it was a bad idea.

"I'm just nervous. I'm glad you are here, but I am also scared of what they will think of me."

"Ell, I can go sit in the car if you want. I just want to be here to support you. I won't be offended by any means if you told me to wait for you."

And therein was the reason I felt myself falling for him. His concern for my feelings over his own melted my heart in more ways than one. I could see the uncomfortable and invading feeling that he was trying desperately to hide from me. The fact that he was even pushing those feelings aside for me was more appreciated that I could ever verbalize.

A tall, thin woman answered the door. Her hair was shorter than I'd last remembered it, but the same blue eyes that I had admired for four years stared back at me. Jeremy's eyes.

"Ellie," was all she managed to say before a small sob came from her mouth and her hands lifted to try and control the emotion.

"Hey, Linda."

I stepped forward into the threshold and wrapped my arms around her, hugging her to my chest as my own eyes began to water.

"It's good to see you, baby girl," Linda said pulling back from me and wiping the tears from her cheeks.

"Look at you. All golden and tanned," she said with a smile, trying to lighten up the mood.

"Yeah, the Keys feel like living on the surface of the sun some days," I joked. "This is my friend Evan. He…he was on the boat the night…"

I couldn't finish my sentence.

"Evan Taylor," he chimed in, extending his hand to Linda.

"Pleasure, Evan."

Linda's eyes looked between us questioningly, as if trying to assess our relationship.

"I lost my wife in the accident. Ellie and I have become good friends and have leaned on each other for support. It is great to meet you. I have heard nothing but great things about your son. I'm incredibly sorry for your loss," Evan said, once again jumping in to save me.

"Likewise. Well, don't just stand out here on the porch. Come inside. I just made sweet tea," Linda replied as she stood back and allowed us to enter the house.

I knew that it would be hard coming here. I knew that about a million memories of Jeremy would hit me all at once as soon as I stepped over the threshold. What I wasn't prepared for were all of the pictures. Pictures of him and his parents. Pictures of him by himself.

Pictures of the two of us. But it was the hardest to see the huge blown up one that sat on the mantle above the fireplace.

Our wedding day.

Jeremy and I stood facing each other with huge smiles on our faces, but the part that stung the most was seeing the love in both of our eyes as we looked at each other like we would never grow tired of doing it.

"Linda, whose rental car is that in the driveway?"

Just as the question passed his lips, Jeremy's dad, Bob, walked into the living room.

"Ellie girl," Bob said, breathing out the nickname he had always called me, as the realization that I was in the room hit him. In three strides he was instantly pulling me into a tight bear hug.

"Bobbie bear," I replied calling him the name I had always called him.

"You sure know how to make an old man choke up baby girl. When did you get home?"

"Uh, just yesterday. I'm only here for a few days. I have to go back."

"What?" He asked as he pulled away from me holding me at the shoulders. I felt comfort with his strong hands on me, so gentle and warm. I always called him Bobbie Bear because the man was huge, yet he was one of the kindest; most gentle human beings I have ever known. Much like Jeremy.

"Maybe we should sit down."

With Evan by my side, I told them all about losing it after the funeral and taking off to Florida. I admitted my guilt to stealing the Jet Ski and that if it weren't for Evan, I could have killed myself out in the ocean that day. I filled them in on how Evan and I have helped each other try to cope with everything by confiding in each other and about the counseling.

What I didn't tell them was that every time Evan touched me, I felt butterflies in my stomach, or that fire ignited within me just from one look. I definitely didn't tell them that I harbored both passion and guilt at the same time for wanting him so much, but still missing Jeremy at the same time.

"Wow," Linda said after I had finished.

"Yeah."

"I think I need a drink after all of that. Anyone want some tea?"

Bob and Evan both smiled as they nodded their affirmation and Linda rose to go into the kitchen.

"I'll help you," I offered, rising up to follow her.

Going to the fridge, she pulled out a large pitcher while I reached for the glasses, familiar with where everything already was in her kitchen.

Linda sat the pitcher down on the counter and sighed before turning to me.

"Is there anything *more* going on between you two?"

I wasn't completely stunned by her question, a little taken aback yes. Even though there wasn't anything accusing in her tone, I still felt scrutinized. I mean, she was the mother of my dead husband, and here I brought another man into their home.

"I, uh—" I stuttered, not quite able to find the words to describe the *more* she was wanting to hear about. How was I supposed to tell her that in a matter of several months, I have mourned my husband, her son, yet found comfort and other things in the arms of another man?

"Ellie, it's okay. I know you loved Jeremy."

"I still do," I admitted, tears springing to my eyes. My heart ached having to admit my feelings to her. The last thing I wanted was for her to think I was insensitive to the fact that I had lost the love of my life only a short time ago, yet now developed feelings for someone new.

"I know that too, sweetheart. When you look at Evan, I see a fire in your eyes. The same you used to have when you looked at Jeremy. But I also see hesitation."

I nodded, my throat feeling tight to the point I didn't think I could speak or the tears would start flowing. Completely ignoring our task of pouring tea, she reached for my hands, rubbing her thumbs on the tops of my knuckles.

"Bob and I love you like a daughter. Hell, you *are* our daughter. But baby, we want you to be happy. Jeremy would want you to be happy. I know you feel guilty. I know it hurts to think about moving on, but sweetheart, you have to."

She nodded towards the living room.

"He looks at you the same way you know. When you aren't watching, he watches you. Studies you. His eyes sparkle, but I also see the hesitation within him too. It is like you both want more, but are too afraid to define it. Afraid to *want* it. Jeremy was my son and I loved him more than anything. I know you did too, but you cannot let his death hold you back from life. You can't let his passing keep you from finding something that is maybe bigger than you ever thought could be possible. I know Jer was your first love, and that you will never get over him. It's impossible. Everyone remembers the very first person they fall in love with. Whether the relationship made it in the end or not, the heart never forgets."

She paused, looking towards the living room and then her eyes met mine once more.

"What if that man in there, what if he was there for a reason? What if it wasn't just coincidence that you two were brought back together? What if he could be your *true* love?"

A wave of dizziness overcame me and I had to grip onto Linda's hands a little tighter to keep from falling to the floor. The breath lodged in my lungs and for several minutes I think I forgot how to breathe.

"Are you alright?" Linda said, concern in her voice as she wrapped an arm around my back to support me.

"Yeah, I think I'm still overwhelmed by it all. Losing Jeremy, the way I feel about Evan. It can all be just—overwhelming."

When she was sure I was steady on my feet, she reached a thumb up to wipe the tears that had trickled down my cheeks.

"No one should have to go through what you have, but that doesn't mean you have to live the rest of your life in turmoil. You deserve happiness just like everyone else, Ellie. If what you feel for the man in there is real, then don't fight it. No regrets. No worries. Jeremy wouldn't want that."

She smiled at me and I nodded my head.

"Now, let's get this tea in there to those men before they think we ran off and left them," she laughed.

Chapter Eighteen

Journal Week Two
SUNDAY

Ellie

How do you feel about yourself today?

If I had to pick a word to describe today, it would be relief. Relief that my guilt and hesitation about the relationship between Evan and I is brought on completely by myself. I am the only thing that has been holding myself back from happiness. I am the one that is putting the wall between my past and my future and blocking me from seeing past anything but the present.

Have you internally punished yourself today?

The beginning of the day, yes, I did. I internally scrutinized myself for my thoughts, feelings, and longing glances at Evan when I was in the childhood home of my husband. But after Linda's reassuring words, I knew that I couldn't do that to myself anymore.

What did you do today to make you feel good?

Today, I let myself breathe I think for the first time in forever. I let the tension roll off my shoulders. I let the guilt and hesitation subside.

I CLOSED MY JOURNAL and laid it on the nightstand. I looked around my old room before I crawled underneath the covers and pulled them all the way up to my chin. No matter how hard I tried, I couldn't shut my mind off. I kept rolling Linda's words around in my thoughts searching for any reason or lie in her words, but in the end I couldn't find one. I could easily see where Jeremy got his good morals and his ability to want others to be happy before himself from. Linda, without me needing to speak a word, could see the longing that simmered just below the surface between Evan and me. She didn't need verbal confirmation to feel the hints of electricity in the air. No, because it could be felt by everyone, including us.

I stared up at the ceiling, trying to imagine what Evan was thinking right now. Even though we were in the same house, separated by one wall, I felt too far away from him. I was in desperate need of his warmth. I felt a great need and desire for him to tell me what I was feeling was okay, as if his permission would give me the catalyst I needed to finally let go.

Throwing back the covers, I decided that I needed to see him. Since arriving in North Carolina, we hadn't had a single moment to be alone. If we hadn't been with my parents, we were with Jeremy's. I needed his comfort.

Tiptoeing out of my room as to not wake anyone, I took the few steps needed to arrive at the spare bedroom next to mine. I didn't knock, not sure if Evan were sleeping or awake. It didn't matter. I just needed to be near him. Just to see his face and be present in the same room would give me the comfort I needed.

The door creaked ever so slightly as I opened it and entered the room. Shutting it, I walked slowly to where his still form lay in the bed. I was positive by the sound of his even breaths that he was asleep, until he rose to sitting and nearly caused me to scream in surprise.

"Ellie?"

"Oh my God," I whisper yelled into the room, clutching my heart and trying to calm my erratic beating heart.

"You scared me. I thought you were sleeping."

"Were you trying to sneak in here and watch me sleep?" He teased, rubbing at his eye with one hand while patting the bed with is other, extending to me an invitation to sit beside him.

Tentatively, I walked over and sat next to him, feeling an instant flood of relief to my system from being so close to him. The springs of the mattress creaked in protest and I sank onto it and instantly laid my head on his shoulder.

"What's wrong?" He asked as one arm snaked around me and he cradled my head against him while reaching for my hand with the other.

"I just needed to be close to you," I admitted, feeling like it was best if I told him the truth.

"It's been a pretty emotional couple of days for you. I didn't intend for this trip to be. I just wanted you to be able to come and see your family. I know you've missed them."

"Yes, it has been, but I think I needed it. I think I needed the reassurance."

Evan pressed a kiss into my hair and I closed my eyes and soaked in the warmth of his gesture, absorbing the affection like the medicine my soul needed.

"Reassurance about what?"

"This, that this is okay."

I lifted my head to turn and look at him. Even though it was dark, I could tell that his blue eyes sparkled. I didn't have to see the brightness of the color to know that what I had said affected him.

"I think I kind of needed it for you as well. I know we are scared. I don't think I've ever been so afraid of anyone or anything in my life."

"You're afraid of me?" I asked a little taken aback by his words.

"Yes, but not in the way you are thinking."

He reached up and pushed a strand of my hair behind my ear, causing tingles to ripple down my jaw and neck as he did so.

"I'm afraid that I could so easily get lost in you. I'm afraid that what I feel for you could easily have me teetering on the edge of falling in love with you, but I'm most scared of what happens when counseling is over and we have to go back to reality. See, these last few months with you have been a fantasy. In the beginning I was living in a dark fantasy world where the love of my life was taken from me. You know how it feels. Like we have been transported into an alternate universe with no way out."

His thumb stroked my cheek as his fingers threaded through my hair, massaging my scalp as he spoke.

"The only thing real in the fantasy has been you. You are the only thing tethering me to the ground, keeping me upright and keeping my heart beating long enough to have another beat. At first I was scared of falling for you. I was scared of what people would think. I was scared of what Lilly would think. I was scared that I started to not feel regret or hesitation because it felt like betrayal. Now, now I'm scared of what is going to happen when I don't have you with me anymore."

For what seemed like the millionth time in this short weekend, tears came easily. He just stated every fear that I was feeling without even knowing it.

"I'm scared too."

Leaning in, Evan pressed his lips to mine, the pressure soft, soothing, comforting. It was slow, deliberate as if he were trying to memorize the way our mouths touched, the way our lips molded together and committing it to memory so that when the time came for us to go back to reality, he could carry it with him always.

Our tongues danced, but it wasn't hurried. Instead we made love with our mouths, taking the time to enjoy the moment, both afraid of what would happen if we were to pull away. His strong hands held my head to his firmly, both thumbs brushing against my cheeks. I held onto his forearms for leverage, getting caught in the high of him, and I feared that if I let go, I would surely float away.

"Evan," I breathed when his lips trailed down my jaw and to my collar bones, creating a million bumps to form on my skin, each one tingling with the need to be touched by him. Caressed by him.

"We're in your parents house," he stated and I wasn't sure if he was trying to remind me, or if he were trying to remind himself.

His hands grazed down my shoulders, the spaghetti traps of my top, slipping off my shoulder. One hand came to cup my breast, instantly fueling my need, driving my desire, and heating me like an inferno from the inside out.

"We should stop," he said as his head dipped and his teeth grazed the hardened nub of my nipple through my shirt. Finally he stopped, resting his forehead on my chest, his breathing deep and long like he was struggling to regain his composure.

When his head lifted, he looked into my eyes. Searching, wanting, needing.

"I'm not ready for this to be over between us. I don't know what it is, but I'm exhausted against fighting it. I don't want to anymore."

His admission hit me in the stomach like nourishment I needed after being on a thirty day fast.

"I'm not ready either."

"Ellie, you better go back to your room or the next thing your parents will hear is you screaming out my name. I want to be respectful so…please."

I nodded, but not before leaning in and giving him one last, hot, searing kiss before I walked back to my room.

Journal Week Three
MONDAY

Evan

How do you feel about yourself today?

Pretty damn good. As soon as the plane had landed, I all but dragged Ellie home and into my bed where I proceeded to lose myself in her not once, but three times.

Have you internally punished yourself today?

No. The weekend of not being able to touch her like I wanted. Feel her like my body craved too all weekend. It was torture all on its own. No need for my own self mutilation.

What did you do today to make you feel good?

Today, when I woke up, it felt like everything was beginning to feel right again. When I opened my eyes, Ellie was laying next to me, her long dark hair fanned out over the pillow and her hand tucked right next to her cheek. If I could wake up every day like that, I think life would be pretty good.

"HELLO EVERYONE. How are the journals coming along?" Sandi asked as she looked around the group. Some murmured that they often forgot to write it or that they didn't really see any patterns to their behavior.

Mine?

All of my entries were centered on Ellie. Well, all except for the letter in the front. The letter where I poured my heart out to my dead wife and admitted my growing feelings for another woman. Ellie was my pattern. She was all of my happy thoughts that had occurred over the last few weeks. Hell, the last few months.

"I'd like to start meeting with you on a one-on-one basis beginning next week. I would like to discuss your journal entries and get a sense for what stage you're in during this process. Some of you may be ready to move on, some of you may not, and that is okay. Everyone processes grief differently. But tonight, I thought we could discuss what I want you to do for next week. I want you to think of a way to memorialize your loved one. This could be anything from a song that you sing, or a CD you play. You could write or read a poem, even share your letter with the group. Come prepared to share next week."

We all chatted about different things we could do in memory of our loved ones. I didn't know what I wanted to do, but I had a few ideas that stuck out to me.

"I—I need the restroom," Ellie announced seconds before she darted out of her chair and out of the room. I stood up quickly to go after her, but Sandi told me that she would go check on her. My brows knitted together in worry as I sat back down and watched Sandi go after her. I had been concerned about her since we arrived back in the Keys yesterday. Trying to reassure me, she told me that she often suffers from vertigo after riding in an airplane. Sometimes to the point that it makes her nauseous. She informed me that it had something to do with the cabin pressure effecting her inner ears and that it usually goes away within a few days. It still didn't stop me from being concerned about her.

After what seemed like forever, Sandi emerged from the bathroom helping Ellie back to her seat. She offered me a small smile, but I could tell by the grey look to her face she still wasn't feeling well.

"Did you guys have a chance to brainstorm about your memorial project?" Sandi asked as she took a seat next to Ellie, I assumed to stay close in case she needed her. I wanted to be the one to sit next to her, but Sandi's rule that we should sit next to someone different every session kept me from doing so.

We all nodded our heads. I knew exactly what I wanted to do, but I needed to find a way to do it. I knew that people were going to find it strange and odd about the way I have chosen to memorialize my dead wife, but I was hoping they could also see and understand the reason why.

SEVERAL HOURS LATER, we were home and Ellie told me she was going to go lay down for a while before dinner, stating that maybe some rest would do her some good in order to help combat the vertigo.

When she wasn't awake more than two hours after we were supposed to have dinner, I went downstairs to check on her.

"Ellie?" I called as I opened the door to her apartment. I didn't hear her respond, only the horrible sound of retching coming from the bathroom.

"Ellie, are you okay?" I asked as I rapped my knuckles on the bathroom door. After several more violent protests of her stomach, she finally answered in a weak voice.

"I'm fine. My stomach is just angry with me."

"Can I come in?"

"No, please. I'll be fine."

More vomiting and I didn't care if she wanted me in there or not. My concern for her as well as my medical brain told me she wasn't fine. Pushing open the door, I saw her flushed face as she sat on her knees in front of the toilet. Her dark hair was plastered to her temples with sweat and her eyes were closed like she was in pain.

"Evan, no. Please," she said lifting a limp arm and trying to shoo me out of the bathroom. Instantly I went into doctor mode and opened the bathroom cabinet to retrieve a washcloth. Turning the water to cold, I wetted the cloth and wrung it out before approaching her.

"Baby, I think this might be a little more than vertigo. You probably caught some bug from someone on the plane," I said as I sat on the floor beside her and began patting the cool washcloth over her flushed skin.

"I—I think you could be right. I'm okay as long as I lay down, but when I stand up, my stomach starts to turn and I instantly feel sick."

I could see a hint of relief on her face as I continued to apply the cool washcloth to her skin.

"You don't feel like you are running a fever. Do you have any other symptoms? Headache? Diarrhea? Funny vision?"

"Ewww, did you have to say diarrhea?" She tried to laugh, but I could easily see it didn't agree with her.

"I'm just trying to see if this could just be a virus, or if I might need to take you in for some tests."

"I'm fine, really. It's just a horrible stomach bug. Nausea and dizziness are all I feel."

"Do you feel like you might get sick again?" I asked as I stood to rinse the cloth to make it cold once again.

"No, I think it has subsided."

"Come on," I said extending a hand to her, "I'll help you get back in bed."

Ellie stood, but was instantly unsteady on her feet. Holding the washcloth in one hand, I bent down and hugged the backs of her thighs while placing the other arm behind her back to pick her up before walking her to her bedroom. I felt a little comforted by the fact she wasn't running a fever which would be a clear sign there could be some infection. Pulling back the covers, I placed her in the bed and covered her up.

"I'll be right back."

Running quickly into the kitchen, I retrieved a bottle of Tylenol out of the cabinet and a large cooking pot. When I returned she saw the bottle of medicine, but her brows scrunched together in curiosity when she saw me carrying the large pot.

"It's just in case you feel like you might get sick again and not be able to make it to the bathroom." I sat the pot down next to the bed and the Tylenol on the nightstand.

"You called me baby," she whispered, snuggling into the pillow.

"Let me get you some water," was all I replied when I realized I had in fact called her 'baby'. I shook it off as habit, often calling Lilly by the same endearment.

When I returned, her eyes were closed and her breathing had evened out. She finally looked so at ease lying in the bed, that I couldn't bring myself to wake her just to take the medicine. Setting the glass down on the nightstand so she would have it when she woke, I tiptoed out of the room, shutting the door slightly behind me. I was too concerned for her to go back upstairs, so instead I pulled the throw off the back of the couch and settled down, trying to get as comfortable as possible.

Chapter Nineteen

Journal Week Three
TUESDAY

Ellie

How do you feel about yourself today?

Overwhelmed, but not in a bad way. Waking up this morning and finding Evan on the couch was a surprise. I remembered being in the bathroom and totally tossing my stomach in front of him, then the next thing I remembered was waking up in bed. My heart swelled knowing that his concern for me meant he didn't want to be too far away.

Have you internally punished yourself today?

At first, I did. I chastised myself insisting that the only reason Evan stayed on the uncomfortable couch was out of medical concern for me. My head telling me that he felt obligated to be sure that I was going to be okay. Yet my heart told me he did it because he truly cared. Then I also scolded myself because this journal is supposed to be about grief. Getting over the pain of losing my husband. But how am I supposed to be feeling guilty and grief ridden over his death, now that just being with or around Evan makes me so happy? That too makes me guilty.

What did you do today to make you feel good?

I sat on the coffee table next to the couch and watched Evan sleep for several long minutes. I enjoyed seeing the content look on his face and the way his brows were smooth instead of squeezed together. I marveled as his full lips were slightly parted as he breathed, and how when he wasn't frustrated, sad, or filled with guilt, he had a very boyish and youthful expression in his calmness. I also may have squealed internally when in his subconscious, it was my name that passed his lips.

"GOOD MORNING, sunshine," I smiled as Evan's eyes fluttered open and adjusted to the light. His blue orbs were unfocused as if he were trapped somewhere between being awake and his dreamy subconscious.

"Morning, baby," he replied as his eyes fluttered closed and back open again, this time more focused.

"You know, that's the second time you've called me that," I smiled.

"Shit, I'm sorry, Ell," he yawned as he sat up. The muscles of his uncovered chest grew taut with movement and I couldn't help but blatantly stare at his body.

"Don't apologize. I—I kinda like it," I reassured him. And it was the truth. Even though he's said twice now, although subconsciously, the endearment still made me feel warm. Happy. A little giddy.

"Did you sleep on the couch all night?" I asked when he was sitting upright and rubbing the muscles in his neck and wincing as if in pain.

"Yeah, I wanted to be sure you were okay if you got sick again. How are you feeling?"

"Better, still a little queasy, but at least I can remain upright."

"You still look a little flushed. You aren't lying to make me feel better are you?" His hand grazed the side of my cheek, sending warm tingles to spread through me.

"I don't feel the greatest, but at least I'm not having to hover around the toilet."

"If that changes, you tell me immediately. Got it?" There was seriousness in his tone and I dismissed it as his doctor side coming out in full force.

"Yes, doctor." I replied, teasing him.

He shook his head at me, but I could see the small smile on his lips.

"I'm going to run upstairs and take a shower. Promise you are okay? I wanted to go out and get what I need for the memorial thing Sandi wanted us to do. Any clue what you're doing?"

I shook my head. I really didn't know what I was going to do. A song felt so impersonal. I'd already written him letters. I didn't have poem writing ability in my body and I definitely couldn't act or sing.

"I'm not sure. And yes, I'll be fine. Go ahead. I might just lie in bed for a while and read a book. I don't want to push myself too hard and not recover from this bug. I don't wish it on anyone. I hope you don't get it."

Standing up, he leaned down to where I was still sitting on the coffee table and kissed me on the forehead.

"I really want to kiss you, but after seeing you last night, I'll let you keep your cooties to yourself until you're better," he teased.

I couldn't stop the smile on my face as he turned around and winked at me before leaving the apartment.

After losing Jeremy, my mind told me that I would never have the ability to care for someone as deeply as I did my husband. It told me that since he was gone, I would never feel the butterflies in my stomach or feel my heart swell when I was completely happy. Happiness would be something that would melt away from my life, leaving me barren and lonely. Well, the head lies. It tells you all kinds of deceitful and dark things. It can take your thoughts and twist them to the point you don't even recognize what your original one was.

But after being with Evan these last five and a half months, I can tell you one thing. Your head will play tricks on you and leave you feeling defeated, but the heart? The heart doesn't lie.

Evan

I'VE BEEN GONE from the house for over an hour now and I must have sent Ellie half a dozen texts. I didn't want to leave her, but I also didn't want her with me when I did what I was about to do. For once, guilt didn't hit me when I thought of the idea, instead my heart drove me to the store I was sitting in front of, telling me that it was okay to do it. It was okay to let go of my past so that I could begin rebuilding my future.

A future that I wanted with Ellie.

She has filled every vacant thought in my head for some time now. She has been the reason I look forward to waking in the morning and the person who I see in my dreams every night. Even though I don't know the outcome of what is going to happen between us, I also know that if I don't take the chance, I'll never forgive myself. Even though a small pang told me that there was a grand possibility that I would be rejected, I knew I had to try.

Climbing out of the car, I went into the small corner shop where an old fashioned bell announced my arrival.

"Evan Taylor, great to see you, son," the old man behind the counter said as soon as I stepped over the threshold.

"Good to see you too Mr. Ellis," I replied, walking over to shake the hand of one of my father's longtime friends.

"I'm terribly sorry about what happened with your wife. Wanda read it in the paper and I didn't want to believe it at first. I mean, I wish it hadn't happened. I spoke to your father not too long after the accident. He told me that you have been down here for a while now."

"Thank you. And yeah, I've been down here for nearly six months now. I'm on a sabbatical from the hospital."

"Any idea when you might return?"

"I'm not sure. It will probably be soon though. I've been doing group grief counseling and I think we are nearing the end."

"That's good son. Therapy has a way of helping tons of people. Have you found it successful?"

I thought about it for a while. Although I had to admit that there were certain aspects of the counseling that had seemed beneficial, I had to give a vast majority of the credit to Ellie. She has been one of the sole reasons why losing Lilly didn't kill me right along with her. Ellie breathed life back into me when I felt like I couldn't stand to take another breath.

"Yeah, it has helped."

"So, what brings you in here of all places?' Mr. Ellis looked around at all the lit up cases in front of him.

"Well, I need you to do something for me. Well, I need to see if you *can* do something for me."

"I'm sure we can, son. What is it?"

I looked down at my hand resting on the case and then back up to him.

"Can you make a piece of jewelry from another piece?"

"Like add diamonds or something?" He asked.

"Well, yes and no. Can you take something like a ring and make it into a pendant or something?"

He looked down at my hand and then back to me.

"You want me to…" he trailed off.

"Yes." I lifted my hands from the cases in front of me and then touched the ring on my left hand. I hadn't taken it off since the day that Lilly put it on me. I never wanted to. Never thought I would *ever* want to.

"I'd like to turn this ring into something. I don't know, like a pendant or something that I could put on a necklace."

"Son, that is your wedding ring, are you absolutely sure you want to do that?"

I took one last look at my ring. I felt a sense of freedom overcome me as if the tension I had been holding onto finally let go. I closed my eyes and whispered to Lilly. I thanked her for the life we had together and for giving me a life to have when she was gone. It's weird and unexplainable, but I swear I could feel her smiling. I could see the happiness on her face through my closed eyes.

"Evan?"

"Yes. I'm absolutely sure."

I asked for a piece of paper and sketched out what I wanted him to do with the metal and the inscription I wanted him to engrave onto it.

When I left, I knew.

I had reached the thing that I have been working towards ever since I lost Lilly.

Acceptance.

But never in the process did I ever expect to find love.

Chapter
Twenty

Journal Week Four
FRIDAY

Ellie

How do you feel about yourself today?

Nervous. Today is the day that we meet one on one with Sandi about our journals and what we have learned in group over the last few months. As I flicked through this book looking at all my past entries, there is one thing that maintain constant in my thoughts and words on the page.

Evan.

Have you internally punished yourself today?

Yes. Because I thought this journal was supposed to be about grieving for my husband. I thought it was to help me get over the fact he is gone and learn to accept it. For the most part it has, but it has become so much more than that. I can see over the last four weeks how I have so easily fallen in love with Evan. And it makes me feel so happy and sad at the same time.

What did you do today to make you feel good?
I woke up in Evan's arms.

"ARE YOU NERVOUS about talking to Sandi?" Evan asked me as we drove to the rec center for our meeting. Over the last week, our relationship had seemed to take a major shift. More often than not, my days were happy. I still thought about Jeremy, but somehow with Evan, I looked back on my life with Jeremy fondly instead of with sadness. I sought some comfort in the fact that I knew he wanted me to be happy.

But as this day had grown closer, I felt an overwhelming sense of sadness fill me. I couldn't help but have that sinking fear that as things got better and we have both come to accept the death of our spouses and learn to move on, that our newfound happiness was soon coming to an end.

Nausea filled me again. It has been over a week since our plane ride and I was still suffering from the vertigo. It had lasted a while in the past, but I don't remember it lasting quite this long. I have learned how to hide it over the last few days from Evan, but it was getting harder to do so. He was a doctor, he knew how to read the signs of pain or discomfort on peoples faces.

"I guess so. I think I'm more afraid to share my thoughts with her."

"I know what you mean."

"Do you think this is it? Do you think she will make us come back for next weeks session?" I asked as the thought of not being here with Evan made me feel even more physically ill. I could feel the saliva pool in my mouth and the bile threaten to rise in my stomach.

He shrugged, acting nonchalant while I was over in my seat feeling like the windows were caving in on me.

"I'm not sure. Do you feel ready? If it weren't for you, Ell, I don't think I would have made it this far."

His hand left the gearshift and came over to clasp mine, threading our fingers together. Even though it were only our palms facing each other, I felt our hearts join. I could feel the pulsing in his veins and it matched my own as if we were one beat. One rhythm.

"I'm not sure."

We rode in silence the rest of the way to the rec center, still connected by the hands and too afraid to say anything else to each other. Emotions threatened to overwhelm me. Several times I had to look out of the window to hide the tears that began to form in my eyes.

"Go on in, I need to use the restroom," I told him and he nodded, kissing me on the cheek before heading to meet with the group. I barely made it into the restroom before the entire contents of my stomach came up. I have heard of people getting physically ill when they were emotionally spent, or nervous.

"Ellie?" The sound of Sandi's voice echoed off the walls of the bathroom. I turned over my shoulder to find her looking down on me with concern.

"I'm okay, just feeling a little nauseous."

"Ellie, you got sick last week too. Are you sure you are okay? You could be really sick, maybe you should see a doctor, or I could go get Evan…"

"No. Please no, don't tell him. I don't want him to worry."

"Ellie, there could be something really wrong, you should see someone."

"I know, I will, I promise. Please, just don't say anything."

"Okay. I'll meet you out with the group. We can do your one-one-one first if you want to leave a little early after the memorial activity."

"I rode with Evan."

"He can go early too."

"Thank you, Sandi."

She nodded, but not without a concerned look on her face. I knew something was wrong, I just didn't want to admit it to myself. This wasn't just any sickness.

It was heartsickness, because I knew deep down, no matter how much I wanted to, it was all coming to an end.

―――――

"ALRIGHT EVERYONE, I'm ready for our meetings. The rest of you can work on preparation for the memorial activity while I speak to you individually. Ellie, will you come and bring your journal with you?" I nodded and reached beneath my chair for my notebook when Evan's hand encircled my wrist.

"Are you okay? You were in the bathroom for a while." His brows were furrowed and his mouth set in a hard line which always gave away that he was worried.

"I'm fine. Sandi was in there, so we chatted for a bit." I said telling the truth. Sort of.

"You'd tell me if you still weren't feeling well, right?"

"Of course, Evan." I lied.

"Okay. Good luck, baby."

I smiled. Ever since I had told Evan that I liked hearing him call me baby, he said it a little more often now. For a few brief moments, it would allow me lock on to the happiness he has brought to my life, so that I could lock it away in my mind. I wanted to memorize every moment, every memory, touch, kiss, every word with Evan, so that when it came time to walk away, I would have them with me always.

Sandi set up in one of the coaches offices of the rec center, with blinds closed and the door shut so that we would have privacy during our individual meetings.

"So, what did you think of the journal activity?" She asked as we both took our seats facing each other.

"I thought it was a great activity," I said honestly. "It definitely helped me to recognize my thought patterns and what went through my head for the last four weeks."

"Good. And what kind of pattern did you find?"

I felt my face flush with heat and a soft sheen of sweat coat my upper lip. The humidity in the small room did nothing to alleviate my anxiety. What would she think of me if I told her the truth? Would I be seen as a horrible person for developing feelings for someone so quickly after my husband's death? I took a deep breath, thinking that telling her the truth may be the best thing for me.

"Evan."

She arched her brows at me, but the small tug at the corner of her mouth told me she was trying to suppress a smile.

"Go on," she said, nodding her head at me.

"Most of the thoughts and things that I experienced in the last month all had to do with Evan. Besides some pain that I would feel about missing Jeremy or fighting an inward battle about my feelings for Evan, most of the words are about how much he's helped me. How much he has been there for me. And how much of the pain I have experienced goes away whenever we are together."

"You've developed feelings for him, yes?"

I nodded, turning my face away from hers towards the door. I wanted to hide, to find sanctuary where I wouldn't be judged for what I was feeling. It wasn't like I could just turn off the feelings for Evan. They weren't a light bulb that I could just switch off and on as I wished. My feelings for him have steadily increased with time to the point that they almost overshadowed the sadness I felt after losing Jeremy.

Almost.

"Ellie, it's okay," she said leaning over and placing her hand on mine where my fingers were knotted in my lap.

I turned to look at her, tears threatening to spill from my eyes and my throat tightening.

"It's okay," she repeated again, looking directly at me as the first tear trickled down my cheek.

"I feel so guilty," I sniffed. "I never meant to fall in love with him. It just...*happened*."

I exhaled long and slow, trying to gain control over my emotions. Subconsciously, my mind and heart have been secretly telling me that I was in love with Evan for a while now, but actually saying the words out loud hit me harder than expected. Not because they weren't true, but because of the guilt.

"You feel guilty because you fell in love with someone that isn't your husband," she said more as a statement than a question.

"Yes," I admitted, removing my hand from under hers and

wiping the tears from my eyes. Sandi reached for a tissue box and handed it to me. My stomach began to turn again and I willed it to go away. The depression and anxiety were starting to take its toll on my body. I haven't taken the best care of myself since Jeremy's death and now I was feeling the consequences of it. I promised Evan I would tell him if I were feeling bad, but I just couldn't. He had done so much for me already. I was so tired of him thinking that I was weak. Even though I knew he truly wouldn't think that about me, I thought it about myself. I want to be stronger. I wanted to be worthy of his generosity and maybe if he felt the same way, his love.

"You and Evan have spent the greater part of six months together. You have helped each other through one of the most difficult times of your life. It's only natural that you two have grown close."

"But how do I know if it truly is love that I'm feeling, or is it just that we feel connected because of what happened?"

"You and Evan are connected because of what happened, but it's more than that. I've gotten to know the both of you over the last few months. Even though most of our exercises were group oriented, the others may as well have been invisible. I would catch him daydreaming and looking at you when you weren't watching. You would always smile or your eyes lit up when he would speak."

"My mom said something very similar," I added.

"Your mom must have seen it as well. So he's met the parents then?"

I nodded.

"I've met his as well. They came down and spent the weekend with us."

"Ellie, know that the guilt you feel for loving Evan is natural too. You lost your husband, the person you thought was your soul mate and someone who you envisioned the rest of your life with. With his life cut so short, your plans for your future were interrupted. You feel like your life stopped the day Jeremy died, but since then you have begun living again. Your heart opened up to someone when you wanted nothing more than to keep it locked away forever."

I sniffled as more tears came. Every word she said was true.

"Close your eyes, Ellie. Now, I want you to try and look ahead into your future. What is it you see? Who do you see in it? Where are you? Take a deep breath. Concentrate, and then tell me."

I inhaled long and slow as I closed my eyes. At first, my mind didn't show me anything but the backs of my eyelids, until suddenly I was surprised to see that it was Evan who came to mind rather than Jeremy.

"I see Evan. We are on the beach somewhere, but it's not here. He's holding my hand as we walk along the edge of the water, which is funny, because I have grown to hate the water."

"Go on," she said when I paused.

"We, we are just happy."

I opened my eyes and saw Sandi staring at me with a warm smile on her face. My eye brows knitted together as I tried to understand.

"Why do you think it was Evan that I saw and not Jeremy?"

Sandi put the papers that were in her lap on the small desk in the room and stood up, reaching out for my hands to follow her. When I was on my feet, she pulled me into her embrace and I welcomed the comfort in which she was offering me.

"Because Ellie, dear, you have come to accept Jeremy's death and can see yourself moving on still loving him, but able to love someone new as well."

Chapter Twenty-One

ACCEPTANCE

Evan

I WAS NEXT TO TALK to Sandi after Ellie had finished. When Ellie and Sandi emerged from the office, Ellie's eyes were red and bloodshot and Sandi was holding onto her as if she were fragile and would crumble to the floor without her support. I wanted to run to her instantly, gather her in my arms and hold her until I knew she was okay. I could tell she had been lying to me about how she was feeling. Normally her skin would shine with radiance, but ever since we returned home from North Carolina, she has had a dull, almost greyish tint to her. I was more concerned than ever having dealt with patients who tried to disguise their symptoms to me at the hospital. What terrified me the most was that Ellie's new look was one that I had seen many times over in the cancer ward. Even though I specialized in pediatrics, I knew a sick person when I saw them.

My mind worked into overdrive with the many different

scenarios of what could be harming her. All of them, the outcomes weren't what I had envisioned for the future. If losing Lilly wasn't devastating enough, I couldn't imagine losing another person I loved without irreparable consequences.

"Evan, are you ready?" Sandi asked as she approached and Ellie excused herself to visit the restroom. I watched her leave until I could no longer see her, questioning whether I should go after her or go speak with Sandi.

"She'll be okay. I promise. Come with me please," she said, resting a hand on my shoulder. Hesitantly, I followed Sandi into the office.

"So, I'd ask you how your journal project went, but I kind of have a feeling I know already. But I guess I want to hear it from you first."

"I think it went well and was a good project. It did help me see where my thoughts have been for the last month."

"And what would those thoughts be?" She asked smiling and arching a brow at me. I smiled slightly. She knew something, but yet was acting like she didn't.

"Well, probably not who the focus of the assignment was supposed to be on."

"Evan, there was no main focus of this assignment other than for you to see the patterns of your thoughts and whether or not you were being harsh on yourself or if you were learning to accept the circumstances and move on," she said. I looked towards the door as if expecting the object of my thoughts to walk in at any time.

"Ellie. Most of my thoughts were of Ellie, but somehow I think you knew that."

"I did."

"Care to elaborate?"

She thought about it for a moment and when I didn't think she was going to tell me, she began to speak.

"I'd be blind if I didn't notice how close you two have gotten. You have been living under the same roof for nearly six months. You've both been bonded by tragedy and developed a deep friendship because you both knew what the other was going through. But you also feel guilty, right?"

I did. But did that also mean that Ellie was feeling guilt as well? Was she regretting our relationship and everything that happened between us even though she told me she wouldn't?

"Guilt, yes. But I think it has grown towards guilt that I don't feel guilt anymore. I don't feel guilty for loving her."

"You're in love with her? So I take it that you have learned to accept Lilly's death?"

"Yes, but Lilly was the one who helped me accept it."

"Lilly?"

"She came to me in a dream. Told me she wanted me to be happy, even encouraged me to develop something with Ellie. Honestly, it didn't take much coaxing on my part. Don't get me wrong, Sandi. I loved my wife. Still love her deeply, but somehow being with Ellie makes me forget the pain. It's like she fills the void left behind by Lilly. I enjoy being with her. I enjoy listening just to hear her speak. I love looking at her because she is so beautiful. I crave being with her because she makes me feel wonderful."

"I'm really glad to hear that, Evan. I've watched you two over these last few months and I could feel the connection. Not only see it, but physically feel the connection. You bonded out of pain and with that, love was bloomed. Have you told her how you feel?"

"No, I mean she knows I like her, but I haven't told her that I'm in love with her."

She tapped her pencil against the notebook in her hand. If anything about Lilly's death had any impact on me, it was realizing the fact that you shouldn't let a day go by without telling someone you love them. You never know when the last time you ever get to say it will be.

"You removed your wedding ring," Sandi said as she pointed the pencil at my hand.

"Yes. I did something with it for the memorial project."

She arched her brows at me in curiosity.

"Most surviving partners tend to cling to their rings as a way to still feel connected to their loved one. Is that the case with you?"

"In a way."

She chuckled.

"I can see you aren't going to tell me until we have the presentation, huh."

"You got it, Doc."

Standing, Sandi extended her hand to me and I stood up to shake it.

"I wish you all the happiness in the world, Evan. I know losing Lilly was extremely difficult, but I can also see that you have accepted it in your heart and are prepared to continue on and live your life happily. That is what Lilly would have wanted, if she loved you half as much as you loved her."

"No doubt. Thank you, Sandi. For everything."

THERE WERE VERY few things in life where I felt teary-eyed, but listening to everyone in the group memorialize their loved one through song, poem, quotes, and many other ways had my throat tightening and tears threatening to form in my eyes. When Ellie and I started coming to these sessions, the pain and anguish in the room was so thick, it could have been cut with a knife.

Finally it was my turn to remember my wife. I was nervous as my palms sweated and I rubbed them against my pants, making contact with the small leather pouch in my pocket.

"Evan, how is it that you want to remember Lilly?" Sandi said to me and I could have sworn she winked at me, trying to offer me the confidence that I was lacking. When I decided on the way I was going to let Lilly live on, I thought it was the perfect idea. Now, I was feeling a little anxious about how people would see me when I did show them.

I stood from my seat and walked up to the front of the group where Sandi had everyone sitting in a semi-circle.

"Lilly was one of the most wonderful, kind, and caring women I have ever met. She was selfless, honorable and an all around amazing person to be around. I felt blessed to be a part of her life no matter how short our time was. There isn't anything about our life together that I would trade."

I shoved my hands in my pockets and fumbled with the pouch in my pocket, trying to draw in Lilly's strength to get my words out. I was terrified to do it, but I finally looked up and met Ellie's eyes.

"I had no clue that stepping on the boat that day would take the love of my life away from me. I never knew that my entire world was going to be ripped apart. You see, not only did I lose Lilly, but our unborn child as well. For a few hours, I was both a husband and a dad, and the high I felt during that time was unexplainable. But just as I never expected to lose someone I loved more than life, I never expected to find someone else who would give my life new meaning. I never pictured falling so completely in love with someone other than Lilly, but I did. I fell hard for this blue-eyed girl who also shared the same pain. She understood me, and just being in her presence made me want to live, when I should have felt like dying."

I pulled the pouch from my pocket and tugged at the string to open it before tipping it over and spilling the contents into my hand. Cold metal rested in my palm. A heart pendant was connected to a chain and I looked down at it, admiring it for about the millionth time.

It wasn't any heart, but a broken one. Cracks zig zagged down the center indicating that the heart had once been shattered. The only thing that was holding it together was the small piece of metal that connected to two pieces. In the center of that strip was a single solitaire diamond.

"I never thought that the pieces of my heart would ever be mended, that they would be broken forever. That is until I had to chase this crazy woman out into the middle of the ocean with a Jet Ski."

Ellie chuckled, but was furiously wiping at her eyes. Sandi reached over and clasped her hand, giving it a small squeeze. Never taking my eyes off Ellie, I walked over to where I was standing in front of her.

"A diamond is one of the strongest natural materials on earth. They are rare, valuable, and very precious. They are built from pressure, and from that pressure a beautiful gem emerges. I can honestly say that coping with the pressure of losing my wife was the hardest thing I've ever had to overcome, but it was the journey I have taken these last few months that has made me more valuable. What made it valuable was that I didn't have to do it alone."

I held up the necklace for everyone to see, allowing the pendant to dangle at the end of the chain.

"This particular diamond is the reason that these two pieces of this broken heart are mended. Although cracks remain, and they always will, the diamond has secured it together, never to be broken apart again."

I knelt down in front of Ellie who was close to sobbing as her hands covered her mouth and tears continued to cascade down her cheeks.

"Ellie, you are the strong diamond that has pulled my broken heart back together. You have mended pieces of me when I never thought it could be possible. Lilly showed me what it was like to love, but it is you who has taught me how to love again. It probably sounds crazy, but Lilly has been your biggest cheerleader from the beginning. I feel as if it were her that brought you to me. There are pieces of her that I see in you. Your kindness, your generosity. Your ability to want me to be happy even when you were dying inside. I never knew that losing one love would lead me to an even greater one. I had this made from my wedding band. I want you to have it. I want you to know that no matter what, it was you who healed me." I handed the necklace to Ellie who took it from me with trembling hands.

"Oh my God," Ellie said as she covered her face and huge sobs erupted. I watched as her shoulders heaved with each breath she took. In that moment, my heartbeat was on hold waiting for her response.

"I—excuse me," she said as she suddenly shot up from her chair and ran out of the rec room. I collapsed into the floor, falling on my ass, not having the strength to stay on my knees any longer. I watched her run away.

I sat there on the floor not sure what to think. All I knew was that my heart was still waiting to start beating again.

Chapter
Twenty-Two

WAITING

Ellie

"ELLIE, ARE YOU okay?" Sandi asked as she knocked on the stall door I was in. Her soft voice could be heard all throughout the bathroom. Luckily, I had gotten sick before she had entered. I didn't want to worry her any more that I already had.

"I'm okay. I just need a moment."

"Honey, Evan wants to talk to you. Want me to let him in?"

"No. I—I can't see him right now. Please. Please tell him I'll meet him at home."

"Okay. Do you need anything?"

"No. I'm fine. I'll be out in a minute."

I heard the door open and close along with the sound of muffled voices. I knew that Evan was hurting by the way I ran off. His words, God, they gutted me. Reached inside of me and secured a permanent place in my heart that no one had ever been able to get to. Not even

Jeremy. But even his words wouldn't be able to ease the heartache I would feel when I finally had to leave him and go back to North Carolina. I wanted to be near my family. He wanted to be near his. His job kept him in Miami, mine Raleigh. As much as I wanted to be with him, needed him, I could never ask him to give up his life in order to be with me. I also couldn't have him continue to take care of me financially like he has been since my savings ran out. Even though he didn't say it, his words felt very close to a declaration of love. The part of me that was in love with him was never happier, but the masochist part of me told me that he just felt sorry for me, or maybe felt obligated. Losing one love was hard enough, I didn't think I would survive losing a second.

And that was the reason why I had to walk away while I still had the courage to do so.

Evan

"SHE WANTS YOU to meet her at home."

"Sandi, I—I need to speak to her please. I need her to understand— "

"She understands, Evan. I think she is just feeling overwhelmed. She loves you too, you know. Just give her a little space to come to terms with your confession, which was beautiful by the way."

"I—I dammit."

Sandi placed a reassuring hand on my shoulder.

"Go home. Wait for her," she smiled and all I could do was nod in return. I looked once more at the bathroom door, begging and pleading with it to open. I was desperate to see her face peek out from the other side and run into my arms, but seconds turned into a minute and when I realized she wasn't coming out, I turned around and walked out to my car feeling defeated.

When I made it home, I sat on the couch for hours in the unlit living room. Each settle of the house or car that drove by had me hoping it was her about to walk in the door. Sandi had told me to come home and wait for Ellie. Little did I know, that's all I would be doing.

Chapter Twenty-Three

BACK TO REALITY

Ellie

I STARED AT THE PHONE that was ringing for the millionth time in the past few weeks. Each ring was like a stabbing pain in my heart, and the silence when it stopped was even worse. The calls had grown less frequent since they first began and I hoped that it was finally helping both him and myself to be able to once again pick up and move on.

"Honey, eventually you are going to have to talk to him."

"It won't do any good, Momma. There's no way it would ever work. His life is there, my life is here."

"Ellison, it doesn't matter if you think it would work or not. When two people love each other, they make it work."

"It's just better this way."

"Yeah, because you clearly look better. Look at you, baby. You are making yourself physically ill from all of this."

I glared at my mother as she handed me a cup of warm tea. It was the only thing I seemed to be able to handle at the moment. My stomach growled with hunger, but I wasn't hungry, not for food anyway. If I said I didn't miss Evan, it would be a complete lie. Being apart from him these last few weeks since I returned to North Carolina have been more than difficult. Amazingly, I was able to return to the home that Jeremy and I shared together without any hesitation or remorse on my part. Sandi was telling the truth when she told me I had finally accepted Jeremy's death, and I had. But accepting walking away from Evan? I don't think I would ever be able to do that.

"It's just a bad virus, " I repeated for the hundredth time over the last few days. I knew my mom's intentions were good, but all I wanted was to be alone to fester in my own thoughts. I wanted my subconscious to crucify me for walking away, I deserved it for not only hurting Evan, but myself in the process.

"Must be some virus to last this long without the symptoms letting up," my mom mocked. My face flushed with heat as anger began to rise.

"It's my decision. I've already lost one love of my life, I couldn't go through that again. I barely survived the pain the first time."

"And what makes you think you would lose Evan? Honey, you spent six months with him. You fell in love with the odds of your pain against you. He fell in love with you when he felt like his heart was broken irreparably. I think that makes you two that much stronger."

I sat my tea down on the table and removed the blanket from my legs. Even though it was still relatively warm outside, my bones were cold, and not entirely from the temperature of the air. I felt the weight of the world on my shoulders, with no way to be able to turn it around. Every time I asked myself what it was that I really wanted, it was Evan who I saw. It was Evan who I needed, and I had no way of knowing how to let that go.

"I've made my choice," I said as I rose quickly to my feet. I loved my mom more than anything, but her daily visits to my house were starting to take their toll on my emotions. It was the same go-around every visit.

"Woah," I said as I placed my hand on the arm of the couch trying to steady myself.

"Ellie, honey? What's wrong?" I could hear my mother ask as she rushed to my side. I tried to look up at her, but just the action of moving my head made me even dizzier. My vision began to cloud over as the world around me was spinning.

"Mom, I don't feel so well," I said just before my muscles gave out and darkness consumed me.

Evan

TWO WEEKS.

I haven't seen or heard her in two weeks. Fourteen days. One-hundred and sixty-eight hours.

The last memory of Ellie I had was when she ran from the room as I all but declared my love for her, leaving my heart aching with the need to know she felt the same way.

I returned to work a week ago, trying to drown myself in work so that thoughts of Ellie didn't consume me. I busied myself by taking extra shifts and extra caseloads so that I didn't have a single moment where my thoughts would pause long enough to think about her. The only thing that it did was leave me exhausted at night, yet still not able to close my eyes because there she was as soon as I did.

My pager went off as I was sitting in my office filling out the paperwork from my earlier rounds. Reading that the main hospital reception was paging me had me questioning why. My parents had direct access to my pager, so all they had to do was put their number in for me to return their call.

Picking up the phone, I dialed reception.

"Good afternoon. University of Miami Hospital, Audrey speaking, how may I direct your call?"

"Hi, Audrey, this is Doctor Taylor returning your page."

"Oh, yes. Dr. Taylor. There is a woman on the main hospital line for you. I told her that you were probably doing rounds and unreachable, but she insisted, saying it was an emergency and that she needed to speak with you."

"Did she happen to tell you her name?"

"Um, yes. Yes she did. It was—hang on let me find the piece of paper—Carolyn. Carolyn Scott."

I tried to think of who this Carolyn Scott could be, racking my brain to try and jog up any memory I could, but I couldn't think of anyone.

"She said it was concerning her daughter. Would you like me to put her through to your extension? Are you in your office?"

Then it hit me.

Ellie's maiden name was Scott.

"Yes, please. Thank you Audrey."

I hung up and waited nervously for the phone to ring, and when it did, I nearly jumped out of my chair.

"University Hospital, Dr. Evan Taylor," I answered, trying to keep my voice as steady as possible.

"Thank God I reached you. I didn't know where I should call or even what hospital you worked at. This was my second try."

"Everything okay? What's wrong?" I asked as my heart rate began to speed up. I couldn't explain it, but I had a bad feeling something wasn't right.

"It's Ellie. I was at her house this morning when she collapsed. She's been sick since she returned home from Florida, but I could never get her to go to the doctor. They are doing tests and stuff now. I—I probably shouldn't have called, but I couldn't not tell you. Ellie may try to push her feelings aside, but she has suffered ever since she came home after leaving you."

I stood up from my chair so fast, the motion sent it crashing into the wall behind me.

"She's still sick?" I asked, suddenly hit square in the chest from the news. It was so obvious now all the times she told me she felt fine, but she was in fact hiding her discomfort from me.

"What do you mean *still?*" Carolyn asked me. Shoving my wallet into my back pocket, and fishing my keys from my drawer, I was ready to dart out of the building.

"She was sick here the last few weeks before she left. Dammit, she swore she was feeling better."

Carolyn grew quiet on the other end of the line and it made me nervous.

"Listen, I'm leaving work now and hopping on a plane. Call me or text me on my cell if you hear anything." I gave her my phone number before I hung up the phone. Shoving files into the drawer of my desk, I grabbed my cell and called Robert, my chief of staff's phone to let him know that there was an emergency and that I had to leave.

By the time I had gotten to the airport my nerves were beyond frazzled to the point my leg was bouncing as I sat and waited to board. So many different scenarios ran through my mind, and none of them had a good outcome.

No matter what news was waiting for me when I got to North Carolina, the one thing I knew for sure was that I let Ellie go once, I'll be damned if I did it a second time.

Ellie

MY HEAD FELT LIKE a sledgehammer had taken residence and proceeded to beat up every part of my brain. When I opened my eyes, the sun was shining brightly from a window, instantly causing me to wince in pain. Finally, I was able to hold them open long enough to notice that I was lying in a hospital bed.

"How are you feeling?" A deep voice said to me from the corner of the room. I was surprised by the sudden awareness of the familiar voice that I had to sit up slightly to look and see if I was just imagining it.

"Evan?" I questioned as I saw him get up from a chair in the corner of the room and come and sit in the one right next to my bed.

"What are you doing here?" I accused, although my voice may have sounded impassive, my racing heart was anything but. It had only been a few weeks since I had seen him, but to me, it felt like an eternity.

"Your mom called me. She told me that you were sick. The surprise was on her when I told her that you were sick before you even came home. Why have you been lying, Ellie?"

His voice was a little angry, but laced with concern.

"It's just a bad virus. I didn't want you to worry. You—you've done so much to help me, I felt like I could have been a burden on you."

"Ellie, I love you, you never have been a burden to me. You have been my saving grace. You have been the only person to keep me going."

Before I had the chance to react to the fact that Evan had just told me that he loved me, a doctor walked in, followed by my mother.

"Good morning, Ellie. How are you feeling?" The middle aged man asked as he came over and shook my hand.

"My name is Adam Clark, I'm the doctor on call today and will be taking care of you."

Evan stood up and extended his hand to Dr. Clark, introducing himself as a doctor as well.

"You gave your family a pretty good scare. Your mom tells me that you've been sick for several weeks now. Is that true?"

I looked at both Evan and my mother before returning my attention to the doctor.

"Y—yes," I managed to croak out.

"How long," He asked as he wrote down some notes on his clipboard.

"Several weeks, now," Evan chimed in, his mouth set in a hard line.

"What have your symptoms been?"

"I've been having dizzy spells and they've been making me sick to my stomach to the point that I vomit," I admitted.

"How often are you having these spells?"

"They come and go, but have been a little more frequent the last few days."

"I see. Well, we definitely want to get some blood drawn to see if we can find out what is going on with you. Once we get those back from the lab, we can make a plan from there."

"Okay. Thank you," I replied politely and the doctor left the room, promising that the nurse would be in shortly to draw my blood.

My mother and Evan both stared at me, and I shrunk into the bed hoping that they would ease up the intensity of their faces.

"So you've been hiding being sick from everyone?" My mother asked. I couldn't hide the guilty look on my face.

"It's just a weird virus, there's no need to anyone to be concerned."

"A virus that has landed you in the hospital, Ellie. You have been sick for a while now. You should have told someone," Evan chastised, concern evident in his voice.

"I'm going to go and get some coffee. Can I get you anything, Evan?" My mom asked as she headed toward the door.

"No, thank you."

"Please let me know anything you learn while I'm gone."

"You got it."

My mom looked at me with concern on her face and then walked out of the room, leaving me trapped with Evan and all the tension radiating off of him.

"Since when do you and my mom act like you are best friends?" I asked with sarcasm, trying to mask the concern brewing in my stomach about why I was feeling the way I was. I didn't want to let my mom or Evan know just how worried I was about me being sick. When one week turned into two and then two turned into more, I knew something was wrong with me, but I didn't want to find out what it was.

"Since when was it you decided that your health wasn't important? You should have come to the doctor a long time ago, Ellie."

He was angry. I could see it in the way he clenched his jaw and in the way his blue eyes darkened when as he didn't take his eyes from me.

We stared at each other for a few minutes, me not knowing exactly what to say to him, when the nurse walked in.

"Hello, Mrs. Morris. I'm going to be taking your blood. Your husband is welcome to stay, I'll just need him to go sit over there," she said pointing the chair in the corner of the room. Nausea turned in my stomach and I winced in pain. Not from physical pain of being sick, but the pain of missing Jeremy coupled with the fact that when she referred to Evan as my husband, I wished it could have been true.

I have missed him to the point that I thought I was sick because of it. I thought maybe the stress of being apart from him made me still get sick just about every day and how my knees would tremble when I walked.

Evan didn't say anything as he went and sat in the chair. Didn't correct her, or say anything about my dead husband, but instead stared at the nurse as she tied the rubber string around my arm to get a good vein.

When she stuck me with the needle and my red blood began filling the vile, I had to turn my head away and try to keep from wanting to lose the contents of my stomach.

"It's okay, Mrs. Morris. A lot of people are turned off by the sight of blood. I'm almost done and hopefully we can find out why you have been so sick. There are a lot of things that can be detected just through your blood work."

She finished up her work and then took the vials to the lab. I watched as Evan held his head in his hands and stared at the ground, his fingers knotted in his hair.

"Evan?" I asked quietly, not sure what kind of mood he was in. It warmed my heart that he was here, made me giddy with the need to have his arms around me.

He looked up, his eyes glassed over with concern, his brows knitted together, and my heart squeezed at the sight.

He got up and walked over to the bed and sat down next to me as he reached for my hand and threaded our fingers together.

"Losing Lilly was one of the hardest things I have ever done in my life, Ellie. You understand more than anyone how that feels. But you, you made it better. You healed me from the inside out. You are the one who kept me sane, and in the process I fell completely in love with you."

He rubbed the back of my hand with his thumb, stroking the skin with tenderness.

"When you walked away, it was like someone had taken the knife of pain from losing Lilly, and re-inserted it into my chest. I couldn't breathe anymore. I couldn't close my eyes without seeing your face. I tried to work, but I couldn't focus on anything but missing you. Never in my life would I ever have imagined that one of the hardest days of my life and losing my very first love, would lead me to find true love. I don't care what this is, Ellie, that is making you sick, but you damn well better fight it, because I am refusing to let you go a second time."

The determination in his voice coupled with the way his eyes softened as he looked at me made the tears swimming in my eyes fall down my cheeks. He lifted his other hand and wiped the tears from my face with the pad of his thumb all the while keeping a secure hold on my other hand with his.

"I love you, too," I whispered just before the doctor returned into the room, breaking the moment.

"Hello, how are you feeling?" Dr. Clark asked as he rubbed some sanitizer onto his hands.

"I'm okay for now," I replied.

"Have you been experiencing any abdominal pain when you get sick or with the dizzy spells?"

"A little, but I thought that it was just from throwing up so often."

"Why don't you lie on back and let me take a look?"

I nodded and Evan moved away from me, releasing my hand. Instantly, I missed the warmth of his touch. The love that only moments ago, overwhelmed me. Saying the words out loud was one of the most freeing, and wonderful moments of my life. I did love him. So much so that thinking about spending another day without him would shatter my heart into pieces that I wouldn't be able to put it back together again.

I leant back as the doctor laid the back of my bed down so that I was no longer in a reclined position. Pulling down the blanket to my thighs, he then lifted up my hospital gown to expose my abdomen.

He rubbed his hands together to try and make them warm before he placed them on my stomach and began small, palpitating movements.

"Let me know if you experience any pain. Does it hurt if I press here?" He asked as he pressed between my rib cage and in the center of my stomach. I shook my head and he continued the same action on nearly every surface of my abdomen until he reached the spot right where my bladder would be.

"Ouch," I winced slightly and as soon as I did, Dr. Clark removed his hands immediately. He reached over to press the button on my bed and in a matter of moments, my nurse was walking back into the room.

"Please have Mrs. Morris scheduled for an ultrasound immediately. It looks like we could have a possible case of appendicitis."

"Yes, doctor," the nurse replied before walking out of the room.

I looked over at Evan whose face was contorted in worry. His hair was wild from the numerous amount of times he had run his hands through it.

"I didn't even think about that. She didn't seem to be in any pain," he sighed.

"It's okay son. You know as well as I do that appendicitis can have many different symptoms. We'll get her checked out and then we will have some answers. It's possible that you will need surgery to remove your appendix if it is on the verge of rupture." He said turning to me.

"Okay," was all I could reply.

"The nurse will be in shortly to take you to ultrasound. I'm going to go check on your labs."

"Thank you, Doctor."

Dr. Clark left the room and Evan once again joined me at my side, taking my hand in his and kissing the back of my knuckles.

"See? Just my appendix. Nothing to be worried about."

His blue eyes lifted to mine, and although they didn't look completely devastated anymore, they still held concern and worry.

"It's still serious, Ell. If your appendix ruptures, it could be fatal, but at least we are here now and can get it taken care of. I need you better so that I can enjoy some time alone with my girlfriend."

"Girlfriend?" I asked, arching my brows at him.

"Yep. I told you, Ellie. This time, there's no walking away. There's no pain or grief. Just two people who under unconventional circumstances, fell in love."

Even though I was elated by his words, I also felt a hollow pain fester in my stomach. How were we going to make it work? I couldn't leave my family in North Carolina and I couldn't ask him to give up his life in Florida. Over the months that Evan and I have spent together, I knew one thing for sure. He loved his job. He loved the kids he got to care for and truly made a difference in the lives of the terminally ill.

"Evan, I don't see how things are going to work—"

I was interrupted by the nurse coming into the room and announcing that she would be wheeling my bed to another part of the hospital for an ultrasound.

Evan leaned down and kissed me on the forehead as the nurse unlocked the wheels of my bed.

"We'll talk about it later," he whispered in my ear and then I was on the move out of the room, and down the hospital hallway.

Chapter
Twenty-Four

REVELATIONS

Ellie

LYING IN MY BED in the darkened room, I looked over at the large machine the technician sat at.

"Can you lift up your gown for me, dear?" She said as she took a small bottle from the side of the machine and shook it. I did as she requested, pulling my gown up and making sure I was covered by the sheet over my hips.

"This might be cold at first," she said as she poised the bottle over my stomach and then reached for a wand and holding it to my abdomen.

"Just lie on back and relax. I may need to you hold your breath a few times in order to get a good shot of you. Hopefully we can find out what it is that is making you so sick."

I nodded as she began moving the wand around on my stomach. She started up high at first, directly under my rib cage.

"It's okay sweetie, deep breath in and hold it."

I did as she asked and we continued the same process on different areas.

"Can you tell anything?"

"Nothing yet, but the doctors will need to review."

She continued to move the wand around as she descended to my lower abdomen and she paused, snapping several pictures with the machine. I watched her brows knit together as she brought her face closer to the screen, her eyes squinting as she reviewed it. I couldn't see the screen from my angle in the bed, but I could tell she saw something just from her facial expressions.

"What do you see?" I asked, nerves starting to stir up within me.

"I'm almost finished. We'll take you back to the room and Dr. Clark will come in and tell you everything."

I blew out a shaky breath, fearing the worst. The serious look on the technician's face didn't do anything to suppress the anxious feeling in the pit of my stomach.

"I don't feel so well," I stated as I covered my mouth. Moving quickly, she turned and reached for a plastic tub and handed it to me mere seconds before I lost the contents of my stomach.

'Are you okay, sweetie?" She asked tenderly while handing me a towel to wipe my mouth.

"I'm okay," I lied, even though I was anything but. My hands trembled from getting sick and the anxiety that overwhelmed me.

"Let's get you back to your room so that Dr. Clark can come and talk to you. Don't worry. Everything will be okay."

She smiled at me sweetly, her reassurance doing nothing to help calm me. I was wheeled back to my room where Evan sat in the corner the room. His blue eyes gazed up at me at the sound of the door opening. He was on his feet and instantly at my side as soon as the nurse locked my bed into place.

"Well?" He asked looking between me and the nurse.

"Dr. Clark will be in shortly to discuss the ultrasound with you. Is there anything I can get you in the meantime?" She asked turning to look at me.

"Maybe some juice or ginger ale to get this horrible taste out of my mouth."

"You got it."

The nurse left, leaving Evan and I alone in the room. He took hold of my hand as he sat in the chair next to my bed, clinging to me as if I would float away.

"Did you get sick again?" He asked, his eyes not looking at me.

"Yeah," I said, tucking my chin and fidgeting with the blanket in my lap with my other hand.

"Evan, I'm—I'm scared," I finally admitted as the tears that had been pooling in my eyes fell down my cheeks.

"Baby, I'm here. I'm not going anywhere. Whatever this is, we'll get through this together."

I melted at his endearment, momentarily forgetting that I was sick. How I ever thought that I could walk away from this man and forget everything we have been through together, everything we discovered about one another, forget how much I loved him, I was sadly mistaken. Even though my stomach turned unpleasantly from being ill, it also fluttered with the thought of getting to see him everyday. Have his arms wrapped around me and seek his comfort, his strength, his love for as long as God will allow.

Since Jeremy's death, I've had the realization that life is too short. We are only given a certain amount of time on earth, so we should live every day as if it would be our last. The torture of not seeing or being with Evan for the past two weeks was nearly my undoing. I want him in my life, and if it meant that I had to move to Miami to be with him, I'd do it. When Jeremy died, I never thought that my heart would feel so full again. Evan didn't just fill up the void that Jeremy left, he healed it. Healed me in ways I never thought I would be able to again. He brought new life to me when it was so tragically ripped away from me.

Evan rubbed his thumb over my knuckles as we sat silently in my room waiting to hear from the doctor. When the door finally opened, both of our heads snapped up simultaneously. I was both disappointed and yet relieved that it wasn't Dr. Clark. I wasn't sure if I was quite ready to hear what was wrong with me. It had to be more than just my appendix from the look on the ultrasound technician's face as she read the monitor.

"Dr. Clark wants me to get this IV of fluids going for you. He said your lab results showed that you are severely dehydrated, which is probably why you passed out and have been feeling dizzy lately. He will be in in just a few moments to speak to you."

She smiled as she said this, and I knew she was trying to be friendly, but I couldn't help but feel like she was trying to hide something from me.

After hooking me up to the IV, Dr. Clark walked in and I could feel the blood drain from my face. I couldn't tell from his expression if the news was good or bad, but at least I had Evan here for support. Shortly after the doctor greeted us, my mom walked back into the room.

"Evan," Dr. Clark said addressing him, "The chief of staff said he could meet with you this afternoon if you'd like."

Evan smiled warmly and thanked him as he shook his hand.

"What's going on?" I asked looking between the two men.

"Good, they got you hooked up to the fluids. We'll probably want to keep you here for a while to make sure that you get plenty of fluids. We have to make sure that body of yours remains good and healthy."

He was smiling at me and it angered me. How could he have such a happy look and attitude when clearly there was something wrong with me? The fact that he seemed to ignore my question pissed me off a little too.

"So, Mrs. Morris. The reason you passed out and was feeling dizzy was because you are severely dehydrated, probably due to getting sick so much. Hyperemesis does that to some women. We'll get you feeling better and I can prescribe some medication to help combat the nausea. It will help you keep food and fluid is so that those babies can continue to grow nice and strong."

Dr. Clark wrote some things down on his clipboard as he looked at all the monitors and I nodded my head in agreement until suddenly all the blood drained from my face and my eyes grew wide.

"Did—did you say baby?" Evan asked looking at Dr. Clark as if he were going to sprout a second head. I couldn't find my voice. Couldn't breathe. My throat tightened and all I could do was stare down at my stomach.

"Indeed. Mrs. Morris is about eight week along. That is why she has been getting sick so much. Hyperemesis usually begins anywhere between weeks four and six, which is why you have been feeling ill for several weeks now," he said turning to look at me. I finally glanced up to find Evan's wide eyes locked onto me, his posture still and motionless as if he were to move, would shatter something.

"I'm pregnant?" I asked, not taking my eyes off Evan.

"You are. Congratulations. "

"But you said babies. Not baby," Evan said turning to Dr. Clark. He smiled.

"Indeed. Mrs. Morris is having twins."

Evan

I COULDN'T MOVE as if my feet were super glued to the floor. My lungs protested against any air I tried to breathe and my stomach bottomed out. Of all the scenarios that ran through my mind as to why Ellie was so sick, being pregnant never crossed my mind. It all made complete sense now. The random times she would run to the restroom. Her lack of any appetite. Being tired so much.

"I'm sorry, but I thought you just said I was having twins," Ellie all but barked into the room, her voice a few octaves higher than normal.

"I did. Twin pregnancies can tend to make the morning sickness more severe due to higher levels of HCG in the system. Congrats, mommy. I'm going to go get you some medicine for the nausea since the nurse told me you got sick earlier. It should help you to keep from throwing up."

Dr. Clark left the room and I stared at Ellie who had both of her hands placed protectively over her belly as if she were holding her babies.

Holding *my* babies.

"Please say something," she begged, not looking up at me.

"Tell me this is all a crazy dream," she added.

Prying my lead-heavy feet from the floor, I took the few steps to be at her side and sank down into the chair.

"We're having twins," I said not taking my eyes from her. She took a shaky breath and then lifted her head to look at me, her eyes shining with unshed tears.

"We're having twins," she whispered.

Love surged through me and I smiled, making my face hurt from the intensity of it. I jumped up from the chair and crashed my lips to hers, never having been more excited in my life. I kissed her with all the love and happiness I felt in my heart. My chest was so full, I felt as if my heart would burst from my chest. My thumbs stroked her cheeks when I pulled back, both of us panting and breathless.

"Well, I guess if this doesn't give me even more reason to move here, then I don't know what does." I smiled, taking in the gorgeous features of her face.

"You're moving here?"

"Without a doubt. I'm meeting with the chief of staff of the hospital later. There is an open position in pediatrics."

"I—I don't know what to say."

"I love you would be pretty perfect right now," I teased.

"I love you," she replied. No hesitation. No fidgeting. Just pure love staring back at me in her eyes.

"We're going to be parents."

"Yes we are," I replied kissing her again.

Epilogue

Evan

"DR. TAYLOR CALL extension four-three-seven. Dr. Taylor, call extension four-three-seven."

My name sounding through the speakers of the hospital room were muffled as I removed the stethoscope from my ears.

"You've got one strong heart there little buddy. I bet you have some super powers, huh?"

The little boy laughed shaking his head as my pager in my pocket went off.

437 read out on the screen.

"Excuse me for a moment. I need to take this," I said to the child and parents who all nodded at me. Stepping out into the hallway, I removed my cell phone from my pocket and dialed the extension.

"Reception, Callie speaking."

"Hi Callie, it's Dr. Taylor."

"Oh, yes. You are needed in maternity as soon as possible."

My heart rate sped up and I nearly dropped the phone from

my hands. Running at a sprinter's pace, I made my way down the hallway, trying to dodge people along the way, to the nearest elevator. I shot out a quick text with shaky fingers to the night shift supervisor letting her know that I was heading to maternity.

I'd only spoken to Ellie a few hours before and she had told me she was experiencing discomfort earlier that evening, but who wouldn't at thirty-six weeks pregnant with not one, but two babies.

This was the day I have waited my whole life for. Working with children, I had always wanted to be a father. On the night that Lilly died and she had told me she was pregnant. I was over the moon, but having to mourn the loss of my child I never got to know, was something I wouldn't wish on anyone. With Ellie, I felt like God was giving me a second chance. Another, or should I say two other, opportunities to be a dad and to love someone more than my own life.

Scanning my badge, I made my way to the maternity ward housed on the sixth floor.

"Ellie Morris? Where is she?" I asked as I stopped at the nurse's station, looking around at all the rooms and trying to find her.

"Room twelve-fourteen, doctor," she smiled and once again, I took off in a mad sprint. When I found her room, I saw Ellie lying on the bed, sweat already beginning to soak her hair, causing it to cling to the contours of her face.

"Evan," she exclaimed just before she squeezed her eyes shut and crinkled her nose in pain.

"I'm here. I'm here, baby," I said taking her hand to help her through the pain of the contraction.

"Why didn't you call me?" I asked when I noticed the pain subsiding and her grip on my hand eased.

"I—There wasn't much time. One minute I was getting up to get a glass of water, the next minute my water broke and the contractions started not long after. I called mom to help me and she drove me straight here."

I stroked her hair out of her face and reached over to the bedside table and brought the cup of ice water to her lips.

"Besides, I knew you were busy with patients so I had mom call the hospital to page you on our way here."

I looked over at Ellie's mother and smiled at her. She looked just as scared as I was but also giddy with anticipation.

"Oh, God!" Ellie exclaimed as another contraction came.

"Hello Dr. Taylor, Mrs. Morris. Are we ready to become parents today?" One of the obstetricians said as he walked into the room, extending his hand for me to shake.

"Can—can I get an epidural?" Ellis asked as she panted out breaths and I stroked the back of her hand with mine to try and offer as much comfort as I could.

"Let's see what your progress is and find out shall we?"

I watched as the doctor examined Ellie, anticipation building within me every second. Ellie and I had decided not to find out the sex of the babies, wanting to be old fashioned and wait to be surprised, and I was more than eager to see what we were having and to meet and hold my children for the first time.

"Ellie, you are at seven and a half, almost eight centimeters. There isn't enough time to administer an epidural. I'm sorry."

"You've got to be fucking kidding me!" Ellie yelled and I couldn't help but chuckle. Ellie was normally controlled, poised and polite to anyone.

"Oh it's funny? This hurts you know!"

"I know baby, I'm sorry," I replied, trying to hide my smile from her. I wasn't happy that she was in pain. Far from it. In fact, it killed me to see her like that.

Over the next hour, things progressed quickly and before I knew it, Ellie was pushing and the cries of my first born child filled the room.

"It's a girl," the doctor said smiling and Ellie paused to take a few breaths in between her contractions.

"Hear that, baby? We have a girl," I said leaning in to kiss the woman who owned me completely. Now there would be two women in my life who would have me wrapped around their fingers.

Seven minutes later, our son was born. Both babies beautiful just like their mother. Both of them with blue eyes just like both of us. Both of them loved beyond comprehension.

When all the commotion was over, the lights were dimmed, and it was only Ellie and our beautiful newborns in the room, I couldn't help but look at the three most important people in my life with all the love I felt inside.

"Think we should name them now?" Ellie asked, her eyes half closed with exhaustion, yet not wanting to go to sleep in case she missed a single moment of their first few hours of life.

"What were you thinking?"

"Well," she said looking down at our daughter who was nursing on her breast. It was one of the most gorgeous images to see, making me wish I had a camera to capture the moment. It didn't matter that I didn't, I would have it committed to memory for the rest of my life. "How about you name him, and I'll name her? Grab a piece of paper and write down the first name that comes to your mind. That is what we should name them. Don't think about it. Just the first name."

I handed her a pen and a piece of paper and picked up my son out of the clear bassinet and took him over to the corner to sit in the chair. Looking into his face, I smiled because the name came so effortless to me and I only hoped that Ellie would like it as much as I did. After writing it down on the piece of paper, I reached in to my pocket, careful to make sure that Ellie wasn't watching and placed something inside before folding it up and waiting for her to finish.

"You ready?" She asked and I smiled at her and walked over to her bedside with our son snuggled in my arms. I was nervous as I handed her the paper and reached for the one she had written on in return. Moving slowly so that she didn't wake our daughter who was now asleep in her arms.

With eager anticipation, I watched as she unfolded the piece of paper and the object I placed inside fell upon her blanket. She looked at it with wide eyes before she looked at what I had written on the paper.

Jeremy Wade Taylor
P.S. He would like to know if you would marry his daddy?

Tears streamed down her face as she looked up at me with more love than I had ever seen come from anyone. It's weird how fate works. God has so many different plans for us that we couldn't even begin to comprehend what is in store for our lives. Even though our love was formed from tragedy, it is how we had gotten here today. More in love than we could imagine possible and with two beautiful, healthy babies to celebrate that love.

"Well, tell Jeremy that his mommy says yes." She smiled as she slipped the ring in her lap onto her ring finger. I leaned in as easily as I could with a sleeping newborn in my arms and brushed my lips across hers.

"Thank you," was all she said and then gestured toward the piece of paper in my hands. Carefully, I opened it to reveal the name she had chosen for our daughter.

Lillian "Lilly" Joseli Taylor.

The End.

When we meet real tragedy in life, we can react in two ways-- either by losing hope and falling into self-destructive habits, or by using the challenge to find our inner strength.

~Dalai Lama

Acknowledgements

I hate writing these things because I am always afraid that I will leave someone out. I have been blessed with a fabulous group of people who have been with me from the very beginning you know who you are and I thank you from the bottom of my heart.

To my 2 best friends in the whole world, Judi and Emma. I can't go a day without talking to either of you because my life isn't complete without a little of you everyday. You inspire me, keep me in line, and love me despite my faults and you praise my accomplishments. More than anything you are just there for me and I love you both dearly.

To my family who never thought I was crazy for perusing this "author thing". Instead, you have always supported me without ever thinking twice. I love you all with all that I am.

To two other really great friends who I have had the pleasure to get to know even better. I enjoy our daily "bestie" chats and the fact that I know you have my back no matter what. Love you Summer and Tyf.

About Cassy Roop:

Cassy is a fitness goddess by day and romance author by night. When she isn't writing furiously on her next novel, she's making books look beautiful inside and out as a graphic designer. She has an unhealthy obsession with peanut butter, pedicures, and all things Les Mills group fitness. She has has on occasion been seen purchasing clothes that aren't athletic apparel (although rare).

She released her debut, The Price of Love, in March of 2014. The Celtic Knot Novels are her first erotic romance series and Books 1 and 2, Ashley's Bend and Figure Eight both reached #1 in Erotic Thrillers on Amazon. Book 3, Triquetra, released September 22, 2014 and book 4 the companion novel, Axel Hitch in December 2014, and VOID in February 2015.

Connect With Cassy Roop Here:

Website: www.CassyRoop.com
Facebook: https://www.facebook.com/cassyroop
Twitter: https://twitter.com/cassyroop
Goodreads Page: https://www.goodreads.com/author/show/7847487.
Cassy_Roop?from_search=true
Amazon Page: http://www.amazon.com/Cassy-Roop/e/B00J1UX9JE/
ref=sr_tc_2_0?qid=1415130653&sr=1-2-ent

Other Books by Cassy Roop

The Celtic Knot Series

Ashley's Bend
Figure Eight
Triquetra
Axel Hitch

Standalones

The Price of Love
VOID

CPSIA information can be obtained at www.ICGtesting.com
Printed in the USA
BVOW06s1858110715

408414BV00013B/393/P